SARAH JAMES

SEEDS
OF
SORROW

MODERN GODDESS SERIES
BOOK ONE

PEYTON DIMITRA HAS ALWAYS
BEEN A GOOD GIRL UNTIL...

SHE MEETS HER WICKED NEW BOSS,

HADINA ADIS

HADINA ADIS HAD NEVER BEEN GOOD... BUT MEETING
PEYTON DIMITRA MAKES HER WANT TO BE BETTER.

THE LONGER PEYTON SPENDS WITH HADINA, THE MORE
SHE IS PROPELLED INTO A LIFE OF SECRECY, CRIME AND
BETRAYAL. LOVING HADINA COMES EASY, BUT TRUSTING
HER DOESN'T.

WHEN HER NEW LIFE IMPLODES, PEYTON HAS TO DECIDE
BETWEEN BEING THE GIRL SHE USED TO BE, OR THE
WOMAN HADINA HELPED HER BECOME.

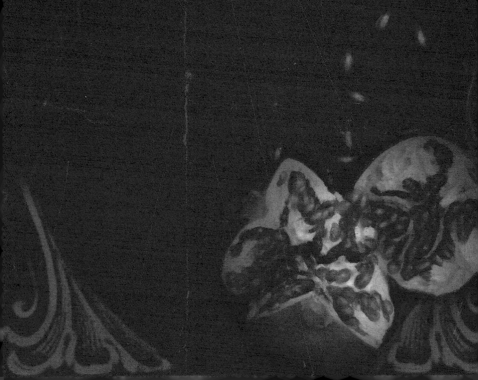

PRAISE FOR SOS

"Jaw meet floor. The madness. The passion. The chaos. This entire book left me reeling and wanting Hadina to burn my world down around me." —Dahlia Reign, author of the *Agostino Crime Family* series

"It's everything we love about Hades x Persephone retellings, but with a delicious sapphic twist!" —@ericasbookshelf, bookish content creator

"A deliciously raw and addictive sapphic mafia romance. Sarah James is an author to watch!" —Jessica S. Taylor, author of the *Seas of Caladhan* duology

"This book was a surprising breath of fresh air. The perfect introduction to dark sapphic romance, with a side of mafia. The Hades and Persephone retelling we deserve." —@corvinascloud, book reviewer

SEEDS OF SORROW | Sarah James

First Edition | Publication Date: October 21, 2023

Paperback ISBN: 978-1-7384105-0-7

Hardcover ISBN: 978-1-7384105-1-4

Ebook ASIN: B0C4RQ8SD6

Ebook & Paperback cover design by @artscandare

Hardcover cover design by V. Domino @3Crows.Author.Services

Formatting by V. Domino @3Crows.Author.Services

Editing by Kat Pagan @kat_m_pagan

AUTHOR NOTE

Seeds of Sorrow is the first book in a dark contemporary romance series, loosely inspired by Greek mythology. Seeds of Sorrow takes inspiration from the Hades and Persephone myth, though it is definitely *not* a retelling.

Seeds of Sorrow also features a queer, Latinx female main character. Coming to the decision to make a main character in the book Mexican-American was not one that I came to lightly. As a White author, I know that I am not the voice of Latinx people. However, I firmly believe that there is a lack of representation in fiction and I strive to help change this.

In order to accurately represent the Latinx culture, I did a lot of research when writing the book. The wonderful author V. Domino (a first generation Mexican-American) was alongside me every step of the way when writing, ensuring that I was writing my characters authentically. I spent time speaking with other Latinx readers and authors, and created a wonderful sensitivity team of diverse readers who beta read Seeds of Sorrow for me and pointed out anything that needed changed or added to create the most authentic characters of my ability. A huge thank you to my team: Andrea @andreagonzalezromance, Anna @annaz.archive, V. Domino @author.v.dom, Reina @reinatellstales, Yvonne @goddess_eve21, Shania @shanias-bookshelf, Stacey @staceyrzreads, Jazmin @jazminslibrary, Líza @the_joyful_closet, Rosy @rosyreadz, and Ana @anachapamillan.

I hope that when you read Seeds of Sorrow, you are able to see the influence of all the wonderful people who helped make the book possible. My aim is not to tell the story of Latinx people, but rather portray them as accurately as possible in my works so that they feel represented in literature. If there is anything at all that you feel is inappropriate, inaccurate or needs to be changed, please do not hesitate to contact me. You can reach me at authorsarahj@gmail.com and I will apply all necessary changes.

TRIGGER WARNINGS

Seeds of Sorrow is a dark romance, which means it contains many triggers such as graphic violence, power control, explicit sexual content including gun, ammunition, knife and blood play. There are also mentions of child abuse and trafficking, kidnapping, and attempted sexual assault. Each book in the series will have different levels of triggers, but all contain the above list. This book is intended for mature readers only.

For anyone in their villain era—
Watch my girls burn the world.

PLAYLIST

Talia – King Princess
Lightning – Mehro
I Fell In Love With The Devil – Avril Lavigne
Don't Blame Me – Taylor Swift
Lilith – Halsey
Numb Little Bug – Em Beihold
Queen of the Night – Hey Violet
Somebody I F*cked Once – Zolita
Achilles Heel – J. Maya
The Tradition – Halsey
She – Dodie
Lady Like – Ingrid Andress
Safe With Me – Gryffin, Audrey Mika
Disfruto – Carla Morrison
Never Seen The Rain (alternative version) – Tones and I
You Broke Me First – Tate McRae
Pomegranate Seeds – Julian Moon
Persephone – Daisy the Great
Boyfriend – Dove Cameron

Rapunzel – Emlyn
I'm Yours – Isabel LaRosa
I'll Be Waiting – Cian Ducrot
Project (acoustic) – Chase McDaniel
For The Girls – ASTON
From Persephone – Kiki Rockwell
Me Quiero Ir – Lusillón
Young Love & Old Money – Elizabeth Girardi

TRANSLATIONS

Tentadora = Temptress
Muñeca = Doll
Mierda = Shit
Pendeja = Stupid girl
Mija = My daughter
Hija = Daughter
Princesa = Princess
Que pasa, papi? = What's wrong, daddy?
El titán de la muerte = The Titan of Death
Lo siento = I'm sorry
Basta = Enough
Bastardo = Bastard
Reina de las sombras = Queen of Shadows
Cariño = Dear
Querida = Darling
Sé a la luz = Be in the light
Grosera = Rude
Hermana / Hermanita = Sister
Hola = Hello

Adíos = Goodbye
No se que hacer = I don't know what to do
Zorra = Bitch
No te creo, pendeja vengativa = I don't believe you, you vengeful bitch
Te creía más inteligente para andar cojiéndote a las sirvientas = I thought you were smarter than to go around fucking the maids
Eres una puta irrespetuosa = She's a disrespectful bitch
Dios mío = My God
Estás pendeja = You stupid girl
Vete para a la casa = Go home
Eres una pinche perra maleducada = You are a fucking rude bitch!
Bastardos = Bastards
Imbéciles = Imbeciles / Idiots
Puta / Puto = Bitch
Dame fuerza = Give me strength
Te cortare las bolas = I'll cut your balls off
Yo creo en ti = I believe in you
¿Estás bien? = Are you okay?
Convertirse en la oscuridad = Become the darkness
Eres la mujer más desordenada del planeta = You're the messiest woman on the planet
Confía en tus instintos = Trust your instincts
Santa mierda = Holy shit
Eres sensacional = You are sensational
Se avecina una guerra = A war is coming
Mi reina = My queen
Veté a la mierda = Fuck off
Por favor = Please
Papel picados = Paper flags
¿Cómo estás? = How are you?
Soy buena, y tu? = I'm good, and you?
Yo tambien soy buena, gracias! = I'm good too, thank you!
Esta es mi novia = This is my girlfriend

Ella es hermosa = She's beautiful

Se ve amable = Looks kind

Sí, sí, ella es = Yes, yes, she is

Ustedes chicas son mi todo = You girls are my everything

Caca = Poop

Cierra la puta boca! = Shut the fuck up!

Cálmate = Calm down

Que mierda estas haciendo? = What the fuck are you doing?

Es complicado = It's complicated

Dónde estás? = What are you doing?

Mi maldita hermana! = My damn sister!

Sí, lo sabia = Yes, I knew

A shadow hand reached out to her,
Beckoning her to the dark.
Her light dimmed in result
Of her newly blacked heart.

Blood was spilled,
And bodies dropped.
Her life grew complicated
But she could not be stopped.

For all she did and saw,
She helped those who had been wronged.
And even when her heart broke in two,
Still she sang her somber song.

In the land of ghosts and ghouls,
She prayed for a better tomorrow.
And when the end note played,
Her tears fell like seeds of sorrow.

Tentadora

CHAPTER 1

PEYTON

A COOL BREEZE HAUNTED THE AIR, TICKLING HER CHEEKS AS SHE CLIMBED out of the cab and handed her fare to the driver. With little more than a grunt in thanks for her generous tip, which she probably shouldn't have given him considering she had no savings, he sped off and left her standing in front of the colonial-style house.

It took her breath away. The estate was large, surrounded by healthy green grass and towering trees that were practically bursting with plump apples and ripe pomegranates. Peyton smiled to herself and inhaled, savoring the fresh air. She couldn't remember the last time she'd been somewhere that was so undisturbed by the rest of the world. The polluted city smog was suffocating.

Straightening her back and tilting her chin up, Peyton grabbed her suitcase off the sidewalk and made her way up the winding driveway. She cursed herself for wearing her heeled leather ankle boots as she struggled up the gravel path, hoping this decision was the right one.

Since finishing her biomedical course at college and working odd jobs that barely paid her rent, Peyton had contemplated her life decisions many times. It was nearly impossible to land an interview, even with a college degree. Her parents had been right about that, at the very least. They knew it was going to be hard for her to move away; she thanked every deity possible for the scholarships that allowed her to attend college in the first place.

Leaving home and deciding not to return to Willowbrooks—especially after it became abundantly clear she could no longer afford to live on her own—well, it was far more difficult than she wanted to admit. Living in a place where everyone knew everything about her and had watched her grow up was stifling. She had been drowning there long before she ever left; however, it didn't mean she didn't sometimes think about going home. But then she'd remember why she left in the first place, and it was clear she was never going back. No, Peyton was determined she could survive on her own.

That thought was what propelled her forward as she climbed the wooden steps and thumped her luggage onto the porch at the door. Spinning around on her heels, she placed her hands on her hips and admired the yard again. Her parents' house in Willowbrooks had been scarcely big enough for her mom and dad and their three kids. Peyton couldn't help the little burst of resentment that fired up inside her as she then pictured her tiny college room with damp walls and flickering lights. How was it fair that she had been forced out of the world's shittiest apartment, and yet there were people who lived in houses like this with more bedrooms and space than they could ever need?

Peyton shook her head and reprimanded her brain for its foolish and selfish thoughts. Life wasn't fair and she knew that—really, she did—and wasn't that why she wanted to become a nurse? To make the world a better place how ever she could?

"Can I help you with something, or do you just make a habit of trespassing on private property?"

Peyton jumped at the steely voice behind her and spun around, almost tripping over her suitcase and falling into the arms of the stranger. The woman's cool fingers caught her around the elbow before she could land on her ass, and Peyton uttered a few profanities.

"Shit, I'm sorry," she muttered as she pulled her arm back and steeled her spine. "I'm, uh, my name is Peyton? I'm supposed to meet Hadina here?"

The raven-haired woman stepped back, her gaze traveling the length of the girl in front of her with a piercing intensity. It made Peyton uncomfortable to be looked at like that. She always felt underwhelming, boring even, but the anxiety working its way through her veins under this scrutiny was something else entirely. While the woman examined her, Peyton found herself doing the same in return.

The stranger had long hair the color of night, and Peyton noticed that the light reflected perfectly on it, the strands glinting like stars. Her full lips were painted blood red and popped against the tan of her skin. Dark lashes framed striking emerald eyes, and Peyton tried not to gasp when they met the Grecian-blue gaze of her own.

"I suppose you better come in then."

The woman turned on her heels—a pair of beautiful Louboutin stilettos that made Peyton insanely jealous as her eyes flicked down to her worn sneakers—and strolled into the house like she owned it. It was only then, after noticing the calm demeanor soaked in self-importance, that Peyton realized her mistake...she had been speaking to Hadina, and had made a complete ass of herself in the process.

"Hurry up, Miss Dimitra. I truly do not have all day," Hadina called over her shoulder, which made Peyton rush inside before closing the door with a click behind her.

Peyton trudged after Hadina through the house, eyes widening in awe at the high ceilings and original beams that added a vintage feel to the place. Leading her into what appeared to be an office area,

Hadina pointed and motioned for Peyton to sit down in one of the olive-colored chairs. Peyton did as requested, groaning at how soft the leather was after such a long cab ride. She watched as Hadina took her seat behind the desk with the poise and grace of an old-timey heiress. She had never been in the presence of someone so beautiful and intimidating before, and Peyton blushed at the thought.

Not that she would be spending much time with Hadina anyway. She was here for sweet old Don.

Tapping her pointed manicured nails against the dark mahogany desk, Hadina glared at Peyton making her shift uncomfortably. *What was with this woman and staring people down?* Peyton thought to herself.

"Let me introduce myself. My name is Hadina and it will be my father, Don, who you will be tasked with caring for—ah, Miss Dimitra, please don't interrupt," Hadina said, and Peyton snapped her lips closed, trying not to seethe at being spoken to like a child. "My father is a very strong and proud man. The fact that he even agreed to have you become his live-in care assistant speaks volumes. He tells me you were extremely polite when he met you at his hospital appointment, but he also told me you didn't get the job you were interviewing for and ended up crying on his shoulder. Let me make it clear to you that you've only been hired at his behest—I do not think you are qualified enough and anyone who cries to an old man in a hospital is not as mentally stable as they should be when caring for another."

Peyton bristled at the woman's tone before sitting a little straighter. "I'm qualified enough for this and please understand that what happened on that day was an extremely rare occurrence. I will care for your father with the respect that he deserves. It's obvious to me that he feels the same, otherwise I would not be here, as you were so kind to point out."

Hadina raised a brow in response, as though waiting for Peyton to continue. But the girl relaxed in her chair once more and motioned for her soon-to-be boss to proceed instead.

Fuck her for trying to belittle me, Peyton thought to herself.

"Your duties are mainly to offer support, company, and assistance to his everyday life. You will be expected to begin work promptly at eight each morning and can clock out at eight each night once my father has decided to retire to his bedroom—he is a creature of habit so this will probably remain your working hours for the foreseeable future."

Hadina spoke without ever taking her eyes off Peyton, her voice commanding respect with every syllable uttered. It made Peyton wonder how someone grew to have so much confidence in themselves that they could garner attention and hold it without a doubt. Peyton certainly could not imagine trying to interrupt again.

"You will have every Thursday afternoon and evening to yourself, as well as the full of Sunday. These are the times I can definitely be here so you won't be needed. Salary is as previously discussed via email but should you need anything or require extra, please do let me know."

Peyton noticed the way Hadina paused, as though contemplating carefully what she was about to say next.

"My father is extremely important to me and your willingness to help my family is greatly appreciated. My sisters and I have busy lives with full schedules, but I will be here as often as I can and if you or my father need anything, I will always answer that call. I would, however, ask that you do not invite strangers into this house or share details of your work with the public."

Peyton startled at that. Was she getting into something she shouldn't be? It was clear she didn't have any other options but unease spiked in her gut.

Hadina, apparently noticing the way Peyton's eyes went wide with concern, relaxed her features a bit and linked her fingers together. "Oh, please don't be alarmed. It's more for your own security. I own a law firm called Adis & Co. Operations. It deals primarily with high-profile cases, so it is extremely important that I keep work separate from any personal business, as I am sure you can understand. Any personal information about my family that is disclosed to the public will result in instant termination. Do you understand, Miss Dimitra?"

A slither of fear continued to linger under her skin, but Peyton knew it was either this job or return to Willowbrooks as a failure. When she thought about it like that, her decision seemed simple.

Peyton offered up her nicest smile—the one that had people telling her that she's so sweet—and nodded. "I completely understand. And please, call me Peyton."

Taking a moment to consider, Hadina nodded her head sharply in return and pushed to her feet. She ran a hand over her silky black blouse, which surprisingly had not a single crease or wrinkle on it, and adjusted the belt on her skirt. It drew Peyton's attention to the curves of Hadina's body and she swallowed audibly. She knew color flushed her cheeks but she couldn't draw her eyes away from Hadina's slender fingers and the way they grazed her waist. She found herself imagining what it would feel like to be touched by those fingertips.

It was rare for Peyton to look at someone and feel the stomach drop of attraction but Hadina was going to get under her skin in more ways than one, it would seem.

She wondered once again how someone like this woman even existed. Hadina oozed importance and brilliance and dominance; everything Peyton wanted to be and never could get near. In her twenty-one years, she was only ever the nice girl, the sweet one, and she loathed it a little. People always wanted to take advantage when they thought you were nice.

Peyton bet no one ever got close enough to take advantage of Hadina.

"Very well, Peyton," Hadina said, breaking the girl's trance. "Let me show you to your room to get settled before dinner. You'll get to say hello to my father then."

Whatever Peyton was feeling faded away when Hadina whisked her around the house in the world's quickest tour, promising she'd find her way easy enough, before depositing the girl outside a bedroom door on the second floor.

"Dinner will be at five o'clock sharp. Please be ready on time. I'll come to get you to make sure you don't get... lost."

Before Peyton could respond, Hadina hurried away and left her standing alone. As she reached out to turn the brass handle, Peyton couldn't help but feel she just stepped into something far more complicated than she first anticipated.

She decided to ignore the rush of exhilaration it gave her. No, she would not allow herself to get caught up in fantasies of adventure and secrets and a life she most certainly could not have.

Peyton Dimitra was a good girl.

That's what she told herself anyway.

Tentadora

CHAPTER 2

PEYTON

PEYTON FELT LIKE SHE WAS LIVING SOMEONE ELSE'S LIFE AS SHE FLOATED over to the four-poster mahogany bed. A bubble of delirious laughter escaped her lips as she examined her new home.

The walls were painted maroon and Peyton surprised herself by looking at them with admiration. It took some severe balls to paint a room red and yet it was beautiful, offset by the black borders and silver accents placed strategically to break up the darkness. All the furniture, including a writing desk and plush chair, was made of the same mahogany as the bed.

It occurred to her that she had been extremely lucky to have met Don that day, when she was lost and at her lowest. To end up here, in a home that was the epitome of extravagance and beauty. It reminded her to be grateful for the chance she was being given.

She lay back on top of the duvet and let herself remember that day. Despite what she had said to Hadina, her boss was right to be concerned about hiring someone who had literally broken down to a stranger. Peyton wouldn't have hired herself either.

PEYTON TAPPED her foot nervously against the metal leg of her chair, resisting the urge to chew on her lip that was already burst and bloodied from her nerves during the drive over.

"*Cariño*, you're going to give me a heart attack with all that fidgeting."

The gruff voice broke her trance. An older man was standing in front of her, looking at her like she was supposed to answer him. Despite the weariness to his voice and the wrinkles of age on his tawny skin, he was handsome. His gray hair was combed back and a light stubble dusted his chin. Dressed in a sharp, tailored suit, he looked like he belonged in a movie.

Peyton mustered a soft smile as he moved to sit in the chair opposite her. "Sorry. Nerves."

The man smiled back. "No apologies necessary. Just wanted to pull you out from under that storm cloud. The name's Don."

Reaching out, Peyton shook his hand and noted the strength of his grip. "Peyton."

Don looked at her, a brow hitched. "What's got you so worked up, Peyton?"

She shrugged and scratched at the back of her hand, which rested on her lap. "Interviewing for a job. I just finished up college and need some sort of medical experience to help me with the next steps."

Nodding, Don listened to her ramble about finishing college and trying to pay rent in her shitty little apartment without a job. Becoming a doctor was what she wanted—Peyton always yearned to help people—but school was expensive and it was going to take so damn long.

"Peyton Dimitra." A stone-faced woman interrupted Peyton's talk with Don, who hadn't said anything as the girl spoke.

She offered him a shy smile in thanks. "Sorry about that. Guess I better go."

Don beamed at Peyton, patting her hand. "Knock 'em dead, girlie. Well, actually, maybe not the best place to do that." He winked at her as she laughed and jogged up to her interviewer.

Interviews always went the same way, in Peyton's mind. Running through your entire background and education, then they started to quiz you. She didn't usually mind the intrusion, but when Doctor Madison asked her why she wanted the job, Peyton found herself stumbling over her words.

"Well, it would be good practice. And the pay seems decent. Not that it's about the money. But it is kind of about money. I need a job so I can finish my degree. I don't want to go home. Willowbrooks isn't where I need to be."

Doctor Madison furrowed her brows and leaned back in the chair. "And you believe this is where you need to be?"

Peyton swallowed and nodded. "I...uh... Look, the job seems really good and stable. I haven't been able to get anything else since finishing up my courses."

"Wouldn't it be a better plan to return home until you're more financially secure before continuing with this career? We take this position very seriously, Miss Dimitra, and you need to be solely focused on it. Seeing as this position is for a research assistant, we really cannot afford for mistakes to be made by staff whose heads are elsewhere."

"I can't go home," Peyton whispered quietly, her voice threatening to break.

The river of blood came to Peyton in flashing images, reminding her of the worst day of her life. Her sister's unmoving, cold hand cradled in her own. That coldness still clung to her skin like an infected wound that refused to heal.

Peyton hadn't realized that tears were streaming down her

cheeks as she struggled to get a grip on her breathing, only noticing when Doctor Madison made her way around the desk to offer her a box of tissues and a glass of water from the dispenser in her office. "Close your eyes and breathe in for me, Peyton. Hold it. Good... Now exhale. Can you repeat that?"

She listened to the doctor's calming voice as the woman guided her out of the first panic attack she had endured since being at Willowbrooks. That place, those memories... It was somewhere even Peyton's mind didn't want to be.

Once she had calmed down, and drank two more cups of water, Peyton offered up an apology to her interviewer. "I don't know what came over me. I'm so sorry."

Doctor Madison smiled empathetically as she perched on the edge of her desk. "No need to say sorry. Panic attacks are more common than you would think."

It made Peyton queasy to recall how often she used to have them —and why did she just have to have one today after so much time had passed?

"Could we start over?"

Again there was that sad smile that made Peyton want to scream. Why couldn't people just act like adults instead of tiptoeing around what they wanted to say?

"I'm truly sorry for whatever you may be going through, Peyton, but I don't think you're the right candidate for this position. I need someone who is all in, focused and alert, and able to deal with whatever I throw their way. I honestly believe you have incredible potential—your grades and recommendations from professors show that —but your head isn't in it right now. That doesn't mean it won't be in the future. But please take care of whatever trauma is haunting you."

If not for that final sentence, Peyton may have kept her emotions at bay long enough to escape the room with some dignity. But tears pushed their way free and she sprinted out the door, muttering apologies and thanks to the doctor.

"Peyton? What's the matter?"

Peyton looked up through blurry eyes and saw Don sitting in the waiting room where she had left him, concern spread across that handsome face. He held his hand out to her, and for some reason, Peyton took a step closer and sobbed into the old man's shoulder.

IT MADE her cringe to think about how much of a mess she had been that day, and just how easily she had let buried memories climb to the surface. If it weren't for Don and his kindness, she would probably have ended up back at Willowbrooks, surrounded by the life she didn't want and smothered by the memories she couldn't escape.

The old man had guided her down to the hospital cafeteria, buying her a cup of herbal tea—good for the nerves, he said—and listened to her once more as she relayed what had happened. He never once asked why she had grown so upset during the interview or pried into what made her appear quite so emotionally unbalanced. Instead, he offered her friendly smiles and placating words of wisdom until she calmed down.

It was then, after they had drunk their tea and eaten far too many chocolate cookies, that Don had said he could use someone to live at the house and take care of him. Peyton had scoffed at the idea, stating she highly doubted he needed looking after, but he simply waved her off and wrote down an email for her to contact.

Peyton set an alarm on her phone, burrowed into a blanket, and smiled to herself. An act of kindness from a stranger had spun her life into a new trajectory, and she was excited to see what came next.

As she slipped into a light sleep before dinner, she wondered if she would figure out a way to get Hadina to warm up to her.

Currently, her boss was ice-cool and Peyton didn't want to think about why that gave her a thrill.

Look after Don... That was her job.

Look after...

"*Hadina,*" Peyton mumbled to herself.

Tentadora

CHAPTER 3

PEYTON

GROANING AS THE ALARM STARTLED HER AWAKE, PEYTON CRAWLED OUT OF bed and made her way into the adjoining en-suite bathroom. She stared at the claw-foot tub in the center of the gray tiled floor. She used to love soaking in a bubble bath when she was younger, letting the heat of the water soak any stress from her bones. But her college apartment only had a shower that went from scalding hot to freezing cold in a matter of minutes—definitely not a fun experience.

Peyton padded into the bathroom, debating whether the half hour she had left herself to get ready for dinner was long enough to draw a bath. Deciding against it, she took a step towards the modernized shower in the corner of the room. Peyton could only imagine that touch was something Hadina must have installed into the house—the extravagant showerhead and various products lined neatly against the shelves.

Did this used to be her room? One of her sisters'?

It made Peyton shiver to think about as she turned on the shower and stripped off the clothes that smelled after such a long drive.

17

Once the water was at the perfect temperature, she stepped into the luxurious shower and let the water coat every inch of her skin. She decided to ignore the heat in her cheeks while she showered, blaming it on the heat of the water and definitely not the recurring thoughts of Hadina in a similar position.

She barely registered how much time had passed before she heard the faint knock on her bedroom door.

"Miss Dimitra, it's five o'clock. I assume you're ready?"

Peyton swore under her breath and turned off the shower, wringing out her hair in the process. "Um, just a minute, sorry!"

By the time she had chosen an outfit—a simple pair of black jeans and a loose-fitting sweater that hung off one shoulder—and made it out of the room, Hadina was leaning against the wall outside, tapping furiously into her phone. She looked up when she heard the door click shut, running her eyes over Peyton before finishing her text.

"You're late."

The coolness in her voice made Peyton shiver and she glanced at Hadina apologetically. "I know. I'm really sorry. I decided to shower and lost track of time."

Hadina hummed and pushed off the wall, walking ahead as Peyton rushed to follow her. Hadina had changed for dinner too, opting to wear a pair of navy sailor pants with a tight black top, complemented by a matching blazer. Peyton gaped after the woman while they walked, wishing she could ask her new boss to teach her how to dress so elegantly.

Leading her into the huge dining room, Hadina pointed for Peyton to take a seat while she poured two glasses of wine from a corked bottle on the side table. Sliding into her allocated seat, Peyton took the glass Hadina extended to her and sipped the sweet alcohol.

"Where's Don?"

"He's coming. He was on a call with my sister," Hadina answered as she took a drink of her own wine. Her phone was on the table and Peyton could see the flood of notifications across the screen.

She nodded at the device. "Do you need to get those?"

The faintest hint of a smile crossed Hadina's lips before she steeled her face into a look of smooth composure once more. "I should, yes. But I rather think the nuisances can wait an hour until we eat."

Peyton hated to admit how impressed she was by that, and almost said so, but a familiar voice filled the room and she couldn't help bouncing from her seat and wrapping her arms around the man who had already given her so much. "Don!"

The old man laughed and patted her back, returning the embrace. "Hello, *cariño*, fancy seeing you here."

Peyton had tears in her eyes when she pulled away to smile at him. "It's really good to see you. I can't thank you enough for having me here."

He chuckled and took his seat at the head of the table, winking at Hadina. "*Hola, mija*. I take it you got Peyton settled in all right?"

Hadina smiled warmly at her father and poured him a glass of bourbon from the decanter on the table. "Quite. But I did have some work to attend to, so it's not like I had time to babysit."

Don 'tsked' at Hadina and gave her a sharp look while Peyton pretended to be very interested in her wine. "Don't be so rude."

Looking over at Peyton, Hadina fixed her with a fake grin, her eyes cold and narrowed. "Peyton knows I was just joking, *Papi*. Don't you, Peyton?"

Trying not to choke, Peyton quickly schooled her features into a polite smile and nodded, patting Don on the back of the hand. "We're adults. A friendly jibe here and there should be expected."

Hadina quirked a brow again and watched Peyton like she was an oddity to be studied. Even when the food was brought out and placed on the table, all three of them scooping greens onto their plates, Peyton could feel that cool gaze focused on her. She tried not to squirm under the woman's obvious scrutiny.

DINNER PASSED by in flashes of food, good wine, and hysterical laughing at Don's anecdotes of life. Hadina, poised and composed, even threw her head back and laughed more than once, her eyes lighting up when she looked at her father. It made food settle weirdly in Peyton's gut as she saw them together, their bond, and remembered that she had lost that with her own father years before. Grief could ruin anything, it seemed.

Don was busy telling Peyton about a moment of Hadina's childhood when she decided to paint all over one of her father's designer suits, Hadina blushing and trying to get him to be quiet before he embarrassed her, when a shrill ringtone broke them out of their bubble.

Hadina glanced down at her phone with disdain, her eyes running over the caller ID. Then she peered up again, her expression automatically returning to that same Ice Queen from earlier, and stood from her chair. "Sorry, I really need to take this."

"Really? Can't it wait until after we finish?" Don sighed.

Hadina pinned him with a glare, pursing her perfectly lined lips. "You know it can't wait. Don't ask me to ignore work."

Her heels clicked off the varnished wood flooring as she left through one of the side doors, yanking it closed behind her. Peyton noticed the way it opened a sliver on a light brush of wind, Hadina's voice carrying through the room. Muffled, but almost audible.

Swigging his bourbon, Don looked at Peyton apologetically and shrugged. "I love her work ethic, but it doesn't mean I don't miss uninterrupted dinners with my baby girl."

Peyton tucked a strand of her golden-colored hair behind her ear. "I'm sorry you have to miss that, Don."

She didn't miss the sadness in his eyes as he took another drink. It made her chest ache; it had been so long since she felt that sort of bond with her parents. Don missed having dinners with Hadina, and yet Peyton hadn't been home in years and still doubted her parents missed her in the slightest. Losing one part of a family was enough to detonate what was left, leaving memories and pain like rubble in its wake.

"So, tell me about your plan for going back to school. Now that you have a job and someplace to stay, it's a possibility, right?"

Peyton smiled sheepishly and folded in on herself a little, remembering just how much of a blubbering mess she had been when Don practically saved her. A job, somewhere to stay, someone to talk to—it was more than she expected.

"I would like to. But I'm going to save up for a while and see what I need to do to survive nursing school. I don't want to repeat history."

Don narrowed in on her with a cutting gaze that could rival his daughter's. "That sounds like an excuse. You'll always have a place here. And if you're worried about the money, I'm sure we could sort something out."

That made Peyton choke on the piece of chicken she was swallowing. She tried not to show her apprehension, at his offer for fear of offending him. Despite his blatant kindness, Peyton couldn't help but wonder why someone—a stranger—would give her such a proposition. It made a chill go down her back.

She battled with herself, unsure what to say. She would be naïve to believe there were no strings attached, and yet, Don seemed genuine. Perhaps she was being too mistrusting, unwilling to believe that someone would want to be kind to her.

Deciding that she was overthinking it, Peyton smiled and shook her head at Don. "That's so sweet, but you're already doing so much for me. I discussed a salary with Hadina and I'm really happy with it —in fact, it's probably way too generous."

As if summoned by the mention of her name, Hadina stormed into the dining room and grabbed her glass of wine from the table. She held her phone against her ear, closing her eyes as she gulped down the deep-red liquid before slamming the empty glass on the table and pouring herself another. Peyton watched the way the woman's throat bobbed as she swallowed, noting the little sigh of relief as she downed another glass.

"Everything okay?" Don inquired.

Hadina shook her head and grabbed the almost-empty bottle, storming out the way she came. She was muttering something about *fucking incompetent idiots* from the doorway when Peyton noticed Don watching her.

"Fucking get rid of him then. It's not difficult to do your job, right!" Hadina yelled down the phone. She leaned against the outer doorframe, the line of her profile the only thing visible. Peyton tried not to watch as Hadina ran a hand across her face, those pointed nails like talons.

"Peyton."

Don's voice brought Peyton out of her weird trance, which consisted of watching his terrifying yet beautiful daughter conduct business. Goosebumps covered Peyton's arms and she couldn't tell if it was from the fear of ever getting on Hadina's bad side, or the way she couldn't look away.

"Whatever is going on in that head, ignore it. You don't want to be dragged into chaos. I can see cogs turning behind those pretty eyes and I don't think it'll end in anything good."

Ignoring the pull in her stomach, Peyton forced herself to chuckle as she smiled at Don in what she hoped would appear to be a reassuring manner. "Sorry, I didn't mean to eavesdrop. She just sounded very stressed is all."

The look he gave her was knowing, almost concerned. "Just be careful. You can't unlearn things in this world. And believe me when I say there are many things you don't want to learn."

Peyton struggled to let her concern and intrigue subside. If there were secrets about the Adis family, she had to unearth them. She refused to work for people she couldn't trust.

"Things like what?" she found herself asking, unable to stop herself.

Don shook his head. "Nothing so exciting, believe me. Lawyers just have extremely high expectations and we find it hard when people let us down. Take it from me—I was the one who helped guide my daughter to where she is today."

Peyton had surmised as much. For Don to have raised someone as strong-willed and imposing as Hadina, she guessed he would have had an edge at some point in his life. She was just glad that he seemed a far cry from who she imagined he once was, someone like Hadina. One cold, scary boss was enough for Peyton to deal with at the moment.

Excusing himself, Don left Peyton sitting at the dining room table alone. The cold food on her plate was only one reason for the way her stomach now churned as she pondered the old man's cryptic words.

"... *get rid of him then.*"

Hadina's statement floated back to Peyton in a way that sent chills down her spine. Why was a lawyer making threats like that?

That question circled in her mind as she made her way to her new bedroom, where she collapsed onto the bed, feeling the alcohol buzz catch up to her. Don seemed so sweet and kind but Hadina was an enigma. Cold, poised, and scary. Two people, so different and yet of the same blood, now in her life permanently for the foreseeable future. As Peyton drifted off into a slumber once more, she continued to question her decisions.

What the fuck was she getting herself into? Who were these people? And why was her fear not enough of an incentive to make her run for the hills?

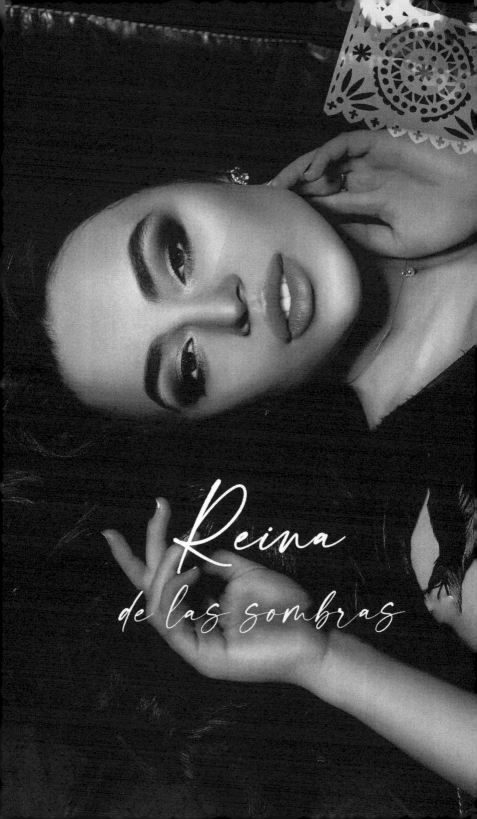

Reina
de las sombras

CHAPTER 4

HADINA

Hadina stormed into the office in her father's home and slammed the door behind her. She took a seat at the desk, remembering how it felt to stare at Peyton from this very chair only a few hours earlier, examining her newest employee and her sheepish demeanor. A bitter laugh was her way of acknowledging just how ridiculous it was that she, Hadina fucking Adis, was hiring the real-life equivalent of a Care Bear to look after her father. The girl did snap back at her, though, which gave her some extra points in Hadina's eyes. Not that she expected her to stick around for long. Nobody ever stuck around here.

She stared at the picture frames lining the walls, showing her lineage throughout the years. While she was second-generation Mexican-American and had been born in the States, Hadina always felt a strong sense of identity and kinship when she looked at these photos. Her *abuela* had passed when Hadina was only five, but she could still remember the comfort she found in one of the older woman's hugs or the smile she'd give Hadina when her *abuela*

25

snuck her extra *galletas* after she complained about still being hungry after dinner. Losing her *abuela* and mama as she grew up was one of the hardest things Hadina had ever had to deal with— which was saying a lot, considering she faced an onslaught of horrors at work.

"Did you get it done or are you really that incapable?" she barked down the phone.

"Ma'am, it's been dealt with as you requested. But..."

Hadina rolled her eyes and swigged from the bottle of wine. She instantly regretted not having grabbed an unopened one. "Spit it out, Harris."

"She won't come with us. One of the crew fucked up, and she managed to push her way past the guys when they were distracted. She saw everything."

Hadina swore under her breath, placing the phone momentarily on the desktop, rubbing at her temples, before picking the phone back up. "I'll be there in ten. Keep things under control until then or so help me, I will have you all buried six feet under before you even know it. Am I clear?"

The tremor in his voice was unmistakable as he whispered, "Yes, ma'am."

THE SLEEK BLACK town car seemed to take forever to reach its destination as Hadina tapped furiously into her phone, warning her employees to keep it together until she got there. The driver was silent, thankfully, but it just made Hadina wish she hadn't had that wine with dinner, or afterwards. She couldn't help but think how much quicker she could have gotten to the warehouse if she had taken her Audi R8.

By the time they pulled up outside the half-demolished building, Hadina was practically shaking—from rage or anticipation, she couldn't really tell. There was some twisted part of her that enjoyed this, took pleasure in the danger of the lifestyle.

Why deny it when she couldn't hide from it?

She sent the driver away, noting the familiar blacked-out SUVs that were given to all of her team. She'd make one of them drop her off when she was done here. Even if some small part of her wanted to go back to her father's and learn more about the too-cheery Miss Dimitra.

As she stormed her way inside the building, thunder clapped in the darkened clouds like some higher power knew what was coming. Hadina once again thought of Peyton. That sunshine disposition that didn't quite match the sadness swirling in Peyton's eyes or the fire whenever she bit back at Hadina. It puzzled her how Peyton had managed to get so far under her father's skin so quickly. What was it about this damn girl that had him hooked, treating her like his new pet project? Old age and boredom didn't seem like enough of a reason for her father to be swept up and ready to play savior to a stranger. She would have to find out *exactly* what the deal was with Miss Dimitra.

Harris met Hadina as she began the descent to the lower levels, untouched by the crumbling walls and asbestos. She knew what horrors she was about to see—it was normally at her own hands—but she still had to steel herself, taking a steadying breath before she nodded for her second to pull the iron doors open.

The stench of piss and shit hit Hadina's senses immediately, pricking her eyes and burning her nostrils. She blinked a few times before stepping inside, those brutal smells almost completely replaced by the familiar metallic scent of blood. Everywhere she looked, blood was splattered across the graffiti-painted walls, pooling around bodies on the floors or staining the discolored mattresses that were placed against the edges of the room.

Hadina looked at her second, who pointed to the far corner, gesturing to the small frame folded into itself. Giving a silent command, she watched as her team silently fell back, only a few remaining at the entrance should she need them. Not that she would. She had been here a thousand times and didn't need anyone to back her up.

Approaching slowly, carefully, Hadina reached the small figure and knelt before her. "Amelia?"

The girl whimpered, raising her head slightly from her crossed arms at the softness in Hadina's voice. It was something Hadina had worked on over the years—removing that iciness and transforming her tone into something sweeter, kinder... something she didn't think was quite possible. Not after everything she had seen.

The girl, Amelia, was dressed in a thin cotton nightshirt, covered in dirt and secretion. Her hair hung in long, matted clumps like a forgotten doll's, hiding half of her face, though Hadina could still make out the distinct myriad of blue and purple bruising on her delicate cheekbones. The icy blue of her eyes was haunting and contrasted harshly with the dirt smeared across her face. Scratch marks and bruises the shape of fingers littered her placid skin and Hadina could feel that fire building inside her chest, the need to destroy the bastard who had made someone suffer in such a way.

"Amelia, my name is Hadina but you can call me Hadi. I'm here to help you."

Amelia's eyes widened as Hadina shrugged out of her coat and placed it on the mattress between them. She nodded for the girl to take it, watching as she reached out reluctantly and wrapped it around herself. Her hands were shaking, her nails coated in blood and muck. Hadina had to curl her own fingers into her palms to channel her anger, trying not to scare the poor girl after what she must have been through.

No, Hadina was here to help her. Even if she wasn't the one to pull the trigger, the man responsible had been dealt with on her orders. Now it was time to follow through with the next steps.

Sitting before the girl with crossed legs, Hadina gestured to the men standing at the doors. "I know those guys scared you earlier and I'm really, really sorry that you had to see what you did. But I need you to know that you can trust me. We know what happened to you, what happened to the others, and I want to help you. That's why my men over there hurt Masters. That's who was keeping you here, right?"

The girl whimpered again, a doe stuck in a lion's sight line. But another small encouraging smile had her nodding her head in response. That was all the confirmation Hadina needed.

"Masters isn't going to hurt you again, Amelia. I can take you somewhere safe, a place where you'll never be hurt again. There will be more people like you—and people who can help you understand what happened. Would you like to come with me?"

Amelia studied Hadina with those piercing, damaged eyes. Her gaze darted over to Bram and Tony, who stood with their tattooed arms crossed, watching everything that transpired. Hadina noticed the way the girl's lip wobbled and tears surfaced as she took in her surroundings, likely recalling what she'd been subjected to. All the girls looked around like that, as though they had to commit it to memory before leaving. Hadina supposed it was their way of recognizing trauma before saying goodbye to it.

"Okay," Amelia whispered, barely audible. Hadina, however, heard her as if she were shouting.

Careful not to spook the girl, Hadina stood ever so slowly and extended her hand. She would never admit it to anyone, but tears formed in her eyes as she felt that small palm slip into hers. "Let's get you somewhere safe, Amelia."

"I'm scared."

Hadina had done this so many times before and each time she believed her heart was incapable of breaking all over again. But Amelia's whispered words confirmed what Hadina already knew—her heart would continue to break. Or maybe it was permanently broken, shards of what used to be there now cutting into whatever remained inside her. She was cold and could be cruel, but she would never be like Masters, and she clung to that.

"I know, *mi niña*. But I'll make sure you never have to be scared again. You're safe with me."

THE SCALDING WATER of her shower wasn't enough to take away the grimy feeling that coated Hadina's body. She scrubbed furiously, lathering up the soap and repeating the process over and over, until her skin was raw and burned. Hadina slid down the wall of her shower, hanging her head under the torrent of water, and finally let her racking sobs free. Gripping her chest, she let her tears wash away with the soapy suds, taking her secrets and pain with them.

Tentadora

CHAPTER 5

PEYTON

THE FIRST WEEK OF WORK PASSED IN A BLUR FOR PEYTON. HER ROUTINE WAS the same each day, drinking coffee with Don and listening to him tell stories about his younger years. His parents had immigrated from Mexico to the States when he was ten, building themselves a new life. He told Peyton how they had struggled for a while but the couple worked hard to provide him with the best life possible, even saving up enough to help put Don through college.

"Now, I'm not saying we were rich," the elderly man said with a half smile. "But we were finally comfortable by the time I went to law school. I had to take out so many student loans, but becoming a lawyer and starting Adis & Co. allowed me to pay my parents back for everything they did for me and I'll always be grateful for that. Not everyone in my family had that opportunity."

It was weird for her to not always be doing something but Don assured her that she wasn't needed for anything except companion-ship and maybe accompanying him to hospital appointments if needed. Prior to her arrival, Peyton had assumed that perhaps Don needed more assistance than he actually did, not that she was complaining. It was nice to feel at ease for once, not having to constantly worry about the next deadline or how she was going to pay for all her expenses.

It was on her fourth day at the residence that Don walked her through his gardens in the backyard. There were so many different types of flowers, at various stages of bloom, creating a sea of multi-colored petals. Peyton smiled and asked Don to help teach her more about his gardening, hoping that it would be an engaging task for them both and also provide her with something to do when Don was napping or didn't need her company.

She'd found it relaxing as she knelt on the grass and busied her hands with digging and weeding. Don praised her, calling her a natural. She lit up at the words, warmth and pride spreading through her veins. Her dad had never complimented her, or even attempted to spend any time with her.

Peyton felt guilty after that bitter thought crept into the crevices of her mind, threatening to blossom into something angry and resentful. She knew her parents had struggled with her, never quite able to understand their daughter's mind or make a true connection. It wasn't her father's fault that he didn't know how to reach her, to form a bond, and she certainly hadn't made it easy on them. Peyton had struggled to try to do the same in return, despite it being what she yearned for most. She found her mother cold and her father distant, even when she tried to bridge the gap of silence between them. It left her feeling lonelier than ever, especially after the loss of her sister.

Leaving her hometown in search of her future was the first time that Peyton had felt free. Now, connecting with Don had helped her find a little part of herself that she'd long forgotten. The little girl searching for a parent's love was what made Peyton's eyes water with unshed tears every time Don congratulated her on the simplest of tasks.

Sweeping the bangs out of her eyes while making a mental note to find a local salon to get her hair trimmed, Peyton poured herself a cup of pomegranate and cranberry tea and took a seat on one of the sleek black stools at the kitchen island. She lifted the steaming cup and inhaled the sweet scent. The kitchen was always fully stocked, with so many different types of tea and coffee that it took her almost three days of constant caffeine drinking to find something that she really enjoyed.

It was already eight thirty in the morning without any sign of Don, which meant he was taking advantage of his Saturday by getting an extra hour or two of sleep. Honestly, Peyton couldn't really blame him. She used to love sleeping in as a teenager but sleep for her was now plagued by nightmares, making her an early riser whether she wanted to be or not.

Even when sleep beckoned her, Peyton struggled to allow herself to be pulled into slumber. She knew that her dreams quickly turned to those night terrors, soaking her memories in blood and tears.

It was always when she fell asleep thinking of her sister that Peyton knew she would be tormented for hours, unless she was able to break free of the grip those nightmares held on her. She would wake on a gasp, covered in sweat, rubbing at her arms as though it would get rid of the gore in her mind. Even as life moved on around her, Peyton's subconscious frequently chose to remind her of Melina's lifeless body and the way her blood soaked into Peyton's skin like tattoos only she could see.

That was why she found it easier to limit the time she spent unconscious—she didn't think she could call it sleep. If her blood had to be made up of fifty percent caffeine, she was willing to pay that price.

The gray marble island faced the patio doors leading to the backyard, and it was one of Peyton's absolute favorite places in the house. The yard stretched on forever, leading to a small cottage right at the edge of the property. Peyton had yet to venture out to see it, but every morning, she sat at the island with her steaming cup and felt like she was part of some secret. She stared at the flowers, the fruitful trees, and the cottage and wondered how she had gotten so lucky. Her life had taken a surreal turn, and she wondered if it was all part of some elaborate daydream. She pinched her skin to see if it was real, smiling at the red welt that appeared.

"Good morning, Miss Dimitra."

Peyton jumped at the voice behind her, spilling tea across the countertop. She quickly hopped off the stool and grabbed a paper towel to mop up the mess.

"Morning, Hadina," she said brightly, saluting her boss with two fingers. Peyton cringed internally at herself, which was only made worse when Hadina stared at her as though she were stupid.

After leaving the dinner table on that first night, Hadina hadn't made another appearance. Don said it was typical for his daughter to rush off for work and spend days at a time at her own place, but Peyton hadn't been able to shake the weird feeling she had after eavesdropping on that conversation between Hadina and her employee. The anger and command in her voice were terrifying— and perhaps a little bit thrilling—but Peyton knew that was just some screwed-up part of her, longing for excitement.

"Where's my father?" Hadina's voice was a cool breeze against Peyton's skin, even if she was standing at the opposite end of the kitchen.

Once Peyton had cleaned the spilled tea and put the towel in the trash, she offered Hadina a slight smile. "Still in bed. I think he's enjoying the Saturday sleeps, haha."

The corner of Hadina's mouth twitched as though she wanted to smile, and Peyton considered it a victory. As Hadina poured herself a cup of freshly brewed coffee, Peyton couldn't help but stare in awe at the flawless outfit the other woman was wearing.

The black wrap dress hung perfectly on her figure, stopping short of her knees and giving everyone a view of her long legs. Hadina had left a few buttons undone at the breasts, the barest hint of cleavage on display. Then matched the blouse with a pair of leather ankle boots and a long black coat. If Peyton ever dared to wear something like that, everyone would think she was going to a funeral—but on Hadina? It just oozed badass boss lady. Looking down at her own plaid pencil skirt and maroon turtleneck, Peyton suddenly felt very insecure being in the same room as her employer.

Hadina took a long drink from her mug. "Do you two have any plans for today?"

Peyton blinked once. Twice. Was Hadina Adis trying to make small talk?

"I think Don mentioned something about wanting to work on the garden? I'm not sure, though. We'll see if that's still his plan when he wakes up."

Nodding, Hadina gulped down the rest of her coffee, poured herself another one, and tapped her fingertips against the counter. "Well, I'll be here most of the day, so if I'm needed, I'll be in the office. Please tell my dad I'm here when he gets up. Have a pleasant day, Miss Dimitra."

Peyton opened her mouth to reply but Hadina sauntered past, leaving her wide-eyed and open-mouthed in her wake.

What the fuck was happening?

Reina
de las sombras

CHAPTER 6

HADINA

Hadina shrugged off her jacket and collapsed into the chair, burying her head in her hands on the desk. *Have a pleasant day, Miss Dimitra.* Was she kidding? Small talk wasn't her forte, and apparently she just sounded like a cold bitch even when she tried.

Not that she minded the icy persona she had adopted since taking over Adis & Co.—that was how you gained and kept the respect of your employees. But the earful she had gotten from her father after that absolutely disastrous dinner the previous week had made her promise to at least try not to be an ass to Peyton. She couldn't fathom why he was so bothered or concerned with Peyton's feelings, but she would do as he asked anyway.

However, she had to admit that annoying little ball of happiness had almost made her blush when her newest employee's eyes raked over her body. It was strange for anyone to look at Hadina with anything but fear or contempt, and she found that she didn't hate it. Not that a glance at an outfit meant anything—it couldn't. Hadina had rules and she was going to follow them.

A normal life wasn't something she thought about often, but sometimes it crossed her mind. She knew it was a waste of time, imagining her life being anything other than what it was, but the daydreams caught her off guard on occasion. In another life, she would settle down with a partner, work a boring nine-to-five job, and discuss the possibility of children. Hadina didn't think any of that was even what she *wanted*, yet she pictured it all the same. It was easier for her to imagine a preconceived happily-ever-after carved by memories of childhood fairy tales, rather than try to envisage a future based in reality.

Nonetheless, Hadina knew that daydreams were just that—a fantasy designed to tempt her into abandoning her path. She had chosen to be who she was, and nothing would stand in her way of continuing the hidden legacy of Adis & Co.

Personal relationships in her line of work were doomed from the beginning, and she wasn't going to get sucked in by fairy-tale thoughts and dreams of a better life. She knew what she signed up for when she agreed to lead the company, and she would never allow herself to regret the work, the importance of what she and her team were doing.

"Get it together, Hadina," she groaned at herself.

Gulping down some more coffee, Hadina walked over to the bookcases lining the walls, removing two of the larger tomes. Tucked behind them was a thin folder concealing a list of names. She brought it over to the desk and opened it up with a sigh.

~~Jeffrey Masters~~

She scored through the tenth name on the list, a single line to acknowledge what she had done—what she had to do. Nobody knew about the physical list. Nobody would understand why she needed to keep it. A way to hold herself accountable, to always remember. Hadina never wanted to lose herself completely, and it was the only way that allowed her to keep those demons at bay.

A list of the scum on Adis's radar.

A list of her victims.

Indirectly or not, the kill orders were signed off by Hadina. Those deaths, how ever well deserved, were her sins to bear. Ten black marks on her soul in exchange for the safety of so many innocent people. It was worth it. She knew it was worth it.

Crossing a name off her list was one of the few times Hadina ever allowed herself to cry, not for the sinner, but the victims. Sometimes she didn't make it in time, and sometimes the survivors believed themselves broken beyond repair. It hurt her soul to know that there were people out there she couldn't and had failed to save. It was for *that* reason that Hadina had to wipe away the tears as she crossed out Jeffrey Masters's name from her file.

Steeling herself and taking a steadying breath, Hadina washed away her emotions and looked at the next name in front of her. Then she quickly dialed a number and returned the folder to its spot on the shelves while the phone rang in her ear.

"Yes, boss?"

"Give me updates on the movements of Kierney and Jacobson. Let's get these bastards."

Tentadora

CHAPTER 7

PEYTON

PEYTON DIDN'T CONSIDER THAT SHE WOULD BE THROWN INTO A WHOLE NEW family dynamic when she accepted her job. As she sat at the dining table and munched on a grilled cheese sandwich, watching as the melted Havarti and cheddar cheese mix oozed onto her plate, she listened to Don chatter idly about the family dinner he was hosting later in the evening. She assumed she wasn't supposed to be part of it, but Don had announced at breakfast that she was expected to attend.

While she had grown accustomed to the beautiful but stern-faced Hadina being around the house, a silent presence that she found weirdly comforting, Peyton had yet to meet Don's other two daughters. From what she could infer, Zellie and Piper were almost as successful as Hadina, which really didn't help lessen the knot of anxiety in her stomach.

"I'm really looking forward to my daughters meeting you, Peyton. You've already been such a huge support for me and I know they're going to love you!"

She chewed nervously on her lip, the sight of the melting cheese souring her stomach. "What are they like?"

Don smiled, his pride in his daughters clear for Peyton to see. It was hard for her to imagine either of her parents looking prideful as they spoke about her—they barely even smiled when they spoke *to* her. "Zellie is a force to be reckoned with. She is driven and extremely fierce, something she shares with Hadi, even if neither of them will admit it. She was always the tough one growing up. I think she felt like she had to take charge."

Pouring herself another cup of coffee and topping up Don's mug, Peyton listened intently. She was nervous to meet the other Adis siblings and she would take all the information she could get if it would help her prepare for the dinner. Making an awkward fool of herself had become her new normal with Hadina, but Peyton was loath to embarrass herself in front of Zellie or Piper.

"What about Piper?"

"Ah, my darling little angel. Piper is a total sweetheart and so unlike her sisters," Don said with a smirk, shaking his head slightly as he added, "She's forever arguing with her siblings about their attitudes. The girl is the kindest one of us all. She's still fearless and an incredible asset to the company—Hadina and Zellie wouldn't have had it any other way, of course—but she really is an angel. You actually remind me of her."

"Oh, Don," Peyton said, trying not to show how emotional the comparison made her. "That's so sweet. Thank you."

Leaving her to her lunch, Don went to read in his office while Peyton sat alone in the dining room with her head spinning. It wasn't just the nerves of meeting new people, but rather the change it brought with it. Don's words were sweet, but Peyton wasn't entirely convinced that Hadina's sisters would welcome her into their family. She knew that she was a paid employee, and she was fine with that, but it was difficult enough with Hadina, never mind her siblings too.

Hadina was a cruel mystery that Peyton couldn't fathom. No matter how hard she tried, she struggled to break through the woman's steely exterior. It was doubly frustrating when she was hot as hell, creating a whole new level of confusion that Peyton wasn't eager to understand.

She dropped her grilled cheese back onto her plate with a sigh. After throwing the remainder of the sandwich in the trash, she rinsed her plate and made her way out to the garden. Don had planted so many different types of flowers across the grounds, the blossoming buds creating a cascade of bright colors that led to a peaceful sitting area situated beneath an oak gazebo. Four hand-crafted chairs were positioned around a bricked fire pit, gray blankets slung across the backs of each one. Peyton had stumbled upon it on her first exploration of the grounds and, after checking it was all right with Don, found herself visiting the spot when she needed a moment to breathe.

She was surprised to find someone else sitting there when she approached, her heart rate already spiking at the idea of her peaceful moment being disturbed. Peyton's anxiety was only heightened by the fact that the visitor perched in one of the seats was Hadina.

"Hadina, are you okay?"

Breaking from her trance, Hadina blinked and shook her head slightly. "Miss Dimitri. Hello."

Peyton claimed the chair opposite her boss, pulling the blanket around her shoulders even though it wasn't cold. She waited for Hadina to say more, or to answer her question. While Hadina still looked powerful as hell—the deep V of her blouse causing Peyton's heart rate to spike tremendously—it seemed as though the woman was not quite herself. Her hair hung loose around her shoulders, a strand tucked behind her right ear, which was incongruous with her character.

"You didn't answer my question."

Hadina furrowed her sculpted brows. "Hm?"

"I asked if you were okay. You don't seem like your usual self."

Hadina scoffed, sitting back in her chair. "And you know me well enough to make assumptions like that?"

"Now that seems much more like the Hadina Adis I've come to know." Peyton cursed herself for being unable to stop talking. She hated awkward silences and did whatever she could to ensure that they didn't happen often; but Hadina didn't seem like the type of person who would appreciate that.

"Maybe you're right," Hadina said with a sigh while running a slender hand through her hair. It made Peyton uneasy to see Hadina so agitated. "There's no need for concern, though. I'm just over-thinking this family dinner."

"You're not looking forward to seeing your sisters?"

Hadina shook her head. She kicked off her heels and propped her feet up on the edge of the fire pit. "My relationship with my family is complicated and slightly strained."

"We should have a fucked-up family club or something then," Peyton said with a sardonic laugh. "Complicated family matters are something I'm well acquainted with."

Her surprise admission caused Hadina to pause, her gaze boring into Peyton's like she was trying to see exactly what she was talking about. Peyton didn't like to discuss her family, the memories too painful for her to manage most of the time. But somehow, sitting under a garden gazebo with Hadina Adis made her want to tell her life story to the relative stranger before her.

"My sister died a few years ago and everything went kind of crazy after that. We were puzzle pieces trying to fit together, only each of us was from a different box. No matter how hard we tried, our grief seemed to separate us instead of bringing us together."

Hadina gave Peyton a weighted look, pursing her lips. "I'm sorry you lost your sister, Peyton."

Peyton's eyes shot up. Hadina had used her name, and the

sincerity of her words brought tears to Peyton's eyes but she blinked them away, forcing a smile onto her face. "I appreciate that. Now, tell me why you aren't looking forward to this evening."

"Put it this way: if you think I'm a cold bitch, you haven't met Zellie."

CHAPTER 8

HADINA

HADINA KNEW IT WAS WRONG TO BE SO RESENTFUL TOWARDS HER SISTER, BUT she truly couldn't help it. Zellie was a cold, calculated asshole. All her life, Hadina had wished to be like her elder sibling, to find a companionship with her kin, but Zellie had never allowed it. She made sure to keep Hadina at arm's length, lest she get too close and figure her out.

The irony wasn't missed by Hadina as she thought about her sister's fears. Zellie had wanted to rule Adis & Co. in whatever way she saw fit, and most definitely without the intervention of their father. Her truth was quickly made clear when Zellie's plans unfolded, leaving Hadina and their father to find out about what Zellie really wanted to do. After all, the only thing Zellie craved more than power was money, and she had planned to corrupt the family business to get her fill of both.

Uncovering that betrayal was the nail in the coffin for Hadina. The little girl inside who so desperately wanted her sister's approval disappeared in that instant, killing any youthful naivety she had left. She knew Zellie was ruthless, but she thought both her sisters respected their father enough to never betray the family. It was how she ended up in charge of the business, leaving her big sister seething.

It had broken their mother's heart that they weren't close, always arguing and bickering over something or other. *"La familia should always stick together!"* she would say, throwing her arms up in the air in frustration. Then she would storm off, muttering in Spanish so that not even Hadina could understand.

Now, as they sat around the dining table with fake smiles plastered on their faces, Hadina had to resist the urge to bitch-slap her sister for the heartache she had caused them all. She couldn't understand how her father had forgiven Zellie so easily, welcoming her back into the family fold. It had pissed everyone off when Hadina had refused to rehire Zellie within the family company, though Hadina had no regrets over her decision. Five years had passed and Hadina was no closer to forgiving Zelina than she was when it happened.

"It's really nice to meet you, Peyton!" Piper sing-songed, clasping Peyton's hand in her own.

Peyton smiled and nodded politely, but Hadina noticed the way she carefully extracted her hand without Piper noticing. There was more to Miss Dimitra than what she presented on the surface, and Hadina *ached* to discover every little secret she had. She'd always loved a tricky puzzle, and Peyton seemed like just that.

Hadina looked at her sisters, offering Piper a small smile. Pip had opted to leave her hair down, the chestnut-brown curls bouncing down her back. Her features were soft, big brown eyes and pouty lips, which had always made her look young and innocent her entire life. It was a stark contrast from Hadina's sharp angles and Zellie's fierceness.

Zellie swiped a strand of her hair from her face, though the black strand bounced back into place on her cheek. She had gotten it cut over the last month, replacing her long locks with an above-the-shoulder feathered bob that framed her face. She had almond-shaped eyes like their father and dark brows that were shaped in a way that made her look permanently angry—which she was.

The three of them looked like their parents in their own way and shared slight similarities, but they were also incredibly different. Hadina was harsh, Zellie fierce, and Piper soft—much like their personalities.

Piper clapped her hands, beaming from ear to ear. "I'm so excited to see everyone. It feels like *forever* since we last had dinner."

"We have dinner every month, Piper. Don't be so dramatic," Zellie snapped, her perfect persona slipping.

She would try her best to make Peyton think she was the prodigal daughter, but Zellie couldn't act to save herself. Her mask would soon be shed to show the vicious bitch she was underneath. She only hoped that Peyton didn't get herself caught in the crossfire.

Hadina could never bear to see her little sister sad, so she glared at Zellie and offered Piper the truest smile she could manage under the tense circumstances. "Ignore her. It's good to see you, Pip. Did you get up to any mischief this week?"

Piper rolled her eyes. It was a running joke within the family that Piper was too innocent, effectively the odd one out in their morally gray family. She had chosen to stray from the career paths of her sisters, choosing instead to become an art dealer. Hadina had often teased that there were plenty of ways to make that into a very lucrative criminal empire, but Piper always scolded her and told Hadina that one of the three had to remain good and lawful.

"Yes, I killed a man for telling me that Picasso was the greatest artist to have ever lived. Like, hello, have you ever *seen* one of Van Gogh's masterpieces?"

Hadina couldn't help but smile as Peyton let out a loud laugh, throwing a hand over her mouth and nose as a snort escaped. Piper sat up a little straighter, looking at Peyton like she had just found her new best friend. Something stirred in Hadina and she resisted the urge to pull Peyton closer to her side while warning her sisters away from her.

The sentimentality and possessiveness of her thoughts made her sick. She shook her head and took a large gulp of her wine, choosing to tune out the conversation rather than letting her newfound emotions take over. She didn't know what was wrong with her, but Hadina swore to bury whatever she was feeling.

When dinner was served, Hadina found herself shoveling food into her mouth to avoid speaking. She didn't cook very often now but she suddenly ached to be in the kitchen, cooking menudo with her mother over the stove while they sang along to Selena. Taking a bite out of the steak in front of her, Hadina had to swallow down a sigh. Family dinner each month always made her horribly nostalgic, grief-stricken, and just plain grumpy.

She could see her father giving her a warning look out of the corner of her eye, but she couldn't make herself care. If he wanted her to be on her best behavior, he was effectively asking her to keep quiet, and that was precisely what she was doing.

Every so often, Peyton glanced at Hadina, offering small smiles and concerned looks. It pissed Hadina off. She had been too open with Miss Dimitra in the garden earlier, lowering a piece of the barrier between them that she wanted kept firmly in place. Peyton was no different from anyone else, which meant Hadina had to keep her distance. But something about that insufferable ray of sunshine kept her talking every *fucking* time.

"Cat got your tongue, Hadina?" Zellie purred, turning that predatory smile on her sister.

Hadina grinned, making sure to show all her teeth. "Sorry, I was just waiting for you to say something interesting enough to require my attention."

At that moment, their father smacked his hands down on the

table, causing the cutlery to clatter against the plates. Hadina winced, looking between her father's angry gaze and Peyton's apprehensive expression.

"Could you all pretend that I raised you with a goddamn ounce of decorum and manners please? You aren't exactly showing our guest any consideration."

Zellie, never one for staying quiet while being lectured, scoffed. "She's not exactly a guest, Papi. You hired her—*solo es una simple sirvienta.*"

The room went eerily quiet as Zellie's words sank in. Peyton stared down in front of her, her fingers playing with a loose thread on the tablecloth. Hadina looked to her father, waiting for him to say something, but he just shook his head. Hadina sighed, resigned that she would have to be the one to call Zellie on her bullshit once again.

"*Eres una pinche perra maleducada!* Apologize to Peyton, Zelina." Hadina's voice brooked no argument, but Zellie laughed in response.

"Oh, am I supposed to be intimidated by your use of my proper name? You don't scare me, *hermanita.* Besides," Zellie continued, "I'm only stating facts. She's not family or a guest—she's just some random girl *Papi* hired to keep him company."

Hadina growled, standing and pushing her seat back. She felt Peyton's eyes on her, but she couldn't make herself look at her. *This wasn't about Peyton,* Hadina told herself, *but rather Zellie's lack of respect in their family home.* That was *all* it was about.

"Get the fuck out," Hadina said, her voice low and deadly calm. "Either apologize to our *guest,* or leave. Those are your only two options."

"*Niñas, por favor—*" Their father tried to interject but was cut off by Zellie pushing to her feet and facing off with Hadina.

"This isn't your house, Hadina. You don't get to tell me what to do."

Hadina looked to her father, imploring him to do something. "*Papi,* please."

53

She tipped her head slightly towards Peyton, who was sitting motionless and silent, an innocent party in the game of power between the Adis sisters. It made Hadina a little sad that someone else had been dragged into their chaotic mess, not that she would admit it to anyone.

"Perhaps your sister is right, Zellie," their father said, sounding defeated. "Maybe you should leave until you calm down. Peyton here doesn't deserve the rudeness you've displayed."

"*Patética!*" Zellie spat. "*Papi*, one of these days you're going to grow a spine and stop letting Hadina run your life."

It caught everyone off guard when Piper let out a frustrated scream, mimicking what she used to do as a child to stop her big sisters from bickering. If the air in the room weren't so tense, Hadina was sure she would have burst out laughing.

"Enough already! This was supposed to be a family dinner, a chance for us to meet Peyton, and yet it turned into a whose-dick-is-bigger contest. I am *so sick* of your power-grabbing bullshit. Why can't you just get along for once?"

The sadness in Piper's voice made Hadina's heart ache. For all the evil she saw and did, there would always be a part of her that remained pure and filled with love, a part that was reserved for the people closest to her. She only ever wanted to protect and provide for Piper, help guide her in the world and stop anyone from hurting her. It broke her to know she was one of the people causing her sister pain.

"Piper, I—"

Piper shook her head, holding her hand up to stop Zellie from continuing. "Just stop, Z. Please, just go."

Zellie looked down at Piper with a warmth she reserved for her baby sister. The only time Zellie felt guilt over her actions was if they upset Piper. She looked like she wanted to say something but instead nodded, throwing one last glare at Hadina over her shoulder before storming from the room. Everyone held their breaths until they heard the front door slam, confirming Zellie's exit.

"Well, that was awkward," Peyton said matter-of-factly, right before she burst into tears where she sat.

Hadina was going to murder her big sister.

Tentadora

CHAPTER 9

PEYTON

SHE LET OUT A STRANGLED LAUGH AS A TORRENT OF TEARS BROKE FREE. It was stupid to cry over something a stranger said to her, but it was the conviction in Zellie's voice that hit Peyton so hard. She didn't even know the Adis sibling, and yet this woman was dismissing her like she was nothing. It was beyond frustrating.

"Peyton, I am so sorry," Don apologized, reaching out to take her hand in his. She could see the sadness in his eyes, which made her feel guilty—seeing as it was Zellie's comments about *her* that caused all the issues.

"It's okay! I don't even know why I'm crying." Peyton sniffled, wiping her eyes with her napkin. "I really am fine."

Piper got up from her chair, floated around to sit beside Peyton, and pulled her into a hug. "You don't need to be brave for us, love. We know how hard Zellie can be to deal with."

Shaking her head, Peyton offered Piper a shy smile. "It's fine. It happened and we can move on now. She wasn't wrong, anyway."

Hadina stepped forward, reaching out a hand to touch Peyton's shoulder before thinking better of it. "She *was* wrong, Miss Dimitra. Zelina has made many mistakes and is most definitely *not* the person to decide who is important in this family. Don't take her words to heart."

Had Hadina Adis really just implied that Peyton *was* important to the family?

Peyton tried not to react, in case it made her boss retreat farther into her shell, but it made her chest beat a little faster all the same.

"Thank you," Peyton whispered, looking between the three Adis family members. She hoped her eyes conveyed just how grateful she was. Unsure what to do next, she shrank back in her chair and wrapped her cardigan tighter around her stomach. She was grateful when Hadina cleared her throat, dragging attention from her.

"If you'll excuse me, I think I'll attend some business now that this dinner is over. Piper, would you mind coming with me so that we may discuss something?"

Piper nodded and the sisters sauntered from the room, confidence exuded in every step. Once they were gone, Peyton slumped in her seat and sighed, tilting her head to peek at Don. He looked so frustrated, which broke her heart. He didn't deserve to be dealing with so much drama.

"Don't give me those sad eyes," he said, shaking his head. "This wasn't the first argument they had and it won't be the last. It's a parent's duty to put up with their children acting like fools."

She was unable to hold in her laugh, some of her anxiety peeling away in the process. "Don…"

The old man chuckled and stood, placing his hand on Peyton's shoulder. "I'm right and you can't convince me otherwise. Fools, I tell you. Now, I think I'm going to go and have a cup of coffee in the garden. I could do with some silence." He reached out a hand to pick up his dinner plate, but Peyton took it from his grasp. "Let me deal with this. Go enjoy your relaxation!"

Scraping the leftovers onto one plate and piling up the rest, Peyton headed into the kitchen. She debated on filling the dishwasher but sentimentality called to her. Whenever she was little and her parents got into an argument, she'd always find her mom washing the dishes by hand in the kitchen. She'd often ask her mother why she was giving herself double the work and Peyton would receive the same response: *it gives me time to think.*

While Peyton wasn't sure she wanted to think about the events of the night, she found herself filling the sink with soapy water and getting to work on the tableware.

It took her far longer than she would have wanted, but Peyton breathed a sigh of relief once the last fork was polished and placed back into the drawer. She figured a bath before bed would soothe both her body and mind, but the light in Hadina's office caught her eye. She assumed that Hadina would have left after speaking with Piper, but Peyton could still hear voices coming from inside. She didn't mean to eavesdrop. It was absolutely accidental when she crept forward and stood outside the office door, thankful they had left it ajar.

"Hadina, you haven't thought this through. You absolutely never go against your own protocols. What's wrong?"

Peyton heard Hadina scoff and slam a drawer shut. "Apart from our royal bitch of a sister? Or the obscene amount of work I have to do, since Zellie can't be trusted and you refuse to be part of the business?"

Piper sighed and Peyton was almost sure she heard her drop into the seat in front of Hadina's desk. "You know that's not fair. I'm not... like you and Zellie. I can't turn it on and off. Besides, that's not the problem anyway. Tell me what's really wrong."

"Pip, I love you, but please stop. I'm not going to tell you every thought I have in my brain. I've asked you to do this *one* thing. Please tell me you'll do it."

"Fine," Piper said, sounding defeated. "But I'm not involved after this. I'll set up a meeting at the gallery so he doesn't suspect anything, but you better make sure my place is spotless when you're done."

"Pfft, I have people for that," Hadina countered.

"I'll call him now."

Hearing Piper move closer to the door—her steps noticeably lighter and less imposing than her sister's—Peyton cursed under her breath and frantically looked around for somewhere to hide. She settled for taking a few steps back, hoping it would appear as though she was only just now approaching the door. However, the look Piper gave her when their eyes connected told Peyton her ruse hadn't been all that convincing.

"Sister, you have a visitor," Piper announced through the open door, winking at Peyton as she passed.

"Dear Lord, *why?*" Peyton whispered.

Straightening her back and steeling herself for whatever mood Hadina was in, Peyton hoped she appeared confident as she entered the room. She was almost sure she would see Hadina sitting behind the desk, paperwork scattered in front of her. She most definitely didn't expect to see Hadina slipping a switchblade into her boot before picking up a gun and emptying a box of bullets onto the desk to fill it.

"What the fuck?" Hadina looked up, her nostrils flaring as she saw her onlooker was Peyton and not Don. Still, she didn't stop her task, loading bullets into the clip. She held Peyton's gaze as she loaded the clip and slapped it into the handle before pulling back the slide to chamber a round.

Peyton gulped, both intimidated and—confusingly—a little turned on by the way Hadina handled the gun, confident and dominating.

"You don't need to be here right now, Miss Dimitra."

Peyton let out a shaky breath, finding that her feet were stuck in place. "Why–what–Hadina, what the fuck?"

Hadina smiled. It was cold, uninviting, and made Peyton shiver. "It's none of your concern."

"You have a fucking arsenal in the same house where I work and sleep! How is that not my concern?"

Rolling her eyes, Hadina slipped the gun into the back of her pants like it was something she did regularly. Peyton's eyes widened at the thought. Fear ran through her veins like ice, keeping her frozen to the spot in the same room as someone who clearly knew how to use a weapon. Or confidently load one, at least.

"If you think this is an arsenal, you'd hate to see my apartment," Hadina quipped.

"Please don't joke about that," Peyton whispered.

Hadina tilted her head, looking at Peyton quizzically. "Who says I'm joking?"

Peyton glanced at the ceiling, inhaling deeply. "Lord, give me strength."

"I'm not going to hurt you, Peyton," Hadina stated, walking around the desk and standing in front of her. "You don't need to pray to a higher power for protection."

"Hadina, please, tell me what's going on. Why do you have a gun? What's happening? I don't feel comfortable being in the same house as deadly weapons."

Hadina shook her head. "As I said before, it is none of your concern. You know your job description, which is *all* that is required of you."

Peyton, unable to control her emotions any longer, pushed forward to close the gap between them. Her fear turned to anger as she tried to comprehend why this woman—a freaking *lawyer*—was strapping up like she was about to go to war. "I deserve to know what's going on. If you expect me to keep working here, I want the truth."

Before she could blink, Hadina had her hand around Peyton's throat, tilting her chin up just enough to cause discomfort. Her nails dug into the tender skin of her neck, but Peyton knew better than to say anything else.

"You will never make demands of me again, do you understand?" Peyton nodded against Hadina's clenched palm. "I am not required to do shit but pay your wage. Whatever you saw here, forget it. And if you think about leaving and running that pretty little mouth, trust that I can find you and make sure you stay quiet." Hadina released her grip, looking down at Peyton as the girl fell to her knees with a hand clasping at her throat. Letting out a sigh as though she was disappointed, Hadina shook her head and made a move as if to leave before adding, "Maybe Zelina was right—you should be reminded that you are *just the help*."

Waiting to hear the soft click of the front door, Peyton panted and crawled until her back rested against the desk. She didn't understand what was happening or what she could do about it. Hadina had made it clear she couldn't leave or tell anyone anything, and she saw the promise of pain in her eyes as she had threatened her.

No, Peyton was alone in this. Whatever was going on, she would discover the truth and find a way to get herself out of it. She *had* to. Her parents couldn't lose another child. But for now, she had to scrub herself clean and make sure no marks were left on her skin. She would take a bath and think of a plan afterward. Which left her with another problem to deal with.

The fact that Hadina had been so close, murderous intent in her eyes as she kept Peyton in a tight grip... Peyton's core contracted at the memory. She could feel the wetness seeping onto her underwear and she threw her head back on a groan. This whole night was confusing as fuck and Peyton didn't know what to make of it.

She did know one thing though: Hadina Adis was a terrifying creature, and Peyton was absolutely intoxicated by her.

CHAPTER 10

HADINA

Once Hadina was in the quiet of her car, she thumped her fist against the steering wheel and let out a frustrated scream. That insufferable, nosy, goddamn *beautiful* little bitch just had to walk in when she was getting prepped for her meeting. Why Piper hadn't told Peyton that she was busy, Hadina would never understand, but it was an inconvenience she didn't have the time for.

But she also couldn't stop herself.

Threatening Peyton had been a mistake, Hadina knew. That being said, the way she had spoken to her like they were equals, well, it boiled Hadina's blood. She had experienced a lifetime of people thinking they were better than her just because she was a woman in charge. She wouldn't let some nobody come in and do the same.

The problem was that Hadina wasn't sure if Peyton *was* a nobody. There was something about her that got under her skin, slowly scratching at the walls she had built. She knew that threatening her reluctant employee was enough to ensure her silence, but it wasn't the look of fear in Peyton's eyes that had Hadina replaying the scene on repeat.

It was the lust.

Hadina was no stranger to hate-fucking, fear-fucking, or any of the other kinds, if she were honest with herself. She knew what she wanted and needed, and she made sure she was satisfied. But business had been busy and it had left her with little time to feed her libido, much to her dismay. So, when she noticed the way Peyton's pupils dilated and her tense muscles relaxed after a fear-filled second, Hadina had to stop herself from slamming her lips against Peyton's and seeing just how much the girl liked to play with fire.

It was so unlike her to feel out of control. She had spent her life learning to hide her emotions behind masks, bury her wants down deep. She gave her life willingly to the company, knowing that they were doing society a service that wouldn't otherwise be provided. But it seemed Peyton was determined to make Hadina's life collapse around her, just by existing. So Hadina would have to further steel herself against the temptation.

Her thoughts were a muddled mess by the time she reached Piper's gallery. She parked around back and cut the lights on her car, making sure nobody would be able to see her in the dark. Once she was safely hidden in the shadows, away from the prying eyes of street cameras, Hadina unlocked the back door and made her way inside the gallery.

She kept the shutters down out front, but switched on the overhead lights within. Firing off a quick text to her team, Hadina made her way into the back office and awaited her visitors by taking a seat. She nodded to Harris when he entered the office, as he sat just beside the door. He pulled his gun from his belt and rested it on his lap. Offering up a devilish smile, he signaled to Hadina that the *guests* had arrived.

"Showtime, boss."

"Clean and quiet, Harris. No mistakes this time."

Hadina found it quite humorous the way she could sense when the target walked in, followed by the sound of his henchmen. White men carried themselves differently—with an air of confidence and superiority, as though they didn't use women to get to whatever position of authority they always wormed themselves into—and it could be heard in their footsteps. Confident, thudding, angry-sounding things, those were the footsteps of the privileged white men. Hadina despised them and chuckled softly to herself, knowing that she was about to rid the world of one more.

"Piper darling, where are you? I'm ready to make you an offer you can't refuse!" The booming voice of Henrik Smith echoed through the empty gallery, making Hadina clench her jaw in annoyance.

She winked at Harris before tilting her head and calling out to Smith. "In here!"

Despite the slight difference in tone, Henrik Smith heard the voice of Piper Adis, but Hadina had always been good at mimicking her sisters. It was a game they used to play growing up, throwing their voices under the guise of a sibling, to confuse each other during hide-and-seek. She was pleased that such a childish fancy had proved to be useful, time and time again.

Henrik swaggered into the office with two men in expensive suits trailing behind him. He had a beige coat slung over his shoulders, a feeble attempt at looking cool and nonchalant. His face dropped when he saw Hadina sitting back in the office chair, her legs kicked up and crossed at the ankles on the desk in front of her.

"Who the hell are you?"

"Your worst nightmare," Hadina stated with a smug smile. "And also Piper *darling*'s sister, Hadina. It's a displeasure to meet you, Mr. Smith."

Harris shifted slightly in his seat, a hand patting the gun on his lap. It drew the attention of the guards and Henrik, who blanched at the sight of the weapon.

"I demand you tell me where your sister is, right this minute!"

Hadina cleared her throat and looked at him pointedly, sure to show him nothing but her gruesome intentions. "I don't think you should be telling me what to do right now, Henrik. You're at *my* mercy. Not the other way around."

She picked up her own gun from where it lay discarded on the desk, motioning for her target to take a seat. He looked over his shoulders at his bodyguards, but both men shrugged. "Time's up, boss."

Henrik fumed, his cheeks turning a furious shade of pink. Balling his fists, he made his way to the chair and lowered himself down with a *thud*. "What the fuck is this? You have my men under your spell now?"

Hadina couldn't help the laugh that escaped her lips as she took in Henrik's anger. What a pathetic waste of life, of power. Henrik Smith had the kind of money and sway to change the world, but instead, he chose to use and abuse people far more vulnerable than most. He was everything that was wrong with the world, and Hadina couldn't wait to destroy him.

"Oh, Henners, you poor, brainless man," she cooed, never once dropping her perfect smile. "Your men aren't under my spell. They're just under the illusion that I'll be giving them a million dollars each if they stand down. But don't worry, they won't be making it out alive either."

Right on cue, Harris shot both bodyguards between the eyes—a single, clean bullet to end them immediately. Blood sprayed across the doorframe, chunks of brain matter and scalp flying across the floor. Henrik watched on in shock as his men fell backward, collapsing in a heap at the door. Their bodies lay in a crumpled mess of crimson puddles that were a stark contrast to the white tiles beneath them.

"Now that they've been dealt with, we should discuss why you're here."

Ignoring her completely, Henrik continued to stare at the bodies of his men, their blood soaking into the suits that Henrik made them wear. Such a waste to see them ruined, but necessary nonetheless.

Snapping her fingers, Hadina commanded the attention of her audience. "Eyes on me, Henrik. You're not here for a show."

"Clearly," he said, finally sitting back in his seat. "I'm here to die."

Hadina smiled, picking up her gun and tapping it against the palm of her hand. "*Technically*, you're here to give me information. Anything that happens afterwards, such as your death, will just be a bonus."

"I don't have anything to tell you. I'm just an art dealer."

"And I'm just a lawyer."

Henrik huffed and shifted in his chair. Hadina stayed silent, waiting for his resignation a moment later. "Fine. What the fuck do you want?"

She knew her smile would have been absolutely feral but she didn't wipe it away. Instead, she bared her teeth, a lioness ready to tear apart her prey. "I want to know where you're keeping the girls you kidnapped. You know, the ones you and your bastard friends have been raping and then selling to the highest bidders. I want a location, then I want a list of everyone you've been working with. If you give me all of that, maybe I'll make your death a fraction less painful than the sheer torture you've been inflicting on those poor girls."

An hour of bodily harm and thorough questioning provided Hadina with all the information she needed. While she knew Henrik was a weak man, she hadn't expected him to break quite so easily. Powerful men were fragile things when confronted by the wrath of a woman.

"Please just kill me," he begged, his swollen, bloodied eyes searching through the haze of red for her. Hadina did the man a favor and moved to stand directly in his line of sight before crouching to his level.

"You didn't think I'd make it that easy for you, did you?" she questioned, shaking her head. Reaching down into her boot, she removed her blade, flicking her wrist to open it. The metal shone under the fluorescent lights, gleaming as it awaited the bloodshed to follow.

Slowly running the sharpened edge across his cheek, Hadina watched as Henrik stopped wriggling where he sat, choosing to sit perfectly still as though it would help him avoid what was about to happen.

"Pieces of shit like you, the absolute *scum* of the earth, always think they can do and take what they want. You steal young girls—fucking *children!*—and ruin their lives. You inflict your cruelty on them, and once you're bored, you throw them at the feet of the highest bidder."

Hadina pressed down on her switchblade, cutting into the skin just under Henrik's jaw. She reveled in the sound of his sharp intake of breath, noting how he gritted his teeth to stop from screaming. Her blood boiled at the thought of what those young girls endured at the hands of men like him, and yet he could barely handle being roughed up. She would try to cause him every bit of pain she possibly could, and when it would threaten to break her, she would let Harris step in and take his fill. Henrik Smith wouldn't get a quick death at her hands—that was for sure.

Her voice was icy as she brought her knife down to his right hand where it was bound to the chair. She scored the blade across his fingertips, back and forth, sawing lightly to cause a slow, burning pain. "Have you ever even considered what you do to them, or does it really not cross your mind?"

He remained silent. The only noise in the room was that of his blood hitting the floor in little crimson droplets.

She heaved a sigh. "I suppose it's the latter, because you would have to care on some level to think about how you treat them. Can you imagine being stolen and abused, men triple your age treating you like their own personal fuck-doll? How would *you* feel, Henrik, to have someone like you tear you apart from the inside out?"

Much to Hadina's dismay, Henrik was mute. His jaw tensed every time she allowed the knife to bite into his skin, but he kept his words locked away.

"You touch and violate these children and get off on their pain. And then you reap the rewards, spending your money on priceless art and meaningless objects. I know you won't be making it out of here alive, but I can't resist the urge to show you what life would be like without your grubby little hands."

Slamming the knife down in one swift motion, Hadina used all her strength to sever Henrik's fingers. She brought the blade down again and again until, one by one, the mutilated digits dropped to the floor and rolled to a stop at her feet. She barely registered his screams as they tore through the small office space, her focus entirely on the horror displayed across his disgusting face.

"You fucking whore!" he roared, thrusting himself back in his chair to try to free himself. But Hadina was confident in Harris's specialized skills and knew there was no escaping those binds.

Hadina cackled, throwing her head back like a madwoman. "I'm most definitely not. But even if I were, there is no shame in that. People like you belittle women to make yourselves feel better about the fact that the only way you can get your dick wet is by paying for it or taking it from someone against their will." She slowly ran her hand down his torso, stopping at the outline of his pants. With a wink aimed at Harris, she grabbed Henrik's flaccid dick through the material of his pants, digging in her nails and twisting. "So, let me return the favor. I'm going to take your most *prized* possession from you without your consent. And while you bleed out as Harris and I watch, I want you to think about how this is *your* doing. You never should have touched anyone without their consent, and now you'll die from the consequences."

Tuning out the shrieking from the flailing meat suit of a man before her, Hadina held out her hand to Harris. He placed a six-inch serrated knife in her open palm, the cool metal of the handle stinging against her hot skin. Torture and murder weren't easy; she always ended up sweaty, overheated, and covered in blood that wasn't her own. Hadina's punishments were as vicious as the actions her targets carried out against the weak and vulnerable, so when the weight of the knife connected with her hand, she didn't hesitate to rip open Henrik's pants and run the jagged edge across the base of his dick.

"Please, don't! Please! I'll give you what you want if you stop. *Please!*"

Hadina glared at her latest target, disgusted by his patheticness. Blood spurted and gushed, covering her hands and face, but her assault continued until Henrik's member lay discarded in his lap, a broken tool for a useless man. His blood continued to pour out of him, pooling beneath the chair like a hellish halo. Hadina made her way back to Piper's desk, sitting in her seat and kicking her bloodied feet up on the table. She watched on with a contented smile on her face as another man on her list bled out in front of her, the world now rid of one more diseased rat.

Vengeance for the innocent felt so fucking good, Hadina thought to herself as the life drained out of Henrik's body. *So fucking good.*

Tentadora

CHAPTER 11

PEYTON

"Peyton, tell me what's wrong," Don asked, sipping from his coffee.

They'd decided to have lunch outside after a long morning of gardening. Peyton had remained silent the entire time, finding comfort in the narcissus bulbs she was planting. Her mind had constantly been replaying the heated interaction she'd had with Hadina last week. No matter what she did, she could feel her fingers wrapped around her throat. She was simultaneously terrified and intrigued, and she didn't know what to do about either reaction.

She knew that finding out the truth of what Hadina was up to, what Peyton had gotten herself involved in by agreeing to take this job, was the most important thing. She would never be able to forgive herself if someone, anyone, got hurt and she could have stopped it. But Peyton had spent her life feeling trapped so all she wanted to do was run. Run far away from Hadina, her fucked-up hobbies, and the rest of the Adis family.

Peyton shook her head and smiled at Don. "I'm okay. Just tired."

Don sighed, setting his mug on the table between them. "This is about the theatrics of my daughters last week, isn't it? I'm so profoundly sorry for how they acted—how they treated you that night, *cariño*."

"Truly, it's fine, Don."

She didn't want to talk about it. Don had been apologizing daily since that night, but Peyton didn't have the energy to deal with any of it. Besides, she could hardly talk to him honestly, considering it was his damn daughter who had her so fucked up.

Hadina hadn't been around the house in days. Peyton was almost sure that her boss was avoiding her, though she could admit that it seemed a bit out of character for Hadina to avoid anyone. The woman oozed power and respect, capturing the attention of every room she was in—there was no way that she cared about how she had scared Peyton to her core.

There was a small part of her that was almost disappointed that Hadina hadn't been at the house. If she were to find out what was really going on, get herself some leverage over the ice queen, Peyton needed Hadina to be around more often. She had tried to come up with plan after plan, finally caving when she realized that she would just have to follow Hadina and spy on her. If she could uncover *something*, Peyton could blackmail Hadina into giving her the freedom she wanted. She would promise to forget everything she witnessed, if she were allowed to leave without repercussions.

But she had to actually witness something first.

Peyton was suddenly struck with an idea steeped in cunning and curiosity. She turned her attention back to Don. "Can I ask you a question?"

"You can ask me anything you'd like, Peyton," Don said affectionately.

"Why did you decide to stop working altogether? I'm sorry if that seems intrusive, but I just don't think you seem old enough and you certainly haven't lost all your faculties. You could still work for the firm as an advisor or something, right?"

Don's eyes slid to hers. It was the first time Peyton had ever seen him look uncomfortable. "The work just became a bit too much for an old man like myself to handle. I'm fortunate enough to be in a position to do so, which is a first in my family. My parents worked themselves to the bone until I was earning enough to take care of them. But I'm tired and retiring was an option I could afford to take. It seemed better to leave it to the girls."

"You must be proud of them," Peyton commented. She could feel the tension hanging in the air but she couldn't stop herself from prying further. "I mean, both Zellie and Hadina becoming lawyers and following in your footsteps? That's pretty impressive."

"They're smart girls—that's for sure. I wanted them to be successful and work hard, just like I did, but seeing them excel fills me with pride." He smiled to himself, running a weathered hand across his jaw. "Piper is doing well on her own too. It wasn't a surprise that she decided against joining the family business; she was always the creative, gentle one."

Peyton eyed Don curiously. Something seemed off but she couldn't put her finger on what it was. She had met Piper, and while she seemed like a sweetheart, Peyton had a feeling that she could be just as headstrong as her sisters. Being a lawyer had to be stressful, but she didn't think that was the reason Piper had decided to branch off on her own.

"Besides," Don continued, his voice breaking Peyton from her thoughts, "I rather like being at home all the time. Just look at how beautiful this garden is! I didn't have time for anything when I was working."

"I'm glad you hired me, Don. Meeting you was a strange streak of luck that I'm extremely grateful for." The lie caught in the back of her throat, making Peyton queasy.

Don took a long drink from his mug. "That it was, *cariño*. But I'm very glad I hired you too. Now, if you'll excuse me, I think I need a shower and a nap. All that gardening tired me out."

Peyton watched Don's retreating figure hurry off inside. There was something weird going on with the entire family she was stuck working for, and she would find out what it was. Even if it killed her.

Peyton Dimitra was no fool, and she wouldn't allow herself to be swept up in whatever fucked-up shit was happening here.

CHAPTER 12

HADINA

Stepping into her family home after almost a week of avoiding it felt strange. Hadina wasn't used to feeling uneasy in her own home, but her last interaction with Peyton had left a bad taste in her mouth. She had caught her preparing to go off and murder people—what the hell was she supposed to do other than threaten her to keep her mouth shut?

That wasn't her only problem though. She couldn't get her mind to stop flashing images of her hand around Peyton's throat, the way she had swallowed thickly and looked at Hadina with dilated pupils... it was really fucking with her head. *La pendeja* should have been terrified, a trembling mess; instead, she looked like she wanted Hadina to devour her whole. Which, she was loath to admit, Hadina had considered.

Mixing business with pleasure was a dangerous game. The issue was Hadina positively thrived in chaos. So she had spent the last week avoiding her father and her home so that she didn't mess up and do something she shouldn't. Even if she really, really wanted to.

But avoidance was no longer an option when Hadina needed to go home and use the office there.

It wasn't like she didn't have her own space. Hadina had an absolutely stunning apartment, furnished with the most beautiful high-end furniture and decorated in different monochromatic styles. It was cool and beautiful, but it also left her empty. She simply slept there when she needed to and used the spare room as her own personal arsenal. At this point, it was basically just a storehouse. She felt uneasy when she was there, lonely almost. So, rather than suffering through another night with her tormented mind, Hadina decided to brave the prospect of seeing Peyton.

"Dad? Where are you?" she called as she closed the front door behind her. She knew it was almost dinnertime and she fully expected him to be sitting in the dining room. The man loved his food and always looked forward to mealtimes.

But Don surprised Hadina by stepping out of the office and motioning for her to follow him inside. "In here, *mija*. Let's have a chat."

Hadina didn't even try to hide her sigh as she complied, flopping down into one of the chairs. Her father took the seat behind the desk and suddenly Hadina was transported back to her childhood, having *serious talks* as he explained the family business to his eighteen-year-old daughter. She had been terrified of her father at that moment, learning about all the things he'd done under the guise of protecting the innocent. Then betrayal reared its ugly head, when she learned that Zellie had known, had started following in their father's footsteps.

It's your turn now, Hadina, he had told her. Hadina had been distraught, screaming and yelling expletives at him. Her young mind couldn't wrap around everything she'd been told, or the expectations that were suddenly upon her shoulders.

Now, at thirty-four and far wiser, Hadina didn't feel anything but love and respect for the man who had taught her everything. She had worked her ass off to prove herself worthy of the Adis name, and she finally felt confident enough in herself to let the fear go. The family may have done bad things, but they protected far more people than they buried.

"*Que pasa, Papi?*" Hadina asked her father what was wrong, her brows furrowed at his serious expression.

Don shook his head, running a hand through his silver hair. "Not really. Peyton has been a mess all week. What happened between you two?"

"Nothing."

"Don't lie to me, *hija!*" He slammed his hand down on the desk, startling Hadina. It had been a long time since she had seen her father embody his nickname of *el titán de la muerte.* He was the god of death, the only person she had ever been remotely afraid of.

Shrugging off her initial shock, Hadina steeled herself and narrowed her eyes at her father. "Why are you so bothered over some random girl? She's just supposed to be the hired help, not an adoptive daughter."

The disdain Don offered in response made Hadina's stomach churn. She wasn't usually the one to upset or disappoint her father and it wasn't a pleasant feeling.

"You sound like your sister. And we both know that isn't a good thing."

Hadina sighed. "You're right. *Lo siento.*"

"Me too. But please, tell me the truth. What happened, Hadina?"

Blowing out a deep breath, Hadina filled her father in on what transpired between the girls. She debated with herself about leaving out the part where she threatened Peyton, but she knew her father would have seen through her lies. Don listened and remained silent through his daughter's narrative. By the time Hadina finished, he was leaning back in his chair, a troubled look distorting his features. It made Hadina agitated to see.

"That was extremely foolish of you. You threatened an innocent, Hadina. It goes against all our rules."

"It was either to threaten, kidnap, or kill her. We can't risk her running away and blabbing that she saw one of the Adis sisters strapping up like she was going to work."

"There was a fourth option, *mija*," Don said softly. He tilted his head and looked at her curiously. "There still is, I suppose."

"Yes?"

The corner of her father's mouth tilted upward with the beginning of a smirk. "You could tell her the truth."

Hadina balked. Staring at her father, she waited for Don to laugh or tell her it was some sort of joke. A beat passed, then another, and another, until the silence was stretched so thin that Hadina thought she could have snapped it just by breathing. "You absolutely cannot be serious! How do we even know if we can trust her?" She knew she was raising her voice, but she couldn't quite stop as her frustration rose. "You're the one who taught me our rules, Dad. How can you suggest risking everything we've built—everything *you* created—so carelessly?"

Don's smirk was on full display now, as he held up his hands. "Because she's different and I know you know that. I see how you watch her, Hadina. There's something about her, isn't there?"

Hadina shook her head. Much like her younger self all those years ago in this office, she couldn't wrap her head around what was happening, what he was suggesting. They never brought anyone into the business without months, if not years, of training and intel. This wasn't like her father. "Are you going senile, old man? I don't know what you're talking about."

"Bullshit, *princesa*." He let out a low chuckle, coming around the desk to perch on the edge in front of her. He reached over and tilted her chin up so that she had to look at him. "I have been your father for thirty-four years and I know you better than you know yourself. Whether you're willing to admit it or not, there's something different about Peyton and you know it. So, I'll say this once more and then I won't mention it again. If you want, you can tell her the truth. No threats or killing. Just honesty." He stood and pressed a soft kiss to his daughter's forehead, exactly like he used to when she was a child. "Let yourself trust someone, *hija*. This can be a lonely world without someone by your side."

Squeezing her shoulder gently, Don left Hadina sitting alone with her head spinning. She knew her father was right—there was something different about Peyton—but the fact her father was willing to break their rules for her sparked curiosity in Hadina's soul. Don was hiding something, and if she wanted to find out the truth, she would have to use Peyton to get it.

Perhaps mixing business with pleasure was the answer this time. Hadina just had to let herself give in to temptation.

Tentadora

CHAPTER 13

PEYTON

PEYTON HADN'T MOVED SINCE DON LEFT THE GARDEN AND WALKED INTO THE house. She wasn't sure how much time had passed, but the sun was still shining, so she was comfortable enough to stay in her spot. She closed her eyes and drifted off into a light sleep, enjoying the quiet of her surroundings.

"Are you so overworked that you must nap during the daytime?"

The voice startled Peyton from her dozing, her eyes opening to a familiar face. She bit her lip and averted her gaze from Hadina, unsure how to act around her after their last exchange. Despite the sun shining in the sky above, Peyton felt an icy chill in the air and wrapped her arms around herself.

"I was just enjoying my free time. Your dad said he was going for a nap."

Hadina claimed the chair opposite Peyton. "He's still awake. I was just talking to him in the office. Maybe he'll go for a nap now."

Peyton shrugged. She wasn't sure how to respond. Conversation between them was always stilted, but now it was awkward on top of that.

"I'm told you haven't been yourself this week. It would seem I owe you an apology."

The laugh that escaped Peyton's lips couldn't be contained. "I didn't think you were the type to apologize. Besides, what are you apologizing for? Grabbing me by the throat, calling me *the help*, or threatening me?"

She watched as Hadina toyed with a small smile. "All the above?"

Peyton stood, her own smirk dropping as she towered over Hadina. "If you want to apologize, try harder. I'm not some stupid kid you can treat like shit, Hadina. You don't even know me."

"Peyton, I–"

Peyton held up a hand, cutting Hadina off mid-sentence. Then, spinning on her heel, she stomped inside. Knowing that Don didn't need her for anything, Peyton made her way up to her bedroom and slammed the door behind her. It was a silly act of petulance, but damn, did it feel good. Flopping onto her back on the bed, she let out a heavy sigh.

She couldn't believe that Hadina didn't see the absolutely *massive* fucking issue with the way she had treated her. Peyton knew that the only reason Hadina was even attempting to apologize was because Don had told her Peyton had been in a funk. Which was almost as frustrating as Hadina was.

The bedroom door opened and Peyton sat up, her eyes widening as Hadina stormed inside and smacked the door closed again. She marched over to the bed, her nostrils flaring as she looked down at Peyton.

"Who the fuck do you think you are to walk away from me, Miss Dimitra?"

Peyton glared at Hadina. "Who the fuck do *you* think you are to storm into my bedroom, Miss Adis?"

"The person who pays for this bedroom."

"And also the person who grabs me by the throat and threatens me so I can't leave," Peyton fired back.

Hadina pressed her lips into a flat line. After a brief stare-off, her mouth twitched into almost a smirk. "I think you liked having my hand around your throat, Peyton."

Her breath caught in her throat as she looked at her boss. How had Hadina known that? It was wrong—even more so to want it to happen again—but Peyton couldn't stop herself from nodding slightly.

"Use your words," Hadina commanded.

Peyton huffed. "Yes, okay? I liked it when your crazy ass was choking me."

Hadina raised a brow. Lowering herself closer to Peyton with one hand holding the headboard to keep herself steady, Hadina stopped only a breath away from her face. Using her free hand, she traced Peyton's jawline with her fingertips. "Do you want me to do it again?"

Peyton swallowed thickly and cursed herself before whispering, "Yes."

Having been granted consent, Hadina wrapped her hand around Peyton's throat, tightening her grip as Peyton gasped. She knew that whatever was happening was a manipulation, just another way for Hadina to be in control. She knew that, *and* she accepted it. If Hadina was this hot when she was in control, Peyton would consider losing all her morals more often.

Hadina climbed onto the bed, throwing a leg over Peyton so that she was straddling her waist. Peyton hated herself for how her body moved against her will, pressing into Hadina, silently begging for more. Hadina tightened her grip, her nails biting into the skin.

Their eyes locked and Peyton watched as Hadina leaned in, until their lips brushed. Peyton pushed into the kiss, opening herself up to Hadina. She tasted like salt and caramel and coffee. Peyton wanted to drown herself in it.

Pulling back slightly, Hadina bit down hard on Peyton's lower lip until she yelped. "You shouldn't have walked away from me."

"You shouldn't have threatened me," Peyton retorted, her tongue peeking out to trace the fresh wound on her lip.

"Oh, sweet girl, you should have listened to my threats. You saw something you shouldn't have and now you're trapped."

A shiver ran down Peyton's spine and she opened her mouth to snark back, only to have it captured in another kiss. This one was rougher and more desperate, Hadina pushing Peyton further into the bed by her throat. Peyton let out a groan as Hadina's tongue pried her lips apart, invading her mouth and overloading her senses.

She knew it was a bad idea, whatever was happening between them, but it felt so good and so she decided she didn't care enough to stop. Peyton had always been the good girl, so maybe it was time to set herself free.

Her hands found Hadina's hips and tugged the woman closer. Hadina ground down, creating a euphoric friction on her sensitive core through their pants. Peyton closed her eyes, losing herself to the kiss while wishing that it could last forever.

Hadina sat back, releasing Peyton's throat so she could remove her shirt. Once she was free of her top layers, Peyton began to feel self-conscious. She lifted a hand to cover herself but Hadina batted it away. "*Basta.* Stop that. I want to see you."

"I feel exposed."

Softening slightly, Hadina shook her head. "Be confident in your beauty, Peyton."

Then sheHadina pinned Peyton's wrists above her head and leaned forward. Hadina pressed her lips against Peyton's collarbones, kissing her way down her sternum. Little red stains left a path in her wake from Hadina's vibrant lipstick.

Peyton couldn't help but wonder what brand Hadina used...

Her back arched as Hadina wrapped her lips around a puckered nipple, swirling her tongue around the bud. She moaned for more as Hadina showered her other breast with just as much attention, teasing slightly with her teeth. Peyton knew she was soaking her panties as Hadina tortured her with pleasure until one of them was a panting mess.

"Are you wet for me?" Hadina asked, her voice deep and sultry. If Peyton wasn't already in bed with her, she thought she may have begged for the chance. Even a look from Hadina was enough to make her wet.

"Soaked," she croaked.

Hadina smiled and released her grip. "Good girl."

Peyton threw her head back on the pillows, unable to watch for fear of finishing right there as her pants were unbuttoned and Hadina slipped a hand inside. Hadina's long fingers reached Peyton's drenched underwear and the woman hummed her approval. Pulling the fabric to the side, Hadina ran a finger through Peyton's dripping folds, causing Peyton to groan loudly.

"Hell, you really are wet, aren't you? Is this what you've been like for me every single time you've looked at me with those fucking eyes?"

Hadina teased Peyton's clit, rubbing the sensitive bundle as she arched her back to press herself into Hadina's hand. She was almost delirious when Hadina slipped a finger inside her, curling it at just the right angle to hit her G-spot.

"You're the one that's been giving me those *fuck me* eyes, Hadi," Peyton ground out, grabbing onto the headboard for purchase as Hadina slipped another finger inside.

"*Hadi?* You really are temptation itself, Peyton. Your moans are a siren song to me, your juice is ambrosia to my lips."

Peyton was too far gone to be able to speak, her body on the precipice of release. Reaching a hand up, Hadina fondled one of Peyton's breasts just as she curled her fingers again, pressing down hard onto Peyton's clit until she was screaming out. She flooded

Hadina's hand, soaking through her panties and jeans until she was nothing but a contented puddle of satisfaction.

Her body slumped onto the bed in a post-orgasm bundle, her breath coming out in heavy pants. Wiping the sweat from her brow, Peyton sat up to find Hadina watching her as she licked the residue from her fingers.

Hadina smirked, brushing a finger around her lips to fix her smudged lipstick. "I trust that sufficed as an apology, Miss Dimitra?"

Peyton barked out a laugh. "You're a cruel, psychotic woman, Miss Adis."

Climbing off the bed, Hadina righted herself and fixed her outfit. Peyton watched longingly—telling herself she was just coming down from a sex-induced high—as Hadina walked to the door. She turned at the last minute, flashing Peyton a devious smile. "You're an enigma, *tentadora*. Perhaps I should threaten you more often."

She slipped out of the bedroom, leaving Peyton to her thoughts as she laid her head back on the pillows and closed her eyes as a yawn overtook her. When sleep beckoned her, Peyton slipped into unconsciousness, dreaming of a certain devil woman and her dangerous ways.

Reina
de las sombras

CHAPTER 14

HADINA

WHAT THE FUCK HAD SHE JUST DONE? SHE HAD KNOWN BARRELING THROUGH the house after Peyton was a bad idea, but her feet had moved of their own accord. It was like her subconscious had taken over, letting her do all the stupid things she would normally avoid.

Like fucking Peyton until they were both exhausted.

Making her way back to the office, Hadina slumped down in her chair and buried her face in her hands. It wasn't like she didn't enjoy it, but *mierda*, it was a mistake. Manipulating Peyton would be easier now, but she knew that wasn't what led her into that bedroom. Her father had been right when he said that Hadina couldn't keep her eyes off the girl—she was beautiful, after all—but she wouldn't let herself give in. She would use Peyton until she got what she wanted, and found out why Don thought their newest employee was so special.

IN THE DAYS that followed their little bedroom escapade, Hadina made sure to remain at the house. She felt Peyton's eyes on her whenever they were in the same room, watching and waiting for their gazes to meet.

Hadina made sure to avoid looking back at her.

It didn't make her feel good about herself, but Hadina was a master in manipulation. She had spent her twenties learning ways to make men fall in love with her and give up their secrets, how to make women so jealous they wanted to be her friend so they could whisper behind her back. It was exhausting, but always worth it.

Manipulating Peyton was different. It made Hadina's stomach churn whenever she felt those eyes on her, and instead of looking up, she'd grab her phone and leave the room. Peyton was peculiar and seemed attracted to Hadina's cold demeanor, which meant a lot of attitude. One-word answers, pretending to be distracted, talking to anyone but her—Hadina had it down to a fine art within the first two days.

But it really, really fucked with her. She ached to taste the little *tentadora* again, even if it was under the guise of business. She found herself more distracted than usual, always aware of where Peyton was and what she was doing. Even Harris had commented on it when he had come to talk to her earlier that morning. It had sobered her up fast enough. Hadina Adis would not show weakness to anyone, least of all one of her employees.

Slumping against the kitchen countertop, Hadina sipped on her coffee and closed her eyes. She was absolutely exhausted but there was a lot of work to be done.

The thing about the family business was that it was never-ending. For every person she killed, another *bastardo* turned up with their sick trafficking rings. Harris had arrived at the house with rumors about a new operation being set up, some of their old informants having heard things through the grapevine. Apparently, the leader was called Regina, a fierce *puta* who kept herself hidden in the shadows. It was stupid of her, really, to be so brazen as to step into Hadina's area and expect to do her business.

Hadina was *reina de las sombras* and she would wield her title like a blade. Nobody would dare come into *her* darkness and expect to live.

"Are you okay?"

Opening her eyes slowly, Hadina locked gazes with Peyton, who stared at her like she was a fragile piece of glass about to shatter. That wouldn't do, not at all.

"That's not your concern, Miss Dimitra," she snapped in response.

Peyton's eyes widened, her nostrils flaring in indignation. Crossing her arms over her chest, which only accentuated her sinful bust in the V-neck tee she was wearing, Peyton glared at Hadina with what looked like an attempt at disgust. "Well, fuck you, then."

If Hadina didn't need to stick to her plan, she may have laughed. "I already did that, *muñeca*. Sex doesn't give you the right to pry."

Hadina could see the anger boiling beneath Peyton's skin as she stepped forward, leaning on the island between them. "Yes, I remember. I'm *just the help*, right? Also, I don't fucking know Spanish. Translate for me if you're going to call me a name."

Hadina raised a brow at that, at the dominance and command in Peyton's voice. It made her want to lean her over the counter and spank the fight right out of her. "*Muñeca* means doll. I figured it was accurate, since you clearly like to be played with, don't you?"

Peyton rolled her eyes. "Oh, fuck off. Making me come one time doesn't mean you get to be a bitch for no reason. You looked stressed so I was asking if you were okay. You know, a very human thing to do."

Ignoring the jab, Hadina gripped her mug tighter and gulped down the rest of her coffee. She knew Peyton was watching her throat as she swallowed, paying particular attention to the small drop that traveled down her chin in a single drip. With a perfectly manicured hand, Hadina scooped the runaway liquid onto her fingertip, bringing it to her lips slowly as she licked it off. Peyton watched the show attentively, her lower lip pulled between her teeth.

Setting the mug down, Hadina winked. "Be a *doll* and wash that for me, won't you?"

Peyton's mouth gaped as Hadina smiled smugly, walking out of the kitchen with a practiced swagger. Being a bitch felt fucking *great* sometimes.

Tentadora

CHAPTER 15

PEYTON

Peyton had no idea where Hadina got off thinking she could treat her like that, where she got the fucking audacity from. Her indignation and anger kept her frozen in the spot, staring after Hadina long after the woman left.

It had been almost two weeks of Hadina being around the house, avoiding Peyton like nothing had happened between them. Peyton knew that it should never have happened anyway, but it didn't stop her pining. People always wanted what was forbidden, and Hadina definitely fell into that category.

She still wanted to find a way out of this mess, to get some sort of leverage over Hadina, so that she could blackmail her way out of this deal. But if she could have fun while she did it, Peyton didn't mind playing with fire. Though Hadina's avoidance dampened the likelihood of that ever happening again. Whether or not either of them wanted it.

The thing was... Peyton wasn't sure *if* Hadina wanted it. The incident in the bedroom was absolutely a manipulation tactic, which meant that she wasn't sure whether Hadina had been into it, or if the objective was purely meant to get Peyton under control. She could pine for her, but Peyton wouldn't make a fool of herself by fawning over Hadina like some lovesick puppy. It was pointless anyway. Hadina didn't show emotion like everyone else.

After cleaning up with maximum grumbling, Peyton went to the living room to find Don. He was seated in a leather recliner, a beautiful hardcover book in hand. He offered a smile as he looked up, sliding a bookmark between the pages to keep his place.

"Hello, *cariño*," he said, gesturing for Peyton to take a seat on the sofa.

She sank down with a sigh. "Are you doing okay?"

"Are you?" he fired back with a brow raised, an expression she had seen on Hadina many times before.

Peyton let out a small laugh. "I tried to be nice to your daughter and she threw it back in my face. I think she hates me, Don," she admitted with a defeated sigh. It was the truth, though. You could hate someone *and* be intrigued or attracted to them. The emotions weren't mutually exclusive.

Don shook his head, reaching to grab Peyton's hand. "Hadina is... She's a very closed-off person. She finds it difficult to let anyone in— she always has—but that doesn't mean she hates you. I think she's just scared to let you in, to accept that you're here."

Peyton tilted her head, pondering the old man's words. "Why would she be scared to let me in? Hadina doesn't strike me as the type of person to be afraid of anything."

"You'd be surprised what my daughter is afraid of, Peyton. She's lost a lot and she's wary of anyone new in her life, or anyone who's close to me. She's protective, that girl."

Peyton held her tongue for a moment before she whispered, "I think I'm the one who's scared."

Don brushed her off with a wave of his hand. "We're all scared of something, Peyton. But you can't let fear rule your life. I've been telling Hadina that for a long time."

"I've never been very brave, Don. Losing Melina only made it worse."

"Fear is natural," Don stated. He gave her a sad smile but the pity in his eyes was like a blow to Peyton's stomach. "You have to make a choice whether you want to let it consume you. Live your life for both yourself and your sister."

Tears blurred Peyton's vision and she sniffled while wiping her eyes with the palms of her hands. She didn't understand how she was still unable to think of Melina without her heart breaking, tears threatening to drown her.

Melina had been the light of Peyton's life and it seemed that she would be haunted by the girl's death forever. They had looked so similar that people had often thought they were twins, despite Melina being Peyton's senior by two years. Peyton didn't think anyone could love their sibling as much as she loved her big sister; they shared a bond that she'd never been able to find again. Melina was her best friend, confidante, and protector. She had always put Peyton first, ensured her safety and happiness were placed above her own, and Peyton felt lost without her.

"Sorry," Peyton apologized to Don, shaking herself back into the moment. "It just doesn't get easier, you know?"

"I do. Losing my wife was like losing the best part of me, half of my heart gone for good. We carry the pain of their deaths to honor them in life, by continuing on like they would want us to, even when it hurts the most."

Peyton blew out a soft breath and gathered herself. "Thank you. I appreciate your kindness."

Don smiled. "The world needs more kindness."

"Indeed it does."

HER TALK with Don had been almost cathartic. Peyton wanted to remember her sister for the bright person she was, rather than dwell on the girl's death and the pain it caused. Melina had wanted the best for Peyton, had helped push her to work hard in school and aspire to go to college. In fact, Melina was the reason behind Peyton's aspirations of becoming a doctor. Peyton just had to focus on saving and getting out from under the thumb of the Adis family—of Hadina—so that she could continue with her life plans.

It was this realization that led Peyton to hide behind the wall, peeking around the corner as she waited for Hadina to leave the office. She had heard her boss telling someone on the phone that she'd be leaving soon to meet with a contact, whatever that meant. Peyton had been waiting almost twenty minutes by the time Hadina clicked the office door shut and made her way down the hallway. Pausing until she heard the familiar *click* of the front door, Peyton crept slowly into the office.

The room was the way it always was: organized and stylish. If she were being honest, Peyton hated just how gorgeous it was decorated and she knew in her bones that it was Hadina's stylistic choice. There was something about the black accents, deep greens, and sharp edges that just screamed Hadina. Peyton was jealous of her employer's eye for decor.

"Focus, Peyton," she whispered to herself, tiptoeing over to the desk.

Papers were stacked neatly in piles, letters deposited into a box at one corner of the desk. As quietly as she could, just in case Don was passing by, Peyton ruffled through the drawers. She wasn't sure what she was looking for, what information she'd have to find to gain her freedom. But she needed to find *something*.

After the drawers proved a waste of time, only previous months' bills and neatly organized research into different laws hidden inside, Peyton moved on to the cabinet in the corner of the room. People always kept important documents in metal cabinets in the movies, so maybe Hadina had done the same.

Pulling the drawers open one by one, Peyton rifled through the folders and papers. Nothing caught her eye, each thing more boring than the last. The bottom drawer, however, was locked, which piqued her interest. She had never tried to pick a lock before, so she rummaged through the desk drawers again in hopes she'd find a key.

"Fuck!" she muttered under her breath, slamming the last drawer closed.

Grabbing a couple of bobby pins from the back of her head, Peyton knelt down in front of the cabinet. They always showed people picking locks in the movies using hairpins, but she wasn't exactly sure *how* to do it. She opened up one of the pins, sticking the ridged side into the lock and twisting it around. When nothing happened, she cursed and tried the flat edge.

Peyton pulled her phone out of her pocket and Googled *how to pick a lock*. She was surprised by just how many tutorials popped up, and how in-depth they were.

"Hell, even locked doors can't protect us, I guess," she said as she watched her third tutorial. It seemed to be the least complex and easiest to follow, so she straightened her bobby pins and tried again while the voice on her phone guided her actions. She glanced down every so often, making sure she was getting it right, and then went back to pressing her ear to the cabinet to listen for the *click* that would tell her she was on the right track.

Peyton could have yelled in celebration when she finally heard the sound of victory before she quickly tugged the drawer open. Seeing a pile of guns, black leather gloves, and a gleaming dagger was not what she thought she'd find, but it sent a shiver down her spine anyway. She picked up the dagger, looking at the carving on the side of the black blade.

Sé a la luz.

Peyton grabbed her phone and opened up the translator. *Be the light.* Her brows furrowed at the translation. Why would anyone own a dagger like this, so sharp that it could cut you with a look, if they were to be the light? It didn't make sense and Peyton didn't understand. Hadina seemed like she thrived in the darkness, her eyes and hair as dark as night, like shadows she could command.

With a sigh, Peyton dropped the dagger back into the drawer and slammed it closed. There was no way she could find anything if she stared at an inscription she didn't understand, trying to figure out what it meant. She needed to find something concrete, something indisputable that she could use to blackmail her way out.

She stood and brushed herself off while her eyes flicked around the room again. She didn't know where else to look, especially since she didn't know what she was looking for. As if guided by some unknown force, her gaze drifted to the bookcases, noting the thin line of dust that layered the shelves. She would have to clean them at some point; she didn't want the books to get damaged.

Stepping closer, Peyton looked over the titles—classics she had never heard of and large leather-bound tomes that looked almost ancient. There were books on law, which didn't surprise her, and books in Spanish, whose titles she had to translate. She ran her fingers across the spines, pausing at two of the black leather tomes with gold calligraphy. Where all the other shelves had undisturbed lines of dust, signifying a lack of cleaning for a few weeks, there was a clean break in the dust in front of the present two.

With great effort, since the things weighed more than she thought they would, Peyton pulled the titles out and set them on the desk. "Jackpot," she whispered as she pulled a folder out from the back of the shelf.

Flipping through the pages, she stopped on a single piece of paper, which was folded and stuffed between the other pages. It was crumpled, the creases from the folds ripped in places. She opened it up, huffing a sigh of frustration when she saw a list of names she didn't recognize. Most were crossed out, a thick dark line struck through the middle, the pen pressed so hard into the paper that Peyton could feel the indentation on the backside of the page.

"Who are you?" she questioned out loud, looking down the list.

All the names were male, first and last names written down in cursive. That was why she found it so weird when a name was added at the bottom, written in bright-red ink and circled three times until the lines overlapped.

Regina

Peyton had a sinking feeling in her stomach as she looked at that name. Why were there so many crossed out, and why were they all men? What was so different about this Regina lady that made her the first woman on the list? Thoughts and questions swam through Peyton's mind and she could sense the rising panic, anxiety clawing its way up her throat until her breath caught.

She had stumbled upon something—something important, just like she had wanted—but she didn't know what it meant yet. She would have to do more digging.

Snapping a photo of the list with her phone, Peyton folded the paper and stuffed it back between the pages where she had found it. It was when she started looking through the rest of the folder, in hopes she'd be able to gather more information, when she heard the front door open, the familiar sound of Hadina's heels clicking against the hallway flooring.

She was about to be caught snooping by the devil woman herself.

Reina
de las sombras

CHAPTER 16

HADINA

THE MOST ANNOYING THING ABOUT BEING THE BOSS WAS THAT *EVERY DAMN thing* fell to you when someone else didn't pick up the slack. Hadina had, reluctantly, asked Zellie to meet one of the informants to see if they could tell her anything about Regina. The eldest Adis girl had said she was busy and hung up the phone, leaving Hadina to meet the informant instead.

Sometimes Hadina really hated her sister.

She was halfway to the meeting point when her phone rang, Zellie's caller ID flashing on the screen. "What is it?"

"*Grosera.* That's no way to answer your big sister, Hadina."

Hadina rolled her eyes, checking her mirror as she signaled to move into the next lane. "What do you want, Z? I'm driving."

She could practically hear the smile in Zellie's voice as she spoke. "Just letting you know that I've canceled my plans and I can cover the meeting now."

"*Mierda.* I'm halfway there!"

"I'm already here, *hermana.*"

"Oh, you *pinche puta*! You just like fucking with me, don't you?" Hadina yelled, smacking her hand on the steering wheel.

Zellie cackled in response. "Maybe. I'll deal with the informant and let you know how it goes. *Adíos*."

Hadina fumed as she turned the car around, driving home with rage brewing under her skin. Zelina was a pain in Hadina's ass and sometimes she wished her father had just cut the woman off for good. Working with her on the rare occasion was torture enough for a lifetime.

Slamming the front door to the house on her way inside, Hadina stormed through the hallway and down to the office. She threw the door open and stopped in her tracks. Sitting in the chair behind the desk, legs thrown up and ankles crossed the way Hadina had done so many times, was Peyton.

"What the fuck are you doing in here?"

Peyton smiled innocently. "Waiting for you, obviously."

"Miss Dimitra, stop fucking around. I don't have the energy for whatever *this* is. Get out of my office."

"Make me." Peyton kept her gaze level with Hadina as she swung her legs down and crossed her arms, the perfect picture of defiance.

Make me. It was stupid to make statements like that to Hadina, especially when she was pissed off and ready for a fight. She pulled her 9mm from underneath her suit jacket, cocking it and aiming at Peyton's pretty face. "Tell me what you were doing in here."

Peyton didn't flinch. "I was waiting for you. I think we need to talk."

Hadina scoffed and moved farther into the room, kicking the door closed with her foot. "I'm not in the mood to talk so get out." She motioned to the exit with her gun before pointing the barrel back at Peyton.

"No."

"What do you mean, *no*?"

Peyton chuckled humorlessly. "I mean, *no*. If you don't want to talk, fine. But you've been a bitch to me ever since we had sex. So either we talk, or you sit in this seat and let me do something else with my mouth."

Hadina blinked. There was no way that Peyton—sweet, almost angelic Peyton—had just propositioned her. In her own office. *And* called her a bitch.

"I won't tell you again. Get out of my office, Peyton."

Peyton sighed and pushed up from the desk, making her way to the door. Hadina was relieved that she wouldn't have to deal with her right now. Thumping her gun on the desk, Hadina reclaimed her office chair, rubbing her temples as she closed her eyes. She could feel a tension headache coming on and she wanted to be alone.

The *snick* of the lock had her lashes prying open again, shock taking hold when her gaze landed on Peyton leaning against the door from the inside. Hadina groaned and shook her head. She didn't have the patience for childish behavior and petulance.

"Miss Dimitra—"

Peyton held up her hand, cutting Hadina off mid-sentence. She stalked forward with heat in her eyes, slowly tying her hair away from her face. Hadina was ashamed by the fact she couldn't look away—she was mesmerizing—and it was infuriating that she was so attracted to Peyton, even if she didn't want to admit it to herself.

"We were past the formalities when you had your tongue in my mouth and your finger in my panties. I told you—if we're not going to talk, we're going to find another way to make you loosen the hell up and stop acting like I'm a piece of shit you can order around."

Hadina swallowed thickly before snapping out of her trance. "I can order you around."

Peyton stepped toe-to-toe with Hadina and smirked. "Maybe, but I'm the one in control right now. Your dad told me that I should stop living in fear."

Sobering at the mention of her father, Hadina tried to stand, only to be pushed into her seat again. Realistically, she could have stopped her easily considering the training she'd had, but Hadina was intrigued by this sudden shift in personality that Peyton was displaying. Her subconscious was eager to find out what she had planned.

"You know what that means, Hadi? I'm not scared of you."

"You should be."

Peyton shrugged, dropping to her knees before Hadina. "But I'm not."

Hadina watched on as Peyton trailed her hands up her thighs, following her actions as she unbuttoned Hadina's pants and motioned for her to move to allow her to pull them down. It felt strange for her to comply, to give up control even for a moment. But Hadina was just so exhausted and didn't have the energy to keep a rein on herself.

Leaning back in her chair, Hadina moved her lower half to the edge of the seat, allowing Peyton easier access. She hissed as Peyton moved her lace thong aside before running a cool finger through Hadina's heated folds.

"Peyton..."

"Shut up. You had the chance to talk," Peyton scolded before parting her with two fingers. "I wonder if you taste as bitter as you pretend to be."

Hadina opened her mouth to reprimand her for talking to her like that, but those thoughts drifted away when Peyton circled her clit, teasing her with a cruel smile on her lips.

"Being a bitch doesn't suit you," Hadina mumbled.

"Perhaps not. But I'm taking a page out of your book," she retorted. Then she ran her fingers through the wetness and pressed against Hadina's clit again, laughing when Hadina groaned.

Leaning forward, Hadina watched as Peyton moved closer, using her tongue to capture the taste of Hadina's pussy. She made no comment as she dove in farther, swirling around the sensitive bud before traveling down to tease Hadina's hole.

"*Mierda*," Hadina moaned, gripping the arms of her chair so tightly that her knuckles turned white.

Peyton continued to work Hadina's hole with that devilish tongue, laughing when Hadina made incoherent noises. Once Hadina was dripping, Peyton pulled back and licked her lips. Hadina was almost ready to beg for release, but her little temptress pressed forward again, using her tongue to circle Hadina's clit as she slipped a finger inside. Then Peyton added a second digit, pumping in and out at a punishingly slow rate.

"Peyton—" Hadina warned, her voice hoarse as her walls started to clench.

"Say please," Peyton mumbled into her pussy, her breath warm and torturous while Hadina was so close to climax. But the Adis sister wouldn't beg.

"No," she managed to croak out through gritted teeth. Peyton extracted her fingers and sat back on her heels, lifting her right shoulder in a shrug. The lower half of her face was coated in Hadina's liquid, shining on her lips like nectar.

"Okay."

Hadina closed her eyes, exhaling slowly. She knew she would regret it, but she had been worked over so fucking good that she needed to come. Leveling her gaze with Peyton, who remained on her knees, Hadina sighed. "*Please.*"

Peyton beamed, leaning forward again and watching Hadina, as she pushed her fingers inside and curled them at an angle she knew made the other woman pulse. When Peyton's teeth brushed against her clit, Hadina felt herself fall off the edge, shattering with a silent scream on her lips.

As Hadina came back down after her high, Peyton pushed to her feet, wiping her mouth with a fingertip and licking the juices off.

"Well?" Hadina asked breathlessly, a smirk toying at her lips.

Peyton schooled her features. "You taste like a bitch who can wash her own damn mug next time. Find me when you're ready to talk."

Hadina was so taken by surprise that she couldn't formulate a response. She just stared after Peyton as she unlocked the door and left Hadina there, with her thong pushed aside and her pants at her ankles.

Perhaps she had misjudged just how well Peyton could play the act of an angel. She would figure out what to do next, after she had cleaned herself up and got the image of her coming apart with Peyton's face buried in her pussy out of her head. Which could take a while, given how much she wanted it to happen all over again.

Tentadora

CHAPTER 17

PEYTON

PANIC HAD SEIZED HER WHEN SHE HEARD HADINA COME HOME. SHE KNEW getting caught snooping was practically a death sentence, so Peyton did the only thing she knew would distract Hadina—fuck with her. She didn't know much about Hadina, but she did know the woman loved to be in control. Peyton had a feeling that messing with her head, forcing her to give up what she loved so much, was a surefire way to divert her attention. Besides, Hadina wasn't the only one who could use sex to manipulate.

Two days had passed since then and Peyton was still overthinking what had happened. She almost felt guilty for talking to Hadina like that, but then she remembered the way Hadina spoke to her, and the list, and the weapons in the drawer...The guilt washed away after that.

Peyton decided to cook dinner to get her mind off everything. She needed to research that Regina woman, but she was facing a mental block and didn't know where to start. She hoped cooking would focus her mind enough for ideas to spark.

Though she could drive, Peyton didn't have a car of her own. There was no need for one when she lived in her student apartment. And she was also a broke bitch. Don had told her she could borrow any of the cars whenever she wanted or needed, so she grabbed a key from the hanger on the wall and made her way into the garage.

She clicked the button to open the door and was shocked to see the keys she'd picked up were for the Rolls-Royce in the corner. The sleek white of the Ghost was beautiful, not a single flaw to be seen on any of the bodywork. Peyton whistled softly. She didn't know much about cars, but she could tell when something was pretty. And expensive.

The driver's seat practically molded to her as she slid behind the wheel, running her fingertips over the polished interior. She was almost scared to move for fear that she would damage it somehow, but the urge to drive such a beautiful car won out.

Peyton was in love by the time she reached the grocery store. Between the purr of the engine and how smooth it drove, she wasn't sure she ever wanted to return it to the Adis clan. The thought of running away, using the Rolls as her bougie getaway car, popped into her mind more than once. She needed an escape and it seemed like the universe had handed her a very fast, reliable way of doing so. But then her common sense kicked in and she realized that if she ran away, Hadina would hunt her down. Especially if Peyton stole from them. With a sigh, Peyton slid from the car, triple-checked that she had locked the doors, and then made her way into the store.

She had decided to cook a moussaka for dinner. It was one of the things Melina had taught her how to cook when Peyton was old enough to be in the kitchen—her sister had loved to cook whenever she got the chance—and Peyton hoped it helped her feel closer to her lost sibling. She made her way around the store with ease, throwing the ingredients into the cart and adding a few snacks for herself. She was in need of comfort food, seeing as her nerves had been shot since the moment Hadina had walked through the office door and found her sitting behind the desk.

The drive home provided her with more time to think, to contemplate her life decisions. Perhaps it had been a mistake for her to run away to college; maybe she should have stayed at home and tried to repair all the broken family relationships she had left behind. Peyton had tried to escape the cage she was raised in, only to find herself trapped in a different and far more confusing prison.

Don greeted her with a huge smile and a hug when she returned to the house, offering to help her carry the bags inside. She waved him off, stating she was more than capable even though she felt like the weight of the groceries was going to tip her over, and shuffled into the kitchen. Peyton dumped the bags on the countertops and sighed, flexing her fingers, which were sore from the handles biting into her skin.

Only a few steps behind the girl, Don leaned against the counter, crossing his arms. Peyton wondered what he had looked like when he was younger. He was formidable now, but she had a suspicion he was a terrifying hot commodity in his youth. Hadina had his strong features—sharp nose, dark brows, high cheekbones—but Piper and Zellie didn't resemble him as much. She would have to pay more attention to the frames hanging on the walls to see if there was a photo of the Adis parents in the years gone by.

"What's for dinner?"

Peyton beamed and danced on her tiptoes excitedly. "Moussaka and garlic spinach."

"Greek food? Yum," Don replied, rubbing his stomach.

"My sister taught me when I was younger. She loved to cook and would go out of her way to find recipes from all over the world. But moussaka was one of my favorites."

Don looked at her knowingly, no doubt thinking of the breakdown she'd had on the day they met. "She sounds like she was a great person."

Peyton's smile turned sad. "She was the best."

She was grateful when Don left her to it after that. She wiped away the tears from her eyes and pottered around the kitchen, shoving her snacks into a cupboard and organizing the ingredients she needed for the dinner. Rummaging through the drawers, she found an old apron with *Queen of the Kitchen* printed on it in white calligraphy. She pulled it over her head and cinched it around her waist with a bow, ready to start cooking her dish.

Peyton could remember the recipe by heart, her hands basically moving on their own as she worked through the steps. She let out a groan when the onions and garlic were added to the pan, the aroma wafting through the kitchen like a comforting blanket. It was an easy enough dish to make once you had practiced a couple of times, and she loved the moment you got to layer all the pieces together.

After she had chopped, sautéed, layered, and covered in sauce, Peyton placed the glass dish in the oven and grabbed the salad ingredients from the fridge. She loved to serve fresh salad with any of her Greek recipes, enjoying the taste of crisp lettuce and the crunch of raw onion. Dicing everything into uniform chunks as much as she was able, Peyton threw the veggies into the salad bowl and tossed in her dressing, adding a squeeze of lemon juice to keep the mixture fresh.

She looked around her and grimaced at the mess she had caused in the kitchen. Dirty chopping boards and utensils were discarded across all the countertops, pieces of vegetables and their skins decorating the floor. She sighed and glanced at the time on the stove clock; she had a few minutes to clean but, damn, was she exhausted.

A smile crossed Peyton's face as she remembered who she worked for—the Adis family was rich as hell and it meant one key thing... They had a dishwasher. She had grown up with the family taking turns handwashing everything, she and Melina alternating between washing and drying. And when she moved out, she could barely afford her rent, never mind an appliance like a dishwasher. It made the tedious process far easier as she tidied her mess, shoving everything inside to get washed and brushing the mess off the tiled floor.

When she was done, an hour had passed and it was time to check on the moussaka. Peyton looked around for oven mitts, hoping a pair was hanging up somewhere. When she couldn't find any, she frantically searched the cupboards and drawers to no avail. She grumbled as she grabbed two dishtowels in her hands and pulled the oven open.

A burst of heat blew into her face and she stumbled back. Her panic that the dish would burn her hands was causing her to be careless. Taking a deep breath, she leaned forward and gripped the pan by its edges, pulling it towards the edge of the shelf. She gripped it tightly and lifted it, kicking the oven shut with her foot. She was about to put the dish on the wooden board on the countertop when her dishtowel slipped from her right hand.

Peyton let out a loud scream as the glass burned her hand. The pain overwhelmed her and she let go, the entire thing dropping and shattering into pieces.

"Fuck!" she yelled as she looked at the floor, her moussaka splattered with glass chucks sticking out of the mixture. She knelt down, wincing as her skin burned, and tried to pick up the larger shards. She inched forward and slipped on a piece of eggplant, her hand landing on a pile of glass as she tried to break her fall.

Tears bloomed in her eyes and fell as she lifted her hand, seeing the blood running down her wrists. Thudding footsteps had her cowering as she looked up, seeing Hadina skid into the room with a gun in hand, ready to shoot whomever was there. She looked around, her eyes wild with panic, before seeing Peyton on the ground, huddled by the corner.

"Peyton? What happened?" Lowering her gun, Hadina crept forward and knelt before Peyton, careful to avoid the glass. If Peyton weren't already crying from the pain and overwhelming embarrassment, she would have cried after seeing the tenderness and concern in Hadina's face. "Are you okay?"

"I was making dinner," Peyton hiccupped, "but I couldn't find oven mitts and the dishtowel slipped when I tried to lift the tray. I burnt myself and then slipped and landed in the glass."

She held her hand up as proof, and Hadina winced through her teeth as she saw the blood pouring, a red welt forming on her palm underneath the cuts.

"*Mierda*, you don't do things by halves, do you?" Standing up, Hadina reached out and helped pull Peyton to her feet, guiding her away from the glass carefully and depositing her in a chair. "Stay here. I'll get the first aid kit."

Hadina disappeared and Peyton closed her eyes, mortified and incredibly sore. She could feel her blood dripping from her hand onto her pants but she loathed the idea of moving, knowing the sting would intensify.

"Don't you dare pass out on me, Miss Dimitra," Hadina said, coming back into the room with a first aid box in hand. "I will leave your ass to bleed out."

Peyton laughed through her tears, wincing when Hadina lifted the wounded hand to inspect it. "I don't doubt that for a minute."

She watched as Hadina fluttered around the kitchen, grabbing a bowl, filling it with water, and sitting down on the floor in front of her. "*Lo siento*," she said before catching Peyton's confused look. "It means *I'm sorry* because this is going to hurt."

Peyton barely had time to process her employer's words before Hadina poured lukewarm water over her hand and wiped away the blood. Hissing and gritting her teeth, Peyton tried to sit still as Hadina cleaned out the small cuts before examining the burn. If she were being perfectly honest with herself, Peyton wanted to punch Hadina so hard in the throat that she'd never be able to call her Miss Dimitra in that *damn* voice ever again. It could be the pent-up anger and fear, or it could be the pain that was talking; either way,

Peyton wanted to hit Hadina despite the woman's present kindness.

"I'm really thankful that you're helping," Peyton ground out, "but I think I'm going to smack you if you keep prodding at my hand."

Hadina tightened her grip on Peyton's injured palm and smirked. "Don't threaten me with a good time."

"You wish."

The silence between them stretched taut as Hadina worked on Peyton's injuries, the latter unable to take her eyes off the former. She really would never get over how beautiful Hadina was. Her dark hair and brows, long eyelashes framing vibrant eyes, a perfectly sculpted face with warm brown skin; Peyton wanted to worship at her feet like the woman was a deity.

Peyton watched as Hadina applied ointment to her burn before pulling some dressings from the box. "How'd you learn to clean wounds?"

Hadina looked up, catching her gaze for a second before looking down again. "My line of work isn't exactly above board, as I'm sure you guessed, given the guns and all."

Peyton snorted. "I gathered, yeah."

Hadina tried to hide her smirk, lowering her head further so that dark hair shadowed her face. "My mom was a nurse. Well, she was before I was born. She thought it was super important for us all to know how to take care of various injuries and stuff, in case there were any emergencies."

"And were there? Emergencies?"

Hadina hesitated before nodding. "More than I can count. It was an invaluable skill to learn."

"What was she like?"

"Who?"

"Your mom," Peyton said softly.

Hadina was silent as she finished tending to Peyton's hand.

Peyton was half-convinced she was going to ignore her when the woman stood, tidying everything back into the box.

"My mom was the best person I've ever known," Hadina replied quietly, before walking out the kitchen.

The sadness in Hadina's voice threatened to send Peyton into another flood of tears. She blinked them away, taking a deep breath as she prepared herself to clear the mess she'd made on the floor. Her eyes widened as Hadina walked back into the room, a dustpan and brush in one hand, and a mop in the other.

"What are you doing?" Peyton asked incredulously.

Hadina scoffed. "I may be a bitch, but I'm not going to make you clean this up when you've already hurt yourself. Just sit there and look pretty, okay? Take a minute to get yourself together."

Peyton's jaw dropped as she watched Hadina sweep, the sight of her doing something domesticated so bizarre that she couldn't formulate words. As a result, she did indeed just sit there and look pretty, staring at Hadina all the while.

Reina
de las sombras

CHAPTER 18

HADINA

IF THERE WAS ONE THING HADINA HATED IN LIFE, IT WAS FUCKING CLEANING. It was tedious and annoying and the bane of her existence. But she couldn't exactly let Peyton try to sweep up and mop away the remnants of the destroyed moussaka.

Hadina could still hear Peyton's scream playing over in her ears, the agony in the sound piercing Hadina's cold heart. She thought someone had broken in and tried to hurt her, so she grabbed her gun and sprinted to the kitchen as fast as she could. The relief she felt to see Peyton there with no attacker in sight was palpable... until she noticed the blood. They say that when bulls see the color red, they charge; Hadina wasn't much different. She saw the girl bleeding and her heart pounded, automatically switching to an act-now-and-think-about-the-consequences-afterwards mindset.

Now she was sweeping up the mess while Peyton's eyes bore into her. It made her hot all over and there was nothing she could do about it. After Peyton had exited the office, leaving her spent and dripping, Hadina had barely seen her. She knew that Peyton asked to *talk* but Hadina couldn't offer the answers she knew the girl needed. Which meant she also knew it would be wrong to kiss away the tears coating Peyton's cheeks, but damn, she really wanted to. She hated herself for it.

"You know, I could have patched myself up and cleaned. You didn't have to do it," Peyton said as her eyes followed Hadina's every action.

Hadina shrugged. "Perhaps, but I wanted to help."

Peyton pursed her lips for a moment and tilted her head slightly, as though she were seeing her employer at a new angle. "Why? Why would you want to help me? Besides the fucking, I'm pretty sure you hate me."

"Hate is a strong word."

"That wasn't an answer, Hadina."

Hadina finished cleaning the floor, considering Peyton's question. She honestly wasn't quite sure why she wanted to help, but she knew she most certainly didn't hate the girl. Hell, Hadina had been beating herself up since the day they met about just how much she *didn't* hate her, even though she should. Peyton was beautiful and infuriating and nosy and far too involved—but she intrigued Hadina beyond measure and that was something she couldn't quite let go of.

Leaning the mop against the countertop, Hadina carefully walked on the wet floor and took a seat beside Peyton. "I don't hate you."

"Are you sure about that? Because it sure as hell feels like you hate me."

Hadina sighed and looked at Peyton from the corner of her eye. Running a hand through her hair, she tucked a strand behind her ear and blew out another long breath. "I definitely don't hate you. You are... interesting, and I find myself being drawn to you far more than I would like."

Peyton laughed bitterly. "So, you like me but you don't *want* to like me? That's a real vote of fucking confidence."

Hadina rolled her eyes. "Don't be so dramatic. It isn't necessarily about you."

Peyton raised a brow and waited patiently for her to continue.

"I'm not a good person, Peyton. I do bad things and I don't feel guilty about it. I will most definitely continue to do bad things, and the only guilt I will feel is if you get caught up in it. Do you understand what I'm saying?"

"I understand your words, Hadina, but I disagree. You're letting fear rule your emotions and, as your dad so kindly reminded me, it's an unhealthy way to live. You don't have to be a bitch all the time just because you don't want to feel. I don't need pretty words and declarations; I just need honesty and a little bit of trust."

Hadina's mouth quirked. "That's quite a few times you've called me a bitch now, you know. If you were anyone else, you'd have a bullet in your skull."

Peyton eyed her for a moment and then burst out laughing, her puffy eyes still red from crying, which made her look delirious. "And that's the third time you've threatened me. I'm still here, aren't I?"

Hadina soured at that. She *had* threatened her cruelly more than once, and yet not much had come of it. Hadina had expected Peyton to run after that first time, to become a problem that she would solve in the only way she knew how. But the girl had defied Hadina's assumptions about her, remaining in the house and digging herself further into their lives. It made her suspicious, and oddly aroused. She imagined a scenario where she had to use extreme methods to find out what Peyton knew, torture her with pleasure until she promised to keep quiet.

Hadina crossed her legs, squeezing her thighs together tightly to apply pressure on her aching pussy. "I think you have a death wish."

Peyton laughed again and Hadina was entranced by how much she enjoyed the sound. "Maybe I do. Who knows? But the point is... I'm here."

"Indeed you are, *tentadora*."

"*Tentadora?*" Peyton repeated, surprising Hadina with how well she rolled the *R*. Hadina schooled her face to stop from showing how impressed she was.

"It means *temptress*. All you've done since we met is tempt me, Peyton, and it's driving me fucking insane."

Hadina felt Peyton's hand tuck under her chin, forcing their eyes to meet. Her tear-stained face was still beautiful, even with the red streaks marring her skin. Before she realized what she was doing, Hadina brushed away a strand of golden hair stuck in Peyton's bangs, clearing her vision. Their touches were gentle and it clogged Hadina's throat to think about it; she couldn't remember being soft and intimate with anyone like she was in that moment, her fingertips skimming across Peyton's pretty cheeks, her eyes taking in those plump lips.

She debated with herself internally. Hadina knew the moment was perfect, a chance to kiss Peyton and *feel*, but it would change things. There was so much tension pent up between them that her resolve would snap, and she would be a lost cause. Her mind battled with the cold, dead thing she called a heart until the decision was taken from her.

Peyton reached out first, cupped Hadina's cheeks, and leaned forward. She tasted like salt and spices as Hadina's tongue entwined with hers, her hand slipping to the back of Peyton's head to grip her hair while pulling her deeper into the kiss. She could feel Peyton's nipples pebble beneath her shirt, her own breasts aching to be touched. She was about to do something about it when Peyton pulled back and smiled softly.

"You may not let the world see the gentle part of you, Hadi, but I see it anyway. I see you."

Hadina felt the absence of Peyton's hands immediately as she let go of her face, leaving her in the kitchen without so much as a goodbye. It felt as though she was always watching her walk away and Hadina cursed the part of her that seemed hurt by that. She was too busy, too important, too independent to have feelings for someone. And yet, she knew that Peyton was peeling away the dead parts of her heart. She had never been *seen* before, never allowed anyone to get that close to her for fear that they would ruin everything she had worked so hard to help build.

Hadina had broken her own rule and allowed herself to be swept up in Peyton, the ruse of manipulation slowly slipping away. The whole situation was getting way too complicated, and for once in her life, Hadina had no idea what to do.

Tentadora

CHAPTER 19

PEYTON

THERE WASN'T A PART OF HER THAT REGRETTED KISSING HADINA THE DAY before. Peyton had felt the air shift between them and a wave of courage swept over her, giving her the bravery she needed to show Hadina how she felt. It was the kind of kiss that she had wanted, had daydreamed about since they met—sweet and passionate and filled with intent.

But that didn't mean Peyton was going to stop trying to figure out what Hadina was up to. She told herself that it was for her own peace of mind, that she would be able to let her feelings go once she realized just how fucked up Hadina was.

Sitting on top of her bed with her laptop open, Peyton searched for *Regina*. Hundreds of thousands of results popped up and she let out a sigh. Filtering by the city and excluding anyone under the age of twenty, Peyton managed to cut the numbers by half, though that still meant there were thousands of results to sift through.

"Think, Peyton," she whispered to herself.

Adding in keywords like Hadina's name, words associated with

133

the business or crime, Peyton searched for hours without a break. Nothing proved important or relevant to what she was looking for—although she didn't really know *what* she was actually looking for—so she closed her laptop with a *smack.*

Peyton could feel herself accepting her current predicament, which she knew wasn't healthy. Perhaps it was some weird case type of masochism, Hadina's threats becoming something alluring in her messed-up mind. She had been told not to leave, that she'd be hunted if she did, and Peyton was close to admitting that she didn't *want* to leave now.

Being in the Adis family home, seeing Hadina almost every day, was a temptation that Peyton found hard to resist. There was a dark cloud that seemed to loom around them, but it was like Hadina was always right there to reassure Peyton that the storm would pass. She knew the woman was dangerous and devious, but the dark part of her that she buried deep was drawn to Hadina anyway.

"Ding-dong!" she heard a voice yell up the stairs, the sound carrying through the empty hallways.

Peyton jumped off her bed and made her way out to the landing, a surprised smile crossing her face when she saw Piper at the foot of the stairs. She waved before gesturing for Peyton to come meet her.

Piper embraced Peyton in a tight hug the moment the two were within arm's reach, reminding Peyton of the way Melina used to hold her. She blinked away tears and pulled back with a grin. "What are you doing here?"

"I came to see if my darling sister wanted to go for lunch. Is she around?"

Peyton shook her head. "She hasn't been around today. Sorry, Piper."

Piper waved a manicured hand. "Nonsense. She's a hard one to get a hold of, is all. I like to check in and make sure she's okay. Hadina's always bottled everything up."

"Your dad said something similar to me about her."

"Dad always did understand Hadina better than everyone else. They're so alike sometimes. *Anyway*," Piper continued, "what are you up to?"

Peyton shrugged and sat down on the bottom stair. "Nothing really. While I'm super grateful for my job, I don't think your dad actually needs me around to help, you know? Most of the time, he lets me do my own thing or we garden. I feel like I'm getting paid for nothing."

Piper sat beside Peyton, bumping her shoulder with a smile. "That's bullshit if I've ever heard some. You get paid for companionship, for my dad to have someone around when he *does* need help. Don't discredit yourself like that, Peyton. He's happy to have someone around who isn't one of his daughters."

Considering that for a moment, Peyton figured Piper was right. Although she didn't have to do much, she knew that she would do anything Don needed if he asked. Still, she was being paid a lot just to sit and talk to an old man.

"Thank you," Peyton said. "I mean it. I appreciate that."

Piper beamed and jumped up, clapping her hands together. "How about *you* come for lunch? I wanna get to know you better!"

Peyton wasn't sure why she felt such a kinship with Piper, but she desperately wanted to be friends with the Adis' ray of sunshine. She found herself nodding and was promptly dragged to her feet.

"Let's go!"

PEYTON FELT SERIOUSLY UNDERDRESSED when they walked into the restaurant, not long after Piper drove them there. *Il Fiore* was a fancy sandstone building in the heart of town. Peyton knew only wealthy people could afford to dine here, with the parking attendant posted outside and the canopy overhead as they entered the front of the building. It was magnificent and intimidating and Peyton felt out of place.

A waiter in a tuxedo led the duo through a sea of marble-top tables, plush suede seats, and charcoal-colored booths to one right in the corner, facing out to the rest of the restaurant. "Your usual table, Ms. Adis."

Piper thanked him and slid into the booth, shirking off her white coat to reveal a beautiful forest-green bodycon dress. It clung to her frame perfectly, a simple V-cut neck revealing just a hint of cleavage. The color suited her complexion and was almost a perfect match for her eyes.

"You look stunning," Peyton said honestly. While she was insanely jealous of how gorgeous the Adis sisters were, she didn't understand the mindset that women should tear other women apart. It seemed absurd to drag someone down out of jealousy and it just wasn't Peyton.

A light blush formed on Piper's cheeks. "Thank you, Peyton."

Glancing at her own ripped jeans and band tee, Peyton grimaced. She was the odd one out in a restaurant full of people who could buy and sell her entire life a thousand times over.

"Wipe that look from your face," Piper commanded with a familiar air of authority. "You look absolutely stunning no matter what you wear, and *nobody* should ever look down on you because of that. If they do, you flash them a pretty smile and tell them to go fuck themselves."

Peyton stared at Piper for a second before bursting out into a rather unladylike laugh, snort and all. "Lord, you sound just like Hadina when you take on that tone."

Piper smirked, throwing Peyton a wink. "Well, us sisters do have to have *something* in common, even if it's an attitude."

"You're really fucking cool." Peyton grinned.

"You're really fucking cool too, Peyton."

A content silence settled between them after that as they

browsed the menu, pursuing their endless options. Peyton had never even heard of half the things listed, and the fact that no prices were displayed next to the items made sweat form under her shirt.

"Do you ladies know what you're having?" A waiter arrived at their table with a smile on his face and a tablet in his hand, ready to take their orders.

"I'll have the Wagyu steak with the truffle mashed potatoes, please," Piper stated, handing the man her menu.

Sweat now dotted Peyton's brow as well, her eyes flicking to the menu again. She hated fancy dining and pompous dishes. Yes, she dreamed of going to places like this and knowing exactly what everything was, but she certainly wasn't at that stage yet. "May I have the lemon and rosemary chicken with the tri-cooked fries?"

The waiter nodded politely and turned on his heel, leaving the women to talk.

"Why do you look like you're about to be sick?" Piper questioned, her brows furrowed in concern.

Peyton leaned forward, whispering so she wouldn't be overheard. "This place is *so* expensive-looking, Piper. I feel so out of place."

Piper laughed, a light sound, which lifted some of the pressure off Peyton's chest. "Girl, please. You look fabulous. Besides, you're an honorary Adis—you don't pay for shit. Always add whatever you want to our tabs and we'll cover it."

Peyton blanched, her jaw falling slightly ajar. "You can't be serious."

Piper shrugged, her lips pulling into a smirk. "You bet your ass I'm serious. My dad told you that you're one of us, and I'll stand by that."

Feeling tears prick, Peyton pressed her napkin against the corners of her eyes. "I really appreciate that, even if I don't understand it."

"You'll understand one day. None of us Adis girls let anyone get close—myself included—but we're fiercely protective of those who break through. If I didn't already want you to be my new best friend," she says with a chuckle, "then the way Hadina acts around you would be reason enough."

Peyton balked at that, almost choking on her water. "I don't—"

Piper held up a hand. "Yeah, yeah. I know how this story goes, Pey. Can I call you Pey? Anyway, y'all have *something* going on, and while I definitely don't need to know details, I am happy to see my sister occupied with *something* other than work."

By the time the waiter brought the decadent meals to the table, Peyton was almost in love with Piper and her cheeriness. She reminded Peyton of Melina a little, with the way she fired off a million questions at once but carried on talking without an answer. She was so bright and fun, and Peyton hoped that they really would be friends. She figured she needed one of those.

They devoured the food on their plates and sat back, both laughing as they patted their full stomachs. "It's unfair that bloating after eating still exists, right?"

"So unfair! Why should we suffer for sustaining our bodies? I call bullshit."

"Oh, Pey," Piper wheezed, a fondness in her voice, "I'm so pleased you said yes to lunch today. This is the most fun I've had in ages. We'll need to keep hanging out." Peyton was about to return the sentiment when Piper clapped her hands together, making her jump slightly. "I know! You should come to the exhibition at my gallery tomorrow evening!"

Art was something that Peyton did enjoy, though she had a sinking feeling in her gut that it would mean facing Hadina. Not that she was avoiding her, but she knew there was plenty to discuss after their kiss in the kitchen, and the floodgate of emotion that had opened between them.

"I don't know..."

"Please!" Piper begged, holding her hands together like she was praying. "It would mean the world to me."

It was weird how swayed Peyton was to say yes, to give in to this newfound friendship in the hopes that it would form a bond between them. But Peyton could be strong—sometimes. "I wouldn't even have anything to wear!" She shook her head when Piper opened her mouth to retort. "Besides, I don't know if I'm ready to see Hadina in a public setting. Her ice-queen persona is terrifying enough at home."

Piper laughed lightly. "*Reina de las sombras.* Queen of the shadows. I suppose it's apt that my sister's nicknames are always associated with queendom, don't you think?"

"She gives *off with your head* vibes for sure," Peyton commented, earning herself a resounding cackle.

"Well, you'll be pleased to know that Hadina has business to attend to tomorrow so she won't be at the event. And I know the perfect place for you to get something to wear!"

Tentadora

CHAPTER 20

PEYTON

PEYTON DIDN'T THINK ANY OF THE ADIS SISTERS HAD EVER BEEN TOLD *NO* IN their lives—and she didn't want to be the one to do it now. Which was how, after finishing their drinks and Piper paying for lunch, Peyton was dragged through town to a beautiful glass building. The sign read "Kloset" in bold, white lettering with a blue light illuminating it from behind.

There was no holding in her gasp as they stepped inside the gorgeous store, mannequins adorned with premium fabrics and accessories that hurt Peyton's bank account to look at. The walls were decorated with large prints of models wearing the outfits on display, or glass shelves piled with stock ready for purchase. In the middle stood a slate-gray circular desk, three different cashiers handing branded shopping bags to the patrons swiping their cards.

"Piper, you gorgeous bitch! Please tell me you're here to get a dress for tomorrow. I have the perfect one set aside for you."

Peyton watched as Piper embraced the woman who spoke to her so casually to the Adis girl that it almost evoked jealousy. The woman was dressed in tight, electric-blue pants with a white halter blouse tucked into the waistband, serving as a perfect contrast to her almond skin. She wore no makeup, which Peyton could only guess was a blessing, considering how gorgeous the woman was without it.

Tucking some of her tight curls behind her ear, she peered over Piper's shoulder and smiled when she saw Peyton. "Oh my *God*! Tell me this is her, Pip. Is this who has Z in a mood and Hadina all fucked up?"

Spinning around, Piper placed her arm around the woman's small waist and nodded. "The one and the same. Peyton, meet my dear friend, Kaira. Kai, this is Peyton Dimitra."

The woman—*Kaira*—pounced forward and tugged Peyton into a hug. Taken aback, Peyton stood rigid, breathing in the scent of rose and sage, before softening into the embrace. "It's nice to meet you."

Kaira pulled back, her smile dazzling as she inspected Peyton from head to toe. "It's my pleasure. Anyone who can get under the skin of one of my girls is someone I'm desperate to meet."

Peyton flashed Piper a warning look, but she simply held up her hands in a mock surrender. "Don't look at me. Kai's been friends with us since we were kids. I'm not the only one who talks to her."

Throwing her arm over Peyton's shoulders, Kaira guided the two girls through the store to an elevator at the back, pressing the button to take them up to the third floor—clearly Kaira's workshop. Mannequins with half-finished dresses and scraps of fabric lay discarded everywhere, with spools of untouched material leaning against whichever wall had space.

Peyton's eyes caught on a dress displayed in front of the windows, the bottle green silhouetted by the sunlight shimmering through. Beside her, Piper let out a soft gasp. "Kaira..."

"I know, I know. I outdid myself," the designer boasted, a playful smirk on her face.

Piper hesitantly reached out to touch the satin gown with trembling fingers. Peyton watched tears blossom in her friend's eyes as she took it all in. It was a work of art in itself. An asymmetric scarf neck fell down the cowl back, accentuating the figure-hugging design of the satin before kicking out into a fishtail at the bottom. Peyton was sure that it would look breathtaking on Piper.

"I can't wear this," Piper whispered, a few stray tears slipping down her cheeks.

"You can and you will," Kaira said with a dismissive wave of a hand. "You've worked really fucking hard on your gallery, babe. You deserve to have your dream dress to showcase that."

Peyton felt her own eyes well up as she watched Piper and Kaira. The only person she had ever been close to like this was Melina, and she felt the magnitude of that loss daily. She was simultaneously jealous of the pair and their friendship, and happy that Piper had someone she was close to. Though, her curiosity was piqued by the fact that Kaira was friends with Hadina too—she didn't think Hadina would be considered a friend to anyone.

"Thank you," Piper sniffled delicately, which almost made Peyton laugh. The Adis sisters even made fucking crying beautiful.

"You're going to look like royalty in that," Peyton said with a fond smile. It was true; the dress was made to be worn by someone like Piper.

Kaira chuckled and slung an arm over Peyton's shoulders again, pulling her close. "That's because she's going to be the queen of her own event. Now, *you*, on the other hand, are going to look like Satan himself sent you to tempt everyone in the room. You'll look positively sinful by the time I'm done with you."

"I can't. I won't even know anyone there."

Patting Peyton's shoulder, Kaira placed a soft kiss on the girl's cheek. "Darling, you'll know me. And besides, it's terribly rude to refuse to let a designer dress you when she offers."

"That's not true," Piper sing-songed.

"Maybe not, but it should be," Kaira replied, sticking out her tongue in response. "Now, Peyton dear, go get undressed in that room over there"—she pointed—"while I fetch the dress for you. We need to see how it fits in case alterations are needed."

Placing her hands on Peyton's back, Kaira gently pushed her forward until they reached the dressing room. Peyton turned to protest some more but Kaira grinned from ear to ear, mischief lighting up her entire face. Peyton couldn't force herself to say anything and instead did as instructed, waiting patiently for Kaira to bring her the dress in question.

"I'm coming in!" Kaira announced as she opened the door and entered the dressing room. Peyton squealed and grabbed her clothes on the floor to cover herself. Kaira laughed, patting Peyton's cheek. "Relax, gorgeous, this is my job. I see tits, ass, and everything else all day long."

Peyton could feel her cheeks burn anyway, but Kaira's attitude was bright and infectious, making her relax slightly. Though she still didn't uncover herself until Kaira's back was turned.

"Take the gown out of the bag carefully and slip into it. I'll help you do up the zips once you're dressed."

Peyton's breath caught as the sleek gown glided from the bag, the black jersey fabric soft against her hands. Undoing the zip at the back and left side, Peyton stepped into the gown and pulled the material up, slipping her right arm into the long sleeve.

"Okay, ready for your assistance."

Kaira's eyes widened when she turned around, her gaze roaming over Peyton's figure. "Fucking hell, you look even better than I thought you would."

Peyton blushed and dipped her head. "Thank you."

Once Kaira had finished zipping her up and making sure that the dress was sitting correctly, the designer moved out of the way and let Peyton examine herself in the mirrored wall.

"*Oh*," she whispered as she took in the sight of her dress in all of its divine glory. The A-line shape wasn't something Peyton ever thought would look good on her, but the gown clung to her curves in all the right places, before trailing down into a long sweep train. She was surprised by how well the ruched one-shoulder suited her too, drawing attention to the small pieces of skin on display, like her exposed shoulder.

Taking a step forward, she let out a happy sigh at the slit in the skirt—which ran from her left thigh to the floor between her feet. It was simple, beautiful, and utterly extraordinary. Peyton didn't feel deserving enough to wear such an extravagant gown.

"This is... *beautiful* isn't even the word, Kai. This is a masterpiece."

The awe in her voice was clear, which earned her a delighted clap. "Let's go show Piper!"

Throwing the door wide open, Kaira grabbed Peyton's hand and pulled her out into the center of room. Piper let out a dramatic gasp before jumping excitedly with Kai. "Look at her! Oh my fucking hell, Kai, you did it. You literally created the perfect dress for her before you even met her!"

"Wait, what?"

Kaira looked nervous for a second before shrugging. "Listen, the Adis family always has events to attend. When the girls started talking about you, I guess I found myself a little inspired. So, I've been making this dress for you for the last couple of weeks, in case you ever needed it."

Peyton didn't know how to feel about that. It was as if she had been pulled into this whole new life without any warning, and the more she tried to pull away, the deeper she sank into it. But the gown was beautiful and Piper and Kai were beaming, and for the first time in a while, Peyton *felt* good.

Staring at herself in the bronze free-standing mirror, Peyton tried to picture her reflection with her hair and makeup done, a pair of heels to match and jewelry too. As if her subconscious was trying to make her suffer, an image of Hadina appeared next to her, the queen and her consort ready to take on the world. Even in her daydreams, Hadina was the most breathtaking person Peyton had ever seen, and it was a cruel cosmic joke that she would never know what it was like to be *hers*.

Shaking her head of all thoughts of Hadina, Peyton turned back to her new friends, forcing a smile onto her face. "Well, Piper, I guess I'll be coming to the event after all."

Piper and Kaira whooped, enveloping her in a crowded embrace, and Peyton didn't pull away this time. Maybe the most meaningful friendships were the ones you didn't see coming.

CHAPTER 21

HADINA

SHE WOULDN'T LIE AND SAY THAT HER HEAD WASN'T COMPLETELY FUCKED after her last encounter with Peyton, but it didn't mean she was happy about it.

I see you.

Three simple words, and she was fucking undone. For days, her mind had been a jumbled mess, a constant switch between worrying about work and worrying about Peyton. She wanted to make the girl promises she knew she couldn't keep, tell her that the thing between them could actually work. But every time Hadina allowed herself to get caught up in her fantasy, a message or call would come through and break the trance.

Like right now, as Harris swore down the phone in frustration. "We can't find a fucking thing, boss. This Regina bitch is a ghost, and all our leads keep coming up dead. A few of the workers down at the docks said there are some special shipments due in, but a whole new staff has been hired to take care of it."

"This fucking broad," Hadina groaned, throwing one of her

knives into her apartment wall. She thought that coming here would help her focus, but all it did was remind her how empty she felt on her own. "Keep digging, Harris. There has to be something that leads us to her before she gets that shipment. Whether it's drugs or girls, we *have* to end her before she gets her hands on it. Do you understand me?"

Hadina heard the sound of scuffling before a gunshot echoed through the speaker. "I got it, boss, loud and clear. We'll find this bitch."

The line cut off and Hadina threw her phone onto the sofa, rubbing her temples. She could sense a tension headache forming, though she wasn't sure that the dull ache had fully disappeared. Every day, more stress was added to her plate and it was becoming harder to pretend she didn't feel the pressure.

It didn't help that she had a barrage of texts from Piper, harassing her to go to the gallery event tomorrow. It wasn't even that she didn't want to go—she'd do anything to support her little sister —but there was a seed of fear planted in her gut, threatening to take root if she didn't find and stop Regina.

Hadina had ended many operations during her years at Adis & Co. but there was something increasingly worrying about the anonymity that Regina had around her. It shouldn't have been possible for her to be a ghost, not with the resources that Hadina had at her disposal. And yet, nobody could find anything out about this woman. It made Hadina uneasy and she detested that.

"*No se que hacer,*" she mumbled to herself with a sigh. She didn't know what she was going to do.

She couldn't remember feeling so out of control since Zellie had tried to undermine their father and take over the company. Zelina had believed their father to be weak, too unwilling to get his hands dirty to get what they wanted. Hadina found it humorous, considering they murdered people regularly, and if that wasn't considered getting your hands dirty, then she didn't know what was.

The rule was no criminal activity that wasn't absolutely necessary. That meant no drugs, trafficking of any kind, murder of the innocent; it was all off-limits. Adis representatives were supposed to tip the balance in favor of the good, help those who couldn't help themselves. They only went after the worst of the worst, and they had a ton of people working for them on *both* sides of the law. None of the employees were good people, not after what they did for a career, but they tried to atone for it where they could.

Zellie had wanted to blur the line that they had promised never to cross. Meeting with dealers and suppliers, she had convinced herself that working *with* them would build bridges within criminal networks and allow Adis & Co. access to worse targets than those in their sights.

Hadina had been furious when she learned of her sister's plans, disbelief filling her system as she tried to understand why Zellie would be okay with slinging hardcore drugs and creating more harm in the process. But then her fury had turned to despair. The betrayal and secrecy of Zellie's actions had caused an irreparable rift, and while their father had forgiven her and moved on, Hadina would never be able to get past it.

Now, as she slumped on the sofa with her head on the wall, Hadina couldn't help but remember the sting of her sister's betrayal. She hoped desperately that the nagging feeling in her gut was nothing more than misplaced anxiety. She didn't think she could cope with another betrayal.

"Your girl is a hottie," Kaira said as she stormed into the apartment, dumping a bag of Chinese takeaway on the coffee table in front of them.

Hadina rolled her eyes. "I should never have given you the code to get in here. And also—she's not *my* girl."

Kaira ignored the comment and grabbed plates from the kitchen, sitting on the floor with her legs crossed. "Bitch, we've been friends for years. I know you like her."

Hadina shrugged and tore into a spring roll. She bit down on the pastry and spoke around her mouthful of food. "That's beside the point. I don't do relationships."

Scooping some chow mein on her plate, Kaira snorted. "You don't do anything but work. It's unhealthy and the lack of pussy is probably why you're such an asshole all the time."

Mouth agape, Hadina stared at her friend. "You did not just say that. You realize I literally kill people for a living, right? You can't talk to me like that."

Kaira looked up, her lip trembling momentarily before she burst into a fit of laughter. "I fucking dare you. You'd be distraught without my wit brightening up your life."

Hadina shook her head, lifting her plate so she could rest comfortably on the sofa while she ate. It had been a while since she'd actually hung out with Kaira, so she felt like she had to say yes when Kaira asked her if they could have dinner together. Hadina wasn't a good friend, her inattentiveness borderline rude, but Kaira had stuck around for years and knew her well enough to not expect anything more.

Hadina did occasionally feel guilty about it though.

"Anyway," she said after she swallowed her piece of salt and chili chicken. "How do you know she's a *hottie*?"

"Piper brought her to the store today. They needed dresses for the event tomorrow."

Hadina's brows furrowed. Neither Piper nor Peyton had said that they were hanging out, and Piper certainly hadn't mentioned that she'd invited Peyton to the gallery event.

"Oh. I hadn't realized they were friends. "

Kaira's grin was devious. "Are we jealous, darling? Worried that sweet little PeyPey will like Piper better than you?"

"*Zorra*," Hadina growled. "I'm not jealous."

"Tell that to the green monster on your shoulder." Kaira laughed. "Speaking of green, I made Pip her dream dress and she looks like a vision."

Hadina pushed rice around her plate with her fork, listening to Kaira describe Piper's gown. It sounded beautiful but she didn't really care. All she wanted to do was ask her about what Peyton would be wearing.

"It's a pity you won't be there. Peyton looks phenomenal in her dress," Kaira commented, stealing Hadina's prawn cracker from her discarded plate.

She knew she was being goaded, and while she abhorred the idea of being manipulated, Hadina couldn't help herself. "What's the dress like? Was she happy in it?"

Kaira smirked, looking pleased with herself. "I'm not telling. I guess you'll just have to come to the event to see it for yourself."

Hadina groaned, throwing a prawn cracker at her friend. She knew that she had more to worry about, things she should have been prioritizing, but all she could think about was what Peyton would look like in an expensive gown. Then she pictured other people being there, *staring*, and Hadina hissed through her teeth. "I'll be there."

Kaira beamed. "Good. Your girl will be happy to see you."

Tentadora

CHAPTER 22

PEYTON

THERE WAS NO REASON FOR HER TO BE NERVOUS, BUT PEYTON FELT SICK WITH anxiety anyway. She finished the wing of her eyeliner with a relieved sigh and sifted through her makeup bag until she found a red lipstick. *Pomegranate Kisses* was a deep, saturated red that stood out against Peyton's pale skin. The color, while beautiful, had always been too striking to wear. She'd bought it on a whim one day when she saw it in the store, the name the major selling point, but it had remained in the bottom of Peyton's makeup bag since then.

"It's a day for being bold," she mumbled to herself as she applied the last swipe onto her lips.

Glancing at the back of her door, Peyton eyed her dress hanging there. She only had twenty minutes to finish getting ready and be downstairs to meet with Kaira. Peyton hadn't even realized when Kaira had entered her number into her phone, but the designer had been texting Peyton excitedly all day. Peyton would be lying if she said she minded, though; having the beginnings of a friendship was more than she thought she'd get after Melina died.

Kicking off her fluffy slippers, Peyton sat on the edge of her bed and grabbed her shoes for the evening. The black stilettos were another gift from Kai, who promised that they were the perfect accompaniment for such a show-stopping dress. Slipping her feet into the five-inch heels, Peyton reached down and wrapped the cords around her calves, tying the ends into a pretty bow. They were definitely statement shoes, and not something she'd normally pick for herself, but they were *gorgeous* and Peyton figured she was indebted to Kai for being so kind to her.

Standing carefully, Peyton stepped into her dress and zipped herself up, smoothing down the skirt so that it was sitting perfectly. She walked over to the mirror and examined her reflection, wondering who the hell she thought she was, looking like such a badass.

Her dress clung to her frame like it had when she tried it on at the shop, though now her cleavage was partially exposed thanks to the strapless bra that Piper had made her buy at Kloset. With her red lips, fierce outfit, and blonde locks sitting in loose waves, Peyton looked like a completely different person. Like the person she *wanted* to be. Bold. Fearless. Beautiful.

Kaira honked the car horn outside and Peyton cursed, wondering how she had lost twenty minutes so quickly. She rushed out of her room and downstairs, surprised to see Don waiting at the front door in a tuxedo.

"*Cariño,* you look stunning," Don said, taking her hand in his.

Peyton blushed from the compliment and pulled him into a half hug. "I didn't know you were coming! Are you riding with Kai and me?"

Don shook his head, opening the front door for her like a gentleman. "Zelina will be picking me up shortly. You go on ahead with Kaira—I'll see you both there."

Slipping into the passenger seat of Kaira's sleek Audi R8, Peyton beamed at her friend, who wolf-whistled in return. "*Damn,* you look hot as hell!"

Peyton took in the blue figure-hugging dress Kai was wearing, admiring the gold chains that overlapped across the entire design. It was gorgeous. "Likewise. That outfit is something else."

"Considering the cost of the material, I better look like a fucking goddess." Kaira chuckled.

She glanced at Peyton once more before pulling out of the driveway and onto the busy streets. Peyton closed her eyes and rested her head back against the seat, enjoying the ride as they zoomed past traffic. Anxious thoughts swirled through her mind, telling her she would look as out of place as she actually was. Each thought was worse than the last, and as Kaira pulled up outside the gallery, telling her they'd arrived, all Peyton could think about was how much she wished Hadina had been able to attend too.

Apparently, the cool silence of her shadow-queen boss had become a comforting blanket for her nervousness. Without it, Peyton felt like a lamb being fed to a pack of rich, aristocratic wolves and there was no escape.

"Welcome to your first Adis party," Kaira said, and Peyton felt her stomach sink as they entered the building.

Her nerves had slowly dissipated after drinking two flutes of champagne that Kaira had swiped from a nearby tray. Hundreds of people were packed into the interconnecting rooms, milling around with their own glasses in hand. Peyton knew that it was a formal event, given the gown that she was wearing, but she didn't expect to see women in fur coats and diamond jewelry that glinted like stars on a clear night sky.

She also hadn't expected the gallery to be as huge as it was. Around ten rooms were filled with artwork, separated by partitions and half walls so that you could easily find your way into the next exhibit. Every room had a different theme and featured a solo artist, displaying their work in turn. As Kaira schmoozed with people she knew, Peyton peeled off and made her way around the gallery, admiring the art.

"Peyton!" Piper called out, pushing her way through a cluster of guests who wanted to chat with her or congratulate her on the event. Her dark hair was curled and pinned at her crown, adorned with tiny pearl pins. With green smokey eyes and a nude lip, Piper resembled beauty as she approached, the green of her dress glinting under the lights.

"You look amazing!"

Piper enveloped Peyton in a hug and pressed a light kiss to her cheeks. "As do you, dear. Are you enjoying the event?"

Peyton smiled, holding up her champagne flute. "There's beautiful artwork and champagne—I'm having the *best* time!"

Piper's answering chuckle calmed Peyton slightly. "I need to go and say hello to some more guests, but I'll try to catch up to you soon. Check out room eight. I think it'll be your favorite."

As Piper was pulled away to talk to the state governor and his wife, who looked to be twenty years his junior with a scowl etched into her face, Peyton caught sight of Zellie and groaned. Catching her gaze, Zellie grinned predatorily. Then the eldest Adis sister marched over, grabbed Peyton by the elbow, and tugged her into the next room, away from Don and Piper's watchful eyes.

"Peyton." Letting go of her arm, Zellie took a step back and looked Peyton up and down. "So nice of you to come to my sister's event. Pray tell, why are you here?"

Peyton stuttered and dipped her head under the cold glare of Zellie's eyes. "Piper invited me."

Zellie scoffed. "Piper always has been kind to the point of foolishness. She's too polite for her own good. So, let me be the one to tell you that you are most definitely not welcome here. Why don't you hurry along to whatever backward Podunk town you come from?"

"Excuse me?" Peyton surprised herself, the alcohol in her system fueling the rage she normally quelled, as she replied, "I was invited here by your sister herself, so I very much think I am welcome. And besides, I don't come from any *Podunk* town, so kindly refrain from making assumptions. What a vile thing to say."

Zellie seethed, stepping into Peyton's personal space. "I don't know who the hell you think you are, or how you've wormed your way into both of my sisters' heads, but I'm not fooled by your innocent, naïve little act. I will kill anyone before I let them fuck with my family."

"I'm not up to anything! I like your family and I'd never do anything to harm any of you!" Peyton hissed back, trying to communicate her sincerity.

"I don't believe you. *No te creo, pendeja vengativa* and I won't let you hurt Piper," Zellie said. Before Peyton could move, Zellie had a fistful of her hair in an agonizing grip. She used her free hand to press a gun—Peyton didn't even know where she had pulled it from—into Peyton's hip. "I'm going to show you to the exit and then I want you to go home, pack your shit, and get the hell out of Papi's house before we return."

Peyton opened her mouth to respond, but a voice interrupted her before she could utter a word.

"I don't think that will be necessary, Zelina," Hadina said, walking into view. "I'd very much appreciate it if you let my date go, put your weapon away before anyone sees, and slither back into your den of snakes before I have to remind you what respect and decorum look like."

Zellie growled but released Peyton, who stumbled forward. Hadina caught her before she fell on her face, maintaining a comforting hold on her arms to keep her steady. She looked at

Peyton with furrowed brows, concern swirling in her eyes. "Are you okay?"

Nodding, Peyton stepped closer to Hadina. Her eyes welled up and she couldn't find the words to express how grateful she was to see her. "I'm all right."

"*Te creía más inteligente para andar cojiéndote a las sirvientas,* Hadina."

Hadina lurched forward and Peyton grabbed at her arm, using all of her strength to pull her back. "What the fuck does that mean?"

Zellie smiled cruelly. "I'm just telling my sister that fucking the help isn't her finest move."

Hadina tried to rush forward again but Peyton stepped in front of her, placing her hands on Hadina's shoulders. "Hadi, stop. Ignore her."

"I can't ignore her. *Eres una puta irrespetuosa* and I won't have her talking about you like that."

Ignoring the way it made her core contract to hear Hadina wanting to defend her honor, Peyton shook her head. "This is Piper's event, Hadi. You can deal with this tomorrow, but let your little sister enjoy her night, huh?"

Throwing a glare over her shoulder at Zellie's retreating figure, Hadina let out a sigh and Peyton felt some of the tension leave her body. A moment passed, and another, before Hadina finally looked Peyton in the eyes. The darkness swirling there was anger mixed with hunger, making Peyton want to cause a different kind of scene right in the middle of the room.

"I didn't think you were coming," she breathed.

Hadina smirked, taking Peyton's hand in hers. "Work can wait. It seems I was going to be missing out otherwise. I have far more pressing matters to deal with."

Peyton grinned as Hadina pulled her by the waist, closing the small distance between them. Leaning down, Hadi caught Peyton's lips in a tender kiss and the fear she had felt before was quickly forgotten. She was suddenly extra grateful to Kaira for gifting her such a wonderful, exposing dress.

"Temptation herself," Hadina whispered against Peyton's lips before pulling her through the gallery. Wherever Hadina was taking her, Peyton would willingly follow.

CHAPTER 23

HADINA

The rage boiling beneath her skin was eclipsed only by the need to devour her *tentadora*. Seeing Zellie's hands on Peyton, her gun pressed to her girl's hip, made Hadina blindingly furious. Had there not been so many witnesses, she wasn't sure that she wouldn't have put a bullet in her sister the moment she saw the scene unfold.

"Where are we going?" Peyton asked, trailing along beside her.

Hadina flashed a grin and winked, loving the way Peyton's pupils dilated in response. "Somewhere private."

After visiting her little sister at work so many times, Hadina practically knew the blueprints of the gallery. Stopping at a side door hidden before the office, she pulled them inside and flicked on the light switch. Then she watched as Peyton's eyes adjusted, taking in the stock room around them. It was small, wall units stacked with tubs of paint and piles of blank canvases.

Pulling her phone from her pocket, Hadina sent a quick text to Harris to tell him where they were. He'd keep watch on Zellie, making sure there weren't any other almost-murders. After the text was delivered, Hadina put her phone on a shelf and turned her attention back to the angel before her.

"Hello."

Peyton smiled sheepishly, lifting her hand in a half-hearted wave. "Hi."

Taking a step closer to her, Hadina allowed her eyes to slowly rake over Peyton, her pulse quickening as she took in the slit reaching up her thigh. Hadina wanted to mark every inch of her exposed skin, showing the world that Peyton now belonged to her. It was wrong to feel such a claim on someone who wasn't hers, *couldn't* be hers, but she told herself she could indulge in the fantasy. Just this once.

"I thought you weren't coming tonight," Peyton whispered, her gaze lingering on Hadina's gown.

She had chosen a figure-hugging velvet dress, which clung to every part of her body before pooling at her feet. With a cut-out underneath her breasts, the design hinted at indecency without actually being improper. Silver sequins decorated the dress in leaf patterns before framing Hadina's hips and thighs in a delicate angel-wing design. It thrilled her to know people would be looking at her dress in the spot where, underneath, she was bare and dripping for the woman in front of her.

Hadina shrugged. "Kaira told me you were coming and I wanted to make sure you were safe. Events like this, especially ones we're attending, bring out the worst kind of people. Like Zelina."

Peyton tilted her head and watched Hadina like she was a puzzle she couldn't quite solve. "I didn't know you cared about my safety. I mean, you have threatened me multiple times."

The air between them became fraught with tension as Hadina smirked. "Consider it my attempt at making sure we don't lose our best employee," she quipped before closing the distance and crushing their lips together.

Peyton sighed as Hadina's hands found her hips, guiding her

backward until they were pressed against one of the shelving units. Hadina devoured the sound, pushing her tongue into Peyton's mouth so she could taste the expensive champagne they had been serving. Underneath the hint of alcohol, Hadina tasted something sweet and it drove her crazy, making her tongue dive deeper as though she could consume it all.

Her fingertips pressed into Peyton's waist firmly before she slipped one hand down to her ass, cupping the voluptuous flesh. Peyton groaned, pressing herself harder into Hadina and grinding against her hip.

"If you ruin this dress, I'll have to dock your wages," Hadina murmured, pressing soft kisses along Peyton's jaw.

Peyton laughed breathily, her hand reaching up to tangle in Hadina's midnight locks. She elicited a shocked, pleasurable gasp from Hadina as she twisted her fingers around some of the curled strands, yanking Hadina's head back so she could look at her. "There are plenty of other ways you can pay me. Dock my pay all you want."

The attitude in her voice made Hadina want to beam with pride, seeing the way Peyton was becoming more sure of herself. Any other time, when she was less needy and desperate to hear Peyton's screams, she may have considered telling her that. But that moment was not now and she had better things to do.

Dropping to her knees, Hadina brushed the slit of Peyton's dress to the side, relishing the easy access it provided her. Underneath, Peyton wore a delicate lace thong, the black material barely covering the front of her swollen pussy. Hadina's mouth watered at the thought of tasting her. She wondered if she should display Peyton in the gallery while she ate her out so that everyone could appreciate the fact that she was a work of art.

Leaning forward, she slowly blew a hot breath against Peyton's sensitive skin, laughing as the girl squirmed above her. Threading her fingers through her hair again, Peyton pushed the back of Hadina's head forward until the woman's lips were almost touching her. "Hadi, stop playing."

"Never," Hadina replied before delving forward, running her tongue through Peyton's wet lips. The answering groan that filled the room had Hadina more determined than ever, her hands curling around the back of Peyton's thighs as she circled the sensitive bud now calling to her.

Peyton's grip on her hair tightened, twisting her fingers at an angle that made Hadina hiss in pain. She retaliated by releasing Peyton's right thigh, instead bringing her hand to Peyton's pussy and teasing her hole with a fingertip. She was soaked and ready, but the game was only just beginning.

"Hadina," Peyton warned, her tone trying to sound commanding but coming out as a whisper when Hadina inserted a finger, teasing her from the inside. "Oh, God, yes! Another one, Hadi."

Setting a punishingly slow pace, Hadina pumped her finger inside Peyton, before finally giving in and adding a second. All the while, she used her thumb to rub and press against Peyton's clit, noting the way her legs shook every time.

Peyton's breath became ragged, her moans louder and longer, the harder Hadina worked her. She was close to climax and Hadina was almost ready to give her release, but then the image of Zellie holding a gun against Peyton, their bodies pressed together, flashed into her mind and another blind rage took over. She knew, logically, that Zelina was unhinged and Peyton had not done anything to warrant it. But the thought of Peyton allowing herself to be so close to someone without fighting to break free—and no, she refused to cut her slack because of the gun—made Hadina want to punish the girl. Teach her that no one else was allowed to put their hands on her body.

Pulling her fingers free, Hadina ignored Peyton's protests as she looked around for something to use. A cruel, domineering smile set across her face as she grabbed two of the paintbrushes at her eye-level, the long and smooth wood exactly what she was looking for.

"Why didn't you fight Zelina?" Hadina asked, running the bristles of the brush over Peyton's swollen sex.

Peyton shivered, her eyes closed and head thrown back. "She had a gun!"

Hadina *tsked* and nudged Peyton's legs farther apart. "Well, this will teach you to get over that pesky fear, won't it?"

Running the wooden handles through Peyton's juices, Hadina made sure the brushes were properly lubricated before she pushed them inside Peyton's entrance, a laugh breaking free as Peyton gasped. Her eyes flashed open and she looked down at Hadina, biting on her lower lip as she moved the brushes out and thrust them back in.

Burying her face between Peyton's thighs, Hadina watched as Peyton lost control, her nails digging into Hadina's scalp as she screamed in pleasure. "Fuck, yes, like that!" she cried as Hadina angled the brushes differently, spreading them wider in her core. She quickened the pace, thrusting them harder each time, while her tongue flicked against Peyton's clit.

"Give it to me," Hadina commanded, feeling her own juices seeping down her thighs and dripping onto the floor beneath. Seeing Peyton so undone was everything she wanted and she would do anything to watch her writhe in pleasure for the rest of her life.

Feeling Peyton tremble against her, Hadina bit down on her sensitive bundle as she thrust the paint brushes once more. Peyton let out a pleasure-induced scream as she slammed back against the shelves, riding out her orgasm. The shelving shook, and Hadina looked up and locked eyes with a delirious Peyton, right as tubs of paint and bundles of brushes fell. The paint clattered to the ground around them, paint splattering and adding a whole new artistic perspective to their gowns.

"Oops..." Peyton laughed as one last tub fell, smacking against

Hadina's shoulder. The scarlet paint covered Hadina's face and chest before dripping between her breasts. The feeling was sticky, which reminded her of the spray of blood after cutting someone's throat— the only difference was the coolness against her skin. While she couldn't see herself, she imagined she resembled the poster child for a *Carrie* remake.

"Well, that didn't go as planned," she deadpanned. Peyton snorted and unwrapped her fingers from Hadina's hair, running her fingers down the other woman's cheek.

"Red looks good on you," Peyton whispered, her eyes darkening as Hadina pulled the brushes from her sensitive pussy.

The brushes were slick with Peyton's cum and Hadina eyed the tips hungrily. Meeting Peyton's gaze, she brought them to her mouth and licked them clean. Once she had lapped up every bit, Hadina tossed the brushes aside, pushed to her feet, and grinned wildly at Peyton.

Slipping a hand around the back of her neck, Hadina brought Peyton in and kissed her deeply. "Taste yourself. Aren't you divine?"

Peyton hummed and cupped Hadina's face, crushing their lips together. Hadina allowed herself to be consumed by Peyton, by that kiss, and prayed that her fantasy could last a little bit longer.

Tentadora

CHAPTER 24

PEYTON

THEIR ANTICS AT THE GALLERY HAD LEFT PEYTON FEELING HOT ALL OVER. SHE was satisfied and sleepy, but her body ached for more. It was like she could never be satisfied by only having *part* of Hadina; she wanted all of her, unhinged mind and all.

One of Hadina's henchman had been waiting for them outside when they left the storeroom, which had made her momentarily embarrassed before a cool acceptance washed over her. She didn't care who heard them, as long as they knew only Hadina could make her lose her mind like that.

"Back exit is clear, boss," Harris told Hadina, flicking his eyes to Peyton with a smirk. "Hope y'all enjoy the rest of your night."

Hadina flashed him a warning look before grabbing Peyton by the hand and pulling her to the car outside. A trail of paint created a map of their path but Hadina assured her that it would get cleaned up, and that Piper wouldn't be mad.

By the time they returned to the house, Peyton was ready to fall into bed and sleep for a week. "Are you staying here tonight?"

Hadina glanced over and saw the mischief in the girl's eyes. "Can't sleep without me?"

"The world doesn't revolve around you, Hadina."

"No, perhaps not, Peyton. But I think yours does." Taking a step forward, Hadina brushed a finger down Peyton's cheek, smirking when she gasped softly at the contact. "Tell me, when was the last time you went to sleep and *didn't* dream of me?"

Peyton sobered and laughed, flipping her off. "I need to go get cleaned." Spinning on her heels, Peyton walked up to her room, casting a glance at Hadina from the banister upstairs. "Thank you for tonight."

A shadow passed over Hadina's face but she quickly wiped it off and smiled back. "I should be thanking you, *tentadora*. I'll speak to you tomorrow."

SLEEP HAD COME QUICKLY and easily to her after her shower. Peyton had scrubbed her skin until every drop of paint was only a distant memory, relishing the soreness between her thighs. Afterwards, she donned a fresh pair of panties and slipped into bed naked, the cool temperature of the sheets soothing her skin. The sound of her bedroom door opening and closing woke her from sleep. Panic rose in her throat as the soft footsteps echoed in the room. Peyton cursed herself for her lack of weapons, suddenly realizing how utterly defenseless she was.

"*Mierda*," the voice cursed as the intruder hit their toe on the bed frame. Peyton smiled into her pillow, warmness spreading through her at the intimacy of Hadina sneaking into her bedroom.

Rolling over so she could make out the looming silhouette, Peyton opened one eye slowly. "Can you stop making so much noise? Some of us are trying to sleep."

Hadina let out a squeal of surprise and Peyton chuckled. It was so out of character for Hadina to be surprised by anything and it made Peyton happy to be the one to do it.

"I thought you'd be asleep," Hadina whispered, awkwardly climbing into the bed. She propped herself up at the headboard, sitting stiffly with her hands in her lap.

Peyton sighed and pulled the covers back in invitation. Hadina's eyes darkened as she took in Peyton's naked figure before schooling her features and slipping under the blankets.

"I was sleeping before someone decided to climb into my bed at" —she glanced at the alarm clock beside her bed—"three in the morning for an adult slumber party."

Hadina pursed her lips as she rested her head on a pillow, her long hair falling over her shoulders. "I'm sorry for waking you then."

"Don't be. I'm not mad about having you in my bed," Peyton replied with a soft smile.

They each lay on their sides, facing each other. Silence clung to the air in the space between them. For once, Peyton didn't need to ask what Hadina was thinking. Without realizing it, Hadina had let Peyton scratch her way through the woman's walls, creating a hole just big enough to let some emotion seep through. Peyton hoped Hadina didn't try to patch it up anytime soon. She was enjoying seeing part of Hadina's vulnerable side.

"Come here," Hadina ordered, holding her arms out for Peyton to slide between them. Hadina enveloped her and Peyton sighed against her chest, resting her head over Hadina's heart. For as much as she pretended to be cold and unfeeling, Peyton could feel the strength of her employer's beating heart beneath her cheek.

Hadina pressed a soft kiss to the top of Peyton's head. "Get some sleep, *tentadora.*"

Peyton yawned, snuggling further into Hadina's warm body. She could feel sleep starting to pull her under again. "Don't leave," she whispered.

Hadina rubbed soft circles along the small of her back. "I'm not going anywhere, Peyton."

Peyton knew that was a lie. Maybe not now, but Hadina would leave at some point and Peyton would be left heartbroken, alone, and angry at herself for ever falling for her in the first place.

She pressed her eyes shut tighter to stop her tears from falling at the thought. She didn't know how or when she had stopped fearing for herself around Hadina, instead fearing a world without this woman in it.

As her breathing slowed and sleep called to her, she heard Hadina speak to her softly. "Are you asleep yet?"

Peyton wasn't sure what it was about Hadina's tone—perhaps the unusual tenderness and slight apprehension behind her question—but Peyton felt the need to stay deathly quiet.

A moment passed before Hadina sighed. "I shouldn't have come here tonight. Or to the gallery, actually." She shifted under Peyton, adjusting herself so she was staring at the ceiling with Peyton in her arms.

"I was supposed to be working. But then Kaira had to go and tell me how fucking incredible you looked in your dress... My jealousy got the better of me."

"You know, I saw you with Zellie and all I wanted to do was put a bullet in my own sister for even glancing in your direction, never mind threatening you. You looked so beautiful and a cruel part of me thought the fear on your face made you even more stunning. I came to the gallery to see you, protect you, but I couldn't help myself from wanting to taste you."

Peyton breathed steadily, but her heart beat ferociously in her chest. She didn't know if she could handle Hadina like this—gentle and honest. It was breaking her damn heart.

"I know I'm not a good person. And that means I don't get to have a good person like you. But, *dios mío*, you have me all twisted up inside and I wish I was a good person so that I could keep you."

Hadina let out a shuddering breath, and Peyton suddenly wished that she wasn't pretending to be asleep so that she could console her. She tightened her arms around her, hoping that it would provide Hadina with a modicum of comfort. Continuing to draw circles on her back, Hadina's touch was delicate as she occasionally let her fingertips drift across other parts of her skin. Peyton had to resist the urge to shiver under the soft caresses.

"Slipping into bed with you tonight was the only way I could think of prolonging this little fantasy of mine for a bit longer. But the time is up, *cariño,* and I can't keep pretending. Pretending that I can be good, that you can be mine." Her fingers stilled on Peyton's back, like she was getting ready to leave and say goodbye. "I need to go now. The business has and always will come first in my life. So, I'm going to leave your bed and go do what I do best. And when you wake up, you'll realize that I lied to you and it'll kill the part of you that has feelings for me. Then, when you lash out at me, I'll tell you that you can leave. No repercussions. It'll be the only good thing I can offer you. We'll go back to our lives the way they were before we met, and I'll shut down my heart once more."

It physically pained Peyton not to open her eyes as Hadina slowly pulled out from under her, pressing a soft, light kiss to her lips.

"For what it's worth, I'm sorry. I know that you'll never know any of this, but I had to say the words. I hope you find someone one day, someone who's good like you. You deserve that, Peyton. You deserve to live and be happy."

———

THE DOOR CLICKED behind Peyton as she tiptoed inside the building, following the path Hadina had taken. She knew she was walking a very fine line between danger and sheer stupidity, but there was no turning back. She had to find out what secrets her employer was keeping.

Holding onto the dagger she had stolen from Hadina's office back at the house, she slowly crept forward into the empty hallway. The old abandoned warehouse groaned, the sound of falling debris making her jump every so often when she was caught off guard. She didn't know why Hadina was here. Fear ran through her veins like ice, a shiver running down her spine.

Following the sound of Hadina's muffled voice arguing with someone, Peyton tried to hurry as she made her way through the creepy building. The voices grew louder until Peyton could hear them speak clearly as she stopped outside an old, rusting door.

"Who the fuck do you think you are? I gave you what you wanted so back the hell off and leave me alone."

Hadina's answering chuckle brought a smile to Peyton's lips. "You're a foolish *pinche puto* if you think you can order me about."

Peyton looked through the glass windowpane on the door. The man was standing with his back to her, though she could see that he was muscled, his coat tight across his shoulders and biceps. He should have been intimidating with his large, towering frame, but Hadina stood her ground and glared up at him like he was nothing more than a nuisance.

The man shook his head, clenching his fists at his sides. "I gave you the details. I could have been killed if she found out. I'm done."

Hadina growled and took a step forward, invading his space. Peyton watched on with rapt attention, fear and intrigue making her heart beat faster in her chest.

"You don't get to decide that. I need more information from you. I know that you're nothing but a fucking coward and don't get to make any decisions, but you can still feed me what I need. Rumor has it that your boss is expecting another shipment soon, and I need to know where I can find it."

"Fuck you!" the man screamed, grabbing Hadina by the hair. He yanked her head back forcefully and Peyton gasped, debating whether she should run in and try to intervene. "I'm not going to risk my life for you. She'll *kill* me if she finds out! Helping you isn't worth it."

Grinning with all her teeth on full display, Hadina was a terrifying beauty. She let out a cold laugh. "That's a pity for you then. Helping me was the only thing keeping you alive."

Peyton hadn't seen Hadina move, but suddenly the woman had a gun in her hand and a loud *crack* filled the air as Hadina pulled the trigger. Peyton felt like everything happened in slow motion after that. First, her ears echoed from the volume of the shot. Next, blood. So much blood. The proximity of Hadina to her target meant that crimson sprayed everywhere, red splatters coating the window separating Peyton from the crime scene in front of her. The man's body dropped to the floor, part of his face now missing.

Now in full view of Peyton, Hadina stood like a poised queen, looking at the dead body with disgust. Blood coated her face and neck, her white blouse now a muddied shade of red. It was wrong, so wrong, of Peyton to be staring at Hadina in awe, but she was. This absolutely terrifying woman had just *killed* a man for putting his hands on her. There was something so innately powerful about it and Peyton felt herself get heated at the thought. She was scared, but her intrigue and hunger overpowered it.

Peyton bit down on her lip just as Hadina looked up. The Adis sister's eyes widened and her satisfied smile dropped, her icy mask sliding back into place.

Peyton was so, *so* fucked.

Reina
de las sombras

CHAPTER 25

HADINA

"*MIERDA*," HADINA MUTTERED, PINCHING THE BRIDGE OF HER NOSE. PEYTON stared at her through a small glass window in the door, biting her lip as if she were fucking turned on by the scene that played out in front of her.

They stared at each other for a beat, the silence an awkward tether between them. Hadina hadn't realized that Peyton had been following her, which was a huge problem. She had allowed herself to get caught up in distractions—in Peyton—and had started to lose her touch.

It was that sobering thought that had Hadina storming through the door. Peyton backed up but Hadina didn't stop until they were toe to toe, so close that she could practically hear Peyton's heart thudding in her chest. "What the *fuck* do you think you're doing?" she demanded, fury lacing her words like venom.

"I--uh–I had to know where you kept running off to." Peyton sighed, shaking her head slightly. "You left me without saying good-bye, okay? You left, and I followed."

Hadina ran a bloody hand through her hair and tapped her gun against her forehead. "How's that curiosity doing for you now? You just watched me murder someone. You've successfully witnessed the shady shit. Are you happy?"

Peyton huffed and straightened her back, steeling herself against Hadina's pissy attitude. "Consider my curiosity only more piqued. Besides, you killed him in self-defense. I literally saw him grab you."

"*Estás pendeja*," Hadina scolded before grabbing Peyton by the throat and shoving her against the door. She let out a small *oof* but Hadina tightened her grip, holding her gun to Peyton's temple. "You don't get to rationalize or make excuses for me. That was a fucked-up thing I did—how can you not be terrified right now?"

Peyton gulped, her pulse jumping beneath Hadina's hand. "He manhandled you. I would have wanted to shoot him if he did that to me. And don't be fooled, I am absolutely terrified. But here's the thing, Hadina... I've been terrified of you since the moment we first met. Seeing you kill someone for putting his damn hands on you doesn't make me more or less scared than I already was. Neither does the fact that you have a gun pressed to my temple, because I don't think you'll actually use it on me."

Hadina wasn't quite aware of the fact she was lowering her gun until it dropped to the ground with a *thud*. "What I did was fucked up, Peyton. *I'm* fucked up. You can't be a part of this."

"That's not your decision to make," Peyton whispered.

Hadina shook her head. "You are devious and infuriating and this will end horribly for you," she replied before smashing her lips against Peyton's.

The kiss was unlike any of the ones they had shared before. There was no sweetness or softness. It was all teeth and tongue and hunger. Hadina's heart hurt at how much she craved Peyton and her touch, how much she wanted to capture her and keep her forever. But she was not a good person and she would never be the type of partner Peyton needed.

Pulling back abruptly, Hadina licked her lips and smirked. Red was now smeared across Peyton's soft skin, beads of blood speckled across her plump lips like pomegranate seeds ripe for the picking. Hadina spun Peyton around and pulled her flush, gripping the girl's chin tightly.

Peyton pressed against her and it took everything in Hadina to stick to her plan. Pointing to their reflection in the glass, she brought her lips to Peyton's ear, biting on the lobe before speaking low. "Look at your pretty face in the reflection, Peyton, and see just how quickly blood can spread. You think you want to be part of this, to be with me, but you don't know what you'd be getting yourself into. I would want to possess you, to ruin you. In fact, I won't just ruin you. If given the chance, I will corrupt your soul."

Releasing her grip, Hadina shoved Peyton forward and created distance between them. When Peyton spun around, there were tears in her pretty eyes. If Hadina were a nicer person, if she had a heart, seeing Peyton cry would break her. But Hadina Adis was not a good person, and she would suffer those tears if it meant that Peyton would stay far away from Hadina's brand of darkness.

"Consider that before you choose to follow me again, Peyton. There would be no going back for you, and I don't think you want that, *tentadora*."

HADINA COULD FEEL the waves of anger rolling off her, threatening to drown anyone who stood in her way as she stormed from the building, leaving Peyton on her own with the very dead body of Adis & Co.'s latest target at her feet.

Well, he wasn't strictly their target. But he deserved to die anyway.

"Fuck!" she screamed into the night, wincing as her voice echoed around the abandoned properties.

She *had* said goodbye. She whispered her truths while Peyton slept and then said goodbye. She wasn't supposed to follow her. She wasn't supposed to still *want* Hadina. There was nothing good that could come from pretending they'd have a happy life together. Hadina and her lifestyle would spoil whatever emotions were between them, festering until it turned into something far more dark and toxic than whatever the fuck it was now. Hadina wouldn't let herself ruin Peyton.

But corruption was her trade and temptation was her downfall.

Hadina's phone rang in her hand, forcing her to bury the overwhelming need to scream again. "What is it?" she barked.

Her right-hand man sighed. Harris was one of the only people Hadina trusted, considered a confidante but not a friend. His loyalty was unwavering and Hadina had never dared to do anything to cross the line of professionalism between them for fear that emotions would overtake them. People thought that love was deadly, but a twisted friendship between those unafraid to murder was just as lethal. Still, the weariness in that sigh made her almost break her own rules and ask him if he was okay. Almost.

"Harris, hurry the fuck up."

"I don't think *Regina* is her name, boss."

"You *what?*"

Harris growled and the sound of a fist meeting bone could be heard through the receiver. "This mark I'm chatting with—he went to call her by a different name. He stopped himself at the last minute, but the boy was confused. Sputtered out *the* Regina before realizing what he did."

Hadina's fingers itched to connect with something, the urge to throw her fist into the nearest wall almost overwhelming. She didn't bother masking the snark in her voice, knowing Harris was probably just as furious as she was. "All these weeks, we've been searching for someone called Regina and she doesn't exist?"

"I think she exists, boss," he grumbled, "But I don't think that's her name. I keep feeling like we're right at the edge of something, but it's never quite within reach. I think this bitch is playing with us, and she's enjoying watching us chase our tails."

"Then we'll make her watch as we bring her entire operation to the ground."

Disconnecting the call, Hadina launched her phone at the wall, watching as it cracked and broke into pieces. She was about to go and inspect the damage when the shuffling of footsteps sounded behind her. Spinning on her heel, Hadina grabbed a dagger from her waistband and held it up, ready to throw.

"It's me!" Peyton screeched, lifting her hands in protest.

Hadina glared, slowly lowering her weapon. "Peyton, go home."

"No."

If Hadina wasn't so ready to kill the next person who crossed her path, she would have found the small act of defiance cute. Especially with the way she jutted out her chin and straightened her back. "I'm not asking. *Vete para a la casa!*" Seeing the confused look on Peyton's face, Hadina sighed in frustration and screamed her translation. "Go home!"

Without waiting for a response, Hadina stomped to her car, ready to leave Peyton abandoned amongst the forgotten shells of offices. She could hear Peyton's crunching footsteps behind her but she ignored them, opening the door instead. Peyton caught up to her, slamming the door closed and pushing into her space.

"Fuck you, Hadina! You don't get to order me around. You don't get to run away just because shit is getting real and you don't want to have to handle your emotions!"

Red blurred her vision and before she knew it, Hadina's hand was around Peyton's throat. She grabbed her and threw her to the side, slamming her against the car. While it wouldn't cause any serious harm, she noticed Peyton wince from the impact. Keeping her pinned with one hand, she grabbed her gun with the other and pressed it to Peyton's neck. She could feel the heat radiating between them, watching as Peyton tried to fight the shiver from the cold metal on her skin.

"And *you* don't get to order me around like I'm some child!" Hadina yelled, making sure Peyton could see how untethered she was now, all restraint abandoned. "You are a foolish girl, playing in the den of wolves. You think you're strong, but you're really prey just waiting to get eaten."

Peyton wriggled, trying to loosen Hadina's hold on her. "You act like you're fifty years old and have one foot in the grave. Being older than me doesn't mean you know better—that you know what I want or need!"

Hadina shook her head, pressing the barrel of her gun harder into Peyton's skin. "And yet, I'm the one here. In control. With a gun."

Peyton laughed and craned her neck. Hadina didn't have a second to think before Peyton used all her strength to push forward and break free. Sweeping her foot out, she managed to throw Hadina off-balance and knock the gun from the woman's hand.

"*Puta*," Hadina cursed, trying to regain her footing. She leaned down to grab the gun but Peyton got to it first, holding it up between them.

While she knew Peyton didn't know how to use a gun, Hadina also knew the danger of the weapon itself. One glance told her the safety was off and that Peyton's finger was on the trigger; she could kill Hadina if she wanted to.

Hadina sneered. "What now?"

Peyton glared back, taking control of the situation. She angled the gun so that it was pressed into Hadina's chest, nudging the other woman forward until she could step around her. Once Peyton was free, she pushed Hadina back, forcing her against the car so that their positions were reversed.

"Now, you listen," Peyton said sternly, invading Hadina's space while mimicking what the woman had just done to her. Hadina hated how much pride flooded her system, how turned on she was at seeing this side of Peyton. "It's my turn to talk." Slowly dragging the barrel down Hadina's torso, Peyton stopped when she reached the bottom of her employer's stomach, pressing the gun into the line above her jeans. Hadina watched with curiosity as Peyton grabbed her by the chin, forcing their gazes to meet. "You think I'm weak and clueless," she said, spitting out the words. "But you're wrong. I know that you're ten types of fucked up. I know that you do bad things and get away with it. And I know that you think you have everything all figured out."

Hadina licked her lips. "I do have everything all figured out, Peyton."

Peyton chuckled, moving the gun a few inches lower. "No, you really don't. Because you think you have *me* all figured out and you don't. You think that I'm good, that I'm innocent. But let me tell you a secret, Hadi," she said, leaning closer to whisper in Hadina's ear. "I'm not good or innocent, and I've just been waiting for someone to ruin me."

Hadina sucked in a breath when Peyton began to rub the sleek metal of the gun against her pussy through her jeans. The friction was divine, though she wouldn't give Peyton the satisfaction of admitting that.

Letting go of her chin, Peyton used her free hand to unbutton Hadina's jeans, yanking them down with a quick tug. She sighed when they got caught on the swell of Hadina's ass, making it difficult to do one-handed. Hadina stilled, watching the scene unfold. Having *her* gun used to bring her pleasure was a new experience, and she knew that moving without being told would end the game. Though the lack of control was challenging.

"You're bad and I'm tainted," Peyton said as she pushed the silk of Hadina's panties to the side, bringing the gun back to press into the woman's exposed flesh. "You kill and I watch it with apathy."

Drawing her arm back, Peyton smirked when the small protruding sight hit against Hadina's clit, causing the other woman to suck in a breath. She repeated the action, watching Hadina with fascination and dilated pupils as she got off. The grooves in the gun provided just enough friction to create an agonizingly slow buildup, teasing and torturing.

"If you want to corrupt my soul, I'll sign it right over to you. You're the devil, Hadina," Peyton said softly, biting on her lip as she tilted the handle, pressing it harder into her dripping cunt. "But I'm no angel. If I'm your temptress, then let me tempt you."

Hadina opened her mouth, but the argument died on her tongue as she looked at her *tentadora*. The girl's hair was a mess, her eyes wide and blown, and it appeared as though *she* was the one who had just been fucked. Hadina was obsessed and if Peyton was offering herself up so freely, knowing everything that Hadina was, then she didn't think she had the strength to refuse her again.

Peyton stepped closer, grabbing Hadina's ass to increase the pressure of the gun. A smile started to creep onto her face as Hadina moaned, threw her head back, and rode the metal with abandon. "You don't know what you're offering. What you're getting into," she hissed, reaching out a hand to grip Peyton's waist for support as she climbed closer to climax.

"Then maybe I'm clueless," Peyton said, pressing her lips to the dip of Hadina's neck. Circling the barrel against her employer's hole, she teased and tested to see how ready she was for more. Hadina groaned, biting down on her lip as the tip of the barrel pushed inside her, scratching against her sensitive skin as it entered.

"Naïve," Hadina called her through gritted teeth, her fingernails digging into Peyton's hip.

"Perhaps. But do you know what else I am?" Peyton asked. She pulled the gun away, slowly, before thrusting it forward again. Hadina screamed and threw her head back. "I'm in fucking control of myself, and *I* make my decisions."

Hadina's breathing came in heavy pants as Peyton continued to assault her pussy, using her wetness to lubricate the gun as she thrust it in and out. Hadina couldn't think straight, couldn't form words or argue. Instead, she ground down against the gun and worked herself harder, loving the stinging bite the sight caused as it scraped against her insides. Lips pressed soft kisses against her neck, sweeping away the sweat beading on her skin. She didn't resist when Peyton brought their mouths together in a passionate, messy kiss. Peyton swallowed up her cries as Hadina felt herself reach the precipice of release, needing to let go.

"Corrupt my soul all you want, Hadina," Peyton said quietly. "You've already ruined me for everyone else."

Hadina blinked back tears as Peyton twisted the handle of the gun and thrust the barrel inside her one last time, hitting a spot she hadn't reached before. Shattering completely, Hadina crashed into Peyton's lips and let herself fall off the edge. As Hadina came apart around her weapon of choice, soaking Peyton's hand, she hoped Peyton could feel everything that was running through her mind.

Peyton had lured her in and now Hadina was ruined too. The queen of shadows and her little temptress.

Tentadora

CHAPTER 26

PEYTON

"Now what?" Hadina asked.

After she had come down from her post-orgasm high, they had picked up the remnants of Hadina's phone and headed back to the house. Hadina had assured Peyton that she'd send one of her guys to retrieve the car that she'd borrowed from Don's collection.

They were sitting in the car in front of the house, Hadina's hand gripping Peyton's thigh, where she rubbed circles with her thumb. Peyton could feel the nervousness rolling off her.

"With us or with everything else?"

Hadina smirked. "Both, I guess."

Peyton thought about it. In all honesty, she wasn't quite sure what came next. Telling Hadina that she wasn't walking away was a big deal that came with even bigger consequences. She just didn't know how everything would play out.

"With us, I'm all in. I wanna know everything, learn everything you have to teach me. After my sister died, my relationship with my family completely disintegrated. I don't have anyone." Peyton took a deep breath before linking her fingers with Hadina's. "You're it, Hadi. This madness you bring out of me is what I want—*who* I want to be."

"I can't tell if the truth will be better or worse than the image you probably have conjured up in your head."

Peyton hated the anxiety underlying Hadina's words. No matter how dark the truth was, nothing would make her want to leave. The moment she had admitted that to herself, she felt free. Free to embrace love and all the tarnished parts of herself that she had been burying for years.

"I'm here either way," she said.

Hadina forced a smile. "Then I think it's time for a history lesson. You should know exactly what we do at Adis & Co."

Peyton took the seat behind the desk as Hadina flurried about the office, grabbing documents and folders hidden behind various pieces of furniture. She stole glances at Peyton every so often, almost like she was checking to make sure she was still there.

"Okay," Hadina said after ten minutes, depositing all the files in front of Peyton. "Are you ready?"

Peyton nodded. "Tell me everything."

Hadina perched on the edge of the desk, opening a folder to reveal a collection of photographs.

Peyton reached for one before dropping it immediately as though it were aflame. "What the fuck?" she said, feeling nausea rise up her throat.

The focal point of the image was a young girl—no older than fifteen or sixteen—lying dead atop a dirty mattress on a stone floor. Her body was beaten and bruised, cigarette burns and cuts dotting her exposed skin. It was the blood covering the dirty white night-dress and fingerprint bruises on her throat that finally caused Peyton to vomit into the trash can beside the desk.

"Keep looking," Hadina demanded, though she showed sympathy by rubbing circles over Peyton's back while she emptied her stomach.

Picking up the piles of photographs with shaky fingers, Peyton forced herself to look through them. It seemed like each one was worse than the last. Poor girls left broken, bloodied, and dead. Her heart ached as she took in the atrocities in front of her. While she knew that these deaths weren't at the hands of Hadina—she knew that with absolute certainty—Peyton couldn't understand why the Adis sister would have such horrid pictures in her possession.

"Hadina..." she choked out, tears streaming down her cheeks. "Why?"

Hadina reached out, swiping away some of the tears with her thumb. "Those girls are who we protect at Adis & Co. We hunt the *bastardas* who terrorize the innocent and abuse those who can't protect themselves."

Peyton looked at her quizzically.

"My mom and dad started the company when they were younger after witnessing some things happen to young girls. It was so horrific that my sisters and I don't even know the full story."

"Then how..."

Hadina tucked a strand of hair behind Peyton's ear. "They both created the company and used the actual business side as a front. *Papi* was already a practicing lawyer, so it made sense."

There was pride in Hadina's voice as Peyton listened to her explain how she and Zellie were recruited by their father when they were eighteen. She hated the knowledge that Hadina had witnessed so much horror at such a young age. But then the image of finding Melina's body in the bathtub, the water colored crimson, came to mind and Peyton realized that moment had changed her so completely. It made sense that Hadina would want to fight for those girls after she saw what would happen if she didn't.

"Did you ever consider saying no? Surely there were other things you wanted to do with your life."

Hadina's lips curled into a sad smile. "You saw those photos. Could you imagine walking away, understanding you had the power to help?"

"No," Peyton responded immediately, knowing there was no turning back now.

"Besides, I still had to train as a lawyer. It was always made clear to us that we could back out if we wanted."

Rolling her chair forward, Peyton took Hadina's hands in hers. There was a slight tremble and she wasn't sure if it was her or Hadina who was shaking. As hard as it was for her to stomach all this information, Peyton knew that it wasn't easy for Hadina to share. Letting someone in was something Hadina wasn't used to, and Peyton just hoped that she didn't get shut out again.

"So, who is hurting the girls?"

"Men with money and power," Hadina answered, disgust written across her face. "They traffic them within their sick little sex rings. Abusing them, beating them, getting them hooked on every type of substance possible. And then they kill them when they're done."

Bile rose to the back of Peyton's throat for a second time but she swallowed it down, refusing to show weakness any more than she already had. "And what do we do? How do we stop them?"

The corner of Hadina's mouth twitched into a half smile. "I like the sound of that. Like we're a team."

Peyton squeezed Hadina's hands. "We *are* a team. We do this together now."

Surprisingly, Hadina leaned forward and kissed Peyton—the gesture more soft than passionate. It was a temporary reprieve from the sadness of their conversation. "We hunt. So many of these *imbéciles* are part of everything. We're lucky because rich *putos* always need a lawyer at their back. We network and situate ourselves until we're trusted."

"And if that doesn't work?" Peyton asked.

"That's where our informants come in." Hadina grinned. "We have a bunch of people in the streets, part of huge companies, in the police... Adis & Co. has a lot of reach."

Nudging Peyton's chair aside, Hadina turned round and logged into the desktop computer in front of her. Peyton watched Hadina tap away at the keyboard while opening up a bunch of tabs. Leaning forward, she gasped when she realized it was camera footage of places around town.

"Is that...?"

Hadina smiled. "Yup." She clicked a few more times, bringing up different angles. "We have access to most cameras, and we can hack into the ones we don't, which allows us to track our targets most of the time. The docks, downtown warehouses, and clubs are where most of the business deals go down, and abandoned buildings have started to get used, too."

Peyton knew her mouth was gaping but she was in awe. It was slightly terrifying knowing that Hadina and her company had access to almost every camera, could follow her wherever she went, but it also gave her a slight thrill. She was sleeping with a woman who was power incarnate.

"Talk me through the process. What happens after you've identified a mark?"

Hadina clicked on a file, opening up a map covered with red Xs. She pointed to one that had a red circle around it. "See this? That's the last place we intercepted a shipment. It was a container in the docks downtown, and when we opened it up, there were thirty underage girls huddled together."

She reached for Peyton's trembling hands, squeezing slightly. The Adis sister was lending her strength to Peyton, something the latter was extremely thankful to receive. While Peyton knew that the atrocities would become less shocking over time, she couldn't shake the sick feeling in the pit of her stomach at that moment.

She nodded for Hadina to go on.

"We have a couple of different avenues we can take. One is to pretend to go into business with them and catch them in the act, letting the target set themselves up. Another is to rely on our intel from informants. Or we can simply follow them, hacking into their shit until we get the details we need to be certain."

Peyton pushed off the desk, pacing around the room as she tried to wrap her head around the seemingly well-organized operation. Her life had been propelled into something completely new, dangerous, and overwhelming. There was no turning back—not that she wanted to—and all these revelations were giving her a headache.

"So, we get the information and then catch them? Do we question them first?"

"Sometimes, if we don't have all the details of their dealings." Hadina made her way to Peyton, reaching out to grip her arms to stop her from pacing. "Are you okay? Are you sure you can handle this?"

That was a question Peyton had been asking herself, but hearing Hadina say it out loud was enough to tamp down her doubts. She was strong and wanted to help save those girls, even if it was the most terrifying thing she'd ever have to do.

"I can do this. I just..." She let out a sigh and leaned forward, pressing her forehead into Hadina's shoulder. "It's so much to take in. And my heart is aching in advance, knowing that whoever we save will already have been subjected to so much."

Hadina ran a hand through Peyton's hair, her fingertips playing with the ends as she soothed her. "I know. It's going to be difficult and it will take a very long time for your heart to catch up with your head. But you have to think of it this way: if we didn't save them, they would face so much worse. We can always strive to do more, but what we do is already life-changing to so many people."

Peyton nodded, pulling herself together. "If we don't need to question them, what happens to the targets?"

"We kill them," Hadina stated bluntly. "We make sure they can never hurt anyone else ever again."

Steeling herself, Peyton squared her shoulders and locked gazes with the woman in front of her. "Then I think you need to teach me how to shoot."

Hadina's answering smile was beautiful and deadly. "It would be my pleasure."

Tentadora

CHAPTER 27

PEYTON

Sleep came to Peyton in short bursts, her mind too focused on being trained to allow her to get proper rest. Hadina had demanded that they both go to bed so that they could start fresh the following day, but as the morning light filtered through her windows, Peyton felt anything but *fresh*.

Perhaps her unrest came from the knowledge that Hadina was still in the house, but not in bed beside her. Peyton had thought they'd go to bed *together* but Hadina had kissed her and said she had to make some calls first. When an hour passed, Peyton had given up waiting for the Adis sister to appear.

Dressing in a pair of khaki cargo pants and a black tee, Peyton tucked her feet into her favorite combat boots before clomping down the stairs and heading to the kitchen. She was surprised to see Don and Hadina sitting together, heads bowed in conversation. Peyton could make out the muffled sound of Spanish, but besides one or two familiar words, she didn't have a clue what they were talking about.

Peyton cleared her throat as she grabbed her mug from the

cupboard, earning herself smiles from the duo. Then she poured herself a cup of coffee and returned the gesture, albeit a little nervously. She couldn't figure out if they had been speaking about her, or something serious—either way, their conversation ceased the moment Peyton entered the room.

"Morning, y'all," Peyton said, taking a gulp from her mug.

"Good morning, *cariño*."

Hadina caught Peyton's gaze and refused to look away, sending excited little chills down her spine. "I cooked breakfast, if you'd like some."

"I'm sorry, what?" Peyton asked, choking on her coffee. "You, Hadina Adis, cooked breakfast? I don't think I've seen you cook since I moved here."

Peyton shrieked when Hadina threw a dishtowel at her with deadly accuracy, a smirk playing on her lips. "She's just trying to impress you," Don chuckled, ignoring his daughter's scowl.

Hadina walked over to Peyton and slid an arm around her waist, pressing a brief kiss to the side of her mouth before creating distance between them. Then she grabbed a plate from the cupboard and handed it to Peyton. "Breakfast."

"What did you make?" Peyton sniffed the air, her stomach rumbling at the smell of eggs.

"The best eggs you'll ever taste in your life," Hadina replied smugly, scooping some onto Peyton's plate. "And black beans. There are some tortillas on the table too." She laughed at the puzzled expression on Peyton's face. "Trust me, just try it. You'll love it."

Taking a seat at the table, Peyton pulled a tortilla from the platter in the middle and looked up expectantly.

Hadina tried to hide her smile as she instructed Peyton on what to do. "Layer them up. Put some black beans in the center, place your eggs on top, and then fold the tortilla over so you can take a bite."

Don and Hadina watched silently, their excitement palpable as Peyton took her first bite before audibly groaning as the flavors exploded on her tongue. Hadina had been right; they were the best eggs she'd ever tasted.

"Holy shit!" she mumbled as she swallowed.

Hadina glanced at her father before they high-fived in victory. "Good job, *mija*."

"You need to cook more often!" Peyton took another bite, then another, until she had cleared her entire plate and sat back to place a hand on her full stomach. She hadn't eaten anything that delicious in a long time, and knowing that Hadina had been the one to cook it made it better.

Don winked, patting Hadina's shoulder before exiting the room. Hadina watched him leave and then turned back around, grinning mischievously. Peyton raised a questioning brow just before Hadina grabbed the girl by the hips and pulled her into her lap.

"Hadina!" Peyton shrieked, throwing her arms over the other woman's shoulders. She glanced at the door, expecting Don to reappear at any minute. "Your dad might see us."

"Then *Papi* will see his very adult daughter openly expressing some emotion for the first time in years. Now hush and let me use those pretty lips to wash away my worries."

Hadina didn't give Peyton a chance to respond, crushing her lips against hers in a hungry kiss. Peyton groaned, pushing herself against Hadina's body while pressing her thighs into the other woman's waist. She could taste a hint of bitter coffee as she explored Hadina's mouth while her hands roamed.

Shivers skittered up her spine as Hadi slipped her palms under Peyton's shirt, her fingertips brushing across the soft skin of her lower back. Peyton closed her eyes and let the sensation run through her body, heating her from the inside out. A low groan escaped her mouth when Hadina moved to pepper kisses along her jawline, dragging her teeth down the column of Peyton's neck. Then she stopped at the dip of Peyton's collarbone, sucking softly on the skin.

"We have so much work to do," Hadina mumbled against her

skin, "But I'd much rather spend the day showing you places in the city that make me feel like home."

Peyton heard a surprising softness in Hadina's voice that took her off guard. Pulling back slightly, she tucked her fingers under Hadina's chin and tilted the woman's face up to eye-level. "What does that mean?"

She watched as Hadina slipped her mask back on, blinking away the softened demeanor that slipped through momentarily. "Nothing. It's not important."

Peyton shook her head and slid to her feet before standing. "It's important to me. Don't start with that cold bullshit again. What did you mean?"

Hadina stood too, looming over Peyton's average five-feet-two height. "That *cold bullshit* is me, Peyton. I said it's not important right now." She brushed past her, making her way out of the kitchen. "Come on. Let's get to work."

THE DRIVE to Hadina's downtown apartment was filled by the sound of Peyton's voice asking a thousand questions about the training plan, while Hadina answered in short sentences that brokered no more querying. Peyton persisted anyway.

"I just want to know what we're going to be doing," Peyton said as she slammed the passenger door shut.

Hadina rolled her eyes as she pressed the lock button. "We're literally about to find out. Why do I have to tell you?"

"You suck."

"And I do it so well, baby," Hadina retorted with a smirk. Peyton turned away to hide her own smile.

Her lack of stamina was cause for concern as Peyton trailed up the stairs in the building after Hadina, wheezing as they passed the second landing. She eyed the elevator on each level, silently cursing

Hadina when they went through the key-carded door on the third floor. While she was a breathless mess, Hadina looked as though she had just stepped out of a photoshoot, not a hair out of place or a bead of sweat to be seen.

Hadina watched Peyton with an amused smile, motioning for her to follow her. She stopped them in front of apartment thirteen, the silver number glinting beneath the stream of sunlight shining through the window at the end of the hallway. A keypad was mounted on the wall beside the door, as well as a card-swiper above the handle. Peyton thought it was a tad overkill as Hadina swiped her card and then keyed in her combination before unlocking the door.

"Doesn't the crazy security make your neighbors suspicious?" Peyton asked.

"No," Hadina said as she pushed open the door. "Anyone who has this much security isn't someone you want to fuck with."

Stepping to the side, Hadina gestured her head for Peyton to go first. There was a tugging feeling in Peyton's gut but she took a deep breath, brushed past Hadina—her fingers deliberately skimming the other woman's—and entered the apartment.

"What in the unholy fuck?" Peyton barked out with an incredulous laugh.

She walked around, examining the living room in fascinating detail. Lining the walls and any available surface was an array of weapons. Knives, guns, fucking *grenades*. Hadina had it all on full display. The white walls were covered by shelves holding AR-15s, pistols, daggers with every length of blade possible. Peyton knew her mouth must have been hanging open as she spun in a circle, unable to comprehend the amount of weaponry amassed in one place.

"This is... Hadina, what the fuck?"

Hadina eyed the girl, almost like she couldn't believe why Peyton was so confused. "What?"

"What?" Peyton mimicked, gesturing around the room. "I get

why you have all these. But why do you have them *here*? You just sleep in a shrine to artillery?"

Shrugging, Hadina took a seat on her sofa and kicked her legs up onto the coffee table, shoving a revolver out of the way with her heel. "Well, I spend most of my time at *Papi's* so it was logical to store them here. Besides, it makes for easy access. The apartment is right in the middle of the city."

Peyton swallowed. "Do you actually *use* all of these?"

"Yes and no," Hadina answered honestly. "I know *how* to use them all, and I keep myself trained, but I have my personal favorites. Everyone usually has something they feel most comfortable handling. But it's useful to be able to adjust in a high-stakes situation."

"Speaking from experience?"

Hadina raised an eyebrow at her. "Perhaps."

Picking up a knife from the kitchen counter, Peyton examined the jagged blade. The handle was made out of steel, a strip of leather covering it to give a good grip. When Peyton looked up again, Hadina was watching her with a heated, hungry gaze. It sent heat pooling to her core, Peyton's body reacting instantly.

"Do you like knives, Peyton?"

Feeling the weight of the blade in her hand, Peyton had to admit that she did like it. Remembering how much more in control she'd felt when she had held the dagger from Hadina's office... She could see why Hadina liked to have a fully stocked arsenal at her disposal.

"Yes."

Hadina's eyes darkened as she licked her lips. "Then let me teach you how to use one."

Reina
de las sombras

CHAPTER 28

HADINA

Teaching Peyton how to use weapons was going to be far more difficult than she thought. Every time Hadina so much as looked at a gun, she pictured how hard she had come when Peyton fucked her with her own gun, and now she wanted to repay the favor. They had far more pressing things to do, but damn, if she wasn't tempted to fuck her against every surface in the apartment with every weapon at her disposal.

From the way Peyton eyed the various daggers, Hadina knew that would be her weapon of choice. Hadina herself was as equally fond of knives as she was of guns, but everyone had their preference. She'd teach Peyton how to use everything but made a note to pay particular attention to daggers.

After they packed up the car with some of Hadina's personal favorites, the duo headed north. Adis & Co. had acquired an old farmhouse on a plot of land far out from the city. While it was dilapidated when they purchased it, Hadina had made sure to turn it into a state-of-the-art training center. From the outside, it looked like an old, unused building; from the inside, it was a spectacular space with a gun range in the backyard, surrounded by a high fence and plenty of security.

She was excited to teach Peyton how to use a weapon, how to stay safe and protect herself. Hadina had never allowed herself to be close to anyone, and now that she had, she wanted to make sure that she'd done everything she could to ensure Peyton's protection.

Peyton was quiet as she pulled up to the house, her eyes darting around to take it all in. The pair exited the car in silence, the gravel crunching under their feet as they walked the path up to the house. "I can't believe the powerful Adis family owns a rundown farm."

Hadina unlocked the door, pushing it open to reveal the large, empty hallway. The walls were painted a pale gray, making the space appear dull and dreary. Hadina had figured it would look less used, and would prevent people from poking around too much.

Kicking the door closed with the heel of her boot, Hadina grabbed her gun cases and opened the last door on the right, which led to the main training room. The walls were lined with floor-to-ceiling bulletproof mirrors, except one at the farthest wall, which was lined with targets.

Peyton gasped. "Holy shit!"

Hadina chuckled at the surprised expression on Peyton's face. "What did you expect?"

"Clearly, not fucking this," she deadpanned. "Do y'all just have secret weapon storehouses everywhere? Damn."

Dumping her equipment on one of the empty tables, Hadina started to unload the various cases she had in tow. She should have sent one of her people to set up, but she liked the idea of being in control of Peyton's first session. She'd probably have been spooked if they turned up and Harris or any other members of the team were still at the house.

"We're fairly equipped, yes." Hadina turned around and crossed her arms, leaning against the table. She watched as Peyton paced, her eyes roving over the various weaponry now on display. "Are you ready for this?"

Peyton laughed feebly. "No."

Hadina's mouth quirked into a half smirk. "Right answer." Taking her hand, Hadina pulled Peyton close. She pressed a featherlight kiss to her lips before spinning her around to face the mirrors. "The most important thing that you need to know before we start is respect."

Peyton rolled her eyes at the reflection. "I do respect you, Hadi."

"Not me," Hadina said, nodding her head towards the table. "The weapons. You should always respect your weapon, Peyton." Picking up her own 9mm, Hadina pulled out the magazine to show Peyton that it was full of bullets. "We respect our guns because we always assume they are loaded. The moment you pick one up, you treat it like the deadly weapon it is."

Peyton's eyes widened as she watched her, her pupils darkening as she swallowed. "Okay. Respect—got it."

"I know you've *held* a gun before," Hadina said, her voice dripping with the memory of being pushed to the edge by the very one she was holding. "But do you actually know anything about them?"

Peyton shook her head.

"Okay. Then the next thing you need to know is that you never point the gun unless you mean to shoot it, understand? The second your hand is on a gun, you make sure it's aimed at the floor—away from everything—unless you plan to pull the trigger."

Setting her weapon back on the table, Hadina swapped it over for the 380 semi-automatic that she'd be showing Peyton how to use. It was smaller and lighter, which made it the perfect gun for a novice to handle. *But it was*, Hadina thought to herself, *every bit as lethal.*

"This is a semi-automatic, meaning every time you squeeze that trigger"—she pointed at it with her free hand—"a bullet will release. Which is why you always keep your finger resting on the guard until you're ready to shoot." Tapping a finger, Hadina demonstrated proper placement. "This is where your index finger should be when you're not aiming to shoot. You'll train yourself over time to keep your hand just like this..." She held the barrel in her left hand before placing the handle of the gun in the web of her thumb and curling her fingers around.

A surge of pride moved through Hadina as Peyton mimicked the actions with empty hands. "Like this?"

"Perfect."

After showing Peyton how to hold the gun, the next thing Hadina had to teach her newest pupil was the basics of a firearm. Peyton listened intently as Hadina taught her what each part was called, drawing particular attention to the thumb safety, which would prevent her from accidentally firing. Hadina was surprised at the speed at which Peyton picked up on the information, repeating the instructions with perfect understanding.

Peyton peered over Hadina's arms when the Adis sister demonstrated how to load and unload the gun. Hadina hadn't been as enthusiastic to learn or understand the mechanics of how weapons worked. The first time she'd been instructed to load a gun, tears had pricked at her eyes as she struggled to apply enough force to shove them in the magazine. Her father had barked at her to try again, and again, and again, until Hadina left in a puddle of tears with tender thumbs. Her mother had comforted her, wiping the girl's cheeks and whispering, "You can try again tomorrow, *mija*," as she ran her fingers through Hadina's hair.

Even now, watching Peyton struggle with that same task brought that feeling of unwanted shame back into focus until it burned its way up Hadina's throat. She wouldn't allow Peyton to feel the way she had.

"Don't be scared of it, Peyton."

"I'm not scared," Peyton replied, straightening her shoulders in indignation, even though the wobble in her voice betrayed her.

Hadina walked up behind her, placing her hands over Peyton's trembling fingers. "You're the one in control," she said softly into Peyton's ear. "All that anger burning inside you? Channel it. You will not be beaten by anything or anyone. You are Peyton Dimitra and you are in control."

Her words had a significant effect, Peyton's whole attitude changing as she steeled herself and pushed in bullet after bullet until the entire magazine was full. Hadina let her hands drop, though she remained behind the girl to whisper encouragement into her ear.

They ran through the basics for an hour and a half before Hadina finally gave in. "Ready to shoot?"

Peyton's mouth slacked as she looked at Hadina, gauging whether the woman was serious or not. An excited squeal escaped before she could stop it, and Hadina had to force herself to keep a straight face. With her hair tied up in a ponytail and that eager expression on her face, Peyton was absolutely fucking adorable and it made Hadina feel an uncomfortable sense of endearment towards the girl. *Her* girl.—well, she didn't actually know what they were, but that was a thought for later.

Grabbing the gun and a pair of earmuffs from one of the cases, Hadina guided Peyton down towards the targets at the edge of the room. While they had practiced stances before, she demonstrated the correct position again and observed Peyton doing the same.

"Now, I know it's exhilarating the first time, but you have to remember everything you just learned, okay?"

Peyton nodded, her ponytail swishing from side to side. Hadina handed her the gun, feeling a pull in her core as she watched Peyton adjust herself and take aim. Peyton looked over her shoulder at Hadina with a playful smile on her lips. "I think I need some guidance."

"*Dame fuerza*, you will be the death of me," Hadina mumbled in reply. Slotting herself behind Peyton, Hadina pressed into her back. "Okay. Hold your arms up like this," she said, her fingertips trailing up Peyton's sides until their hands met. She held her breath as

Peyton shivered and pressed closer. "Whatever you do, don't pull back, okay? You'll hurt yourself. You need to hold strong against the recoil, even though it's our natural instinct to pull away."

She could hear the smile in Peyton's voice as she said, "I don't pull away easily."

"That's my girl," Hadina whispered into her ear before she slipped the protectors over her ears and dropped her hands to Peyton's waist. Nervous energy was swirling around Hadina's body and she squeezed her fingers into Peyton, telling her pupil she could finally pull the trigger.

As the loud *pop* filled the air, Hadina felt all her pent-up energy burst free to follow the path of the bullet. She was mystified by Peyton's restraint, her heart tugging as she watched the girl hold the gun, in complete control of herself with confidence emanating in waves.

One thing was for sure: Hadina Adis had sorely underestimated Peyton Dimitra.

Tentadora

CHAPTER 29

PEYTON

HER ARMS ACHED AS SHE LOWERED THE GUN TO HER SIDE, MAKING SURE TO point it at the floor. She spun around to face Hadina, beaming from ear to ear. Surprisingly, the Adis sister was also smiling, her eyes tender when she gazed at Peyton's excited expression.

"I did it!" Peyton said, though the earmuffs stopped her from regulating volume, which meant it came out as more of a yell.

Hadina's brows furrowed, but she let out a laugh and removed the protectors for her. "Well done, Peyton."

There was clear emotion in Hadina's voice and it made tears burn at the back of Peyton's eyes. She surged forward, locking lips with Hadina, who let out a sigh against her mouth. Peyton felt Hadina take the gun, freeing up her hands to cup Hadina's cheeks and deepen their kiss. Adrenaline was flowing through her and she wanted to use it for pleasure, chasing the ultimate high that only Hadina could give her.

Sensing the shift, Hadina picked Peyton up, holding her by the ass as Peyton wrapped her legs around the other woman's waist.

Hadina walked them back to the table, depositing the gun with one hand before backing them against the mirrors, pinning Peyton in place.

"Seeing you shoot one of my guns drove me insane," Hadina whispered, moving her lips to Peyton's jaw. "I couldn't stop thinking about how good you are with a weapon, how hard you made me come when you used mine against me. I want to torture you, Peyton, just like you torture me."

Peyton's breath hitched when she felt Hadina's lips skim her throat, soft pressure and the light grazing of teeth against her tender skin. Hadina's hair was like silk through her fingers as Peyton played with it, grappling with the desire to yank it back and fight for control. But this was what she liked, what she *craved*—Hadina driving her insane and showing just how powerful she was.

"What do you have in mind?" Peyton asked breathlessly, struggling to form coherent words as Hadina gripped her ass tighter.

Pulling away from her neck, Hadina turned her gaze to the table. "You see that big one there? It's an AR-15."

Peyton balked at the huge, lethal-looking weapon. "Hadina, absolutely the fuck not!"

Hadina barked out a laugh, throwing her head back and showing off all her pretty teeth. "Oh, not the gun itself, baby. The bullets."

"The bullets?"

Carefully setting the girl on her feet, Hadina grinned wickedly while Peyton watched the Adis sister return various weapons to their cases, clearing off one of the tables. When she looked back at Peyton, there was nothing but mischief and desire in the woman's eyes. It made Peyton hot all over, hunger spreading through her veins like wildfire.

"Get on the table," Hadina commanded.

Peyton blew out a breath and did as she was told, shivering when Hadina pressed a hand against her torso, forcing her to lie flat on her back. It was thrilling to see Hadina like this, domineering and flirtatious. Peyton wanted to bottle up all these moments, keeping them forever so she would be able to relive them whenever she wanted.

Propping herself up on her elbows, Peyton watched Hadina walk to the end of the table, her hand fisted around something. A delighted spark burst in her chest when Hadina opened her palm, revealing the biggest bullet she'd ever seen. The gold metal glinted against the tan of Hadina's fingers, her red nail tapping against the pointed tip.

"You're going to...?"

Hadina licked her lips, moving her gaze from the bullet to Peyton. "Torture you with this, yes. You see, these bullets have a spectacular trait that I think will drive you insane."

"Oh?"

"These particular bullets are cold to the touch, Peyton," she said, running her hands up Peyton's legs. "And it's going to drive you fucking wild when I use one to fuck you."

"Oh, God, please," Peyton moaned.

Lifting her hips, she helped angle herself so Hadina could pull Peyton's pants down to her ankles. Peyton tried to kick them off but Hadina tutted and shook her head. It took a second for Peyton to realize Hadina wanted her to feel trapped, her legs forced closer together. The ache between Peyton's thighs increased at the thought.

Her mind was a chaotic, wordless thing while Hadina climbed onto the table on top of her to straddle her legs. Hadina's lipstick was smudged slightly, a red smear at the corner of her mouth, and Peyton wanted to lick it.

Leaning forward, Hadina pressed her lips against Peyton's left thigh, peppering red-stained kisses against her skin. Each one made the fire inside her burn brighter, the hunger inside her more desperate for nourishment the higher Hadina got. Peyton's breath hitched when Hadina reached the line of her panties, only to pull away and pay attention to her right thigh instead. Peyton let out a long, slow groan, which made Hadina chuckle against her leg.

"I did promise to torture you," she said, her voice promising devilish things.

The response died on Peyton's tongue when Hadina licked a path up the rest of the girl's thigh, before wrapping her teeth around the thin material of her panties. Peyton gasped when Hadina pulled back, ripping away the material with her teeth in the process. The sharp sting was only fuel to the fire, making Peyton's nipples pebble beneath her shirt.

"They were in my way. I'll buy you another pair," Hadina muttered with a wink.

"Fuck me," Peyton croaked out in disbelief.

Hadina smiled. "I plan on it."

She coaxed another gasp from Peyton when she parted her, running two fingers through her seeping pussy. She was always wet and ready around Hadina, it seemed—not that she minded. If anyone was deserving of having Peyton permanently turned on, it was Hadina Adis.

Coating her fingers in the wetness between the girl's thighs, Hadina rubbed against Peyton's clit before pulling free to examine the juices dripping down. "The sweetest nectar," she whispered before sucking them clean, making Peyton's eyes flutter as she watched.

Her body was already trembling, the foreplay enough to have her ready. But she knew Hadina was having fun, and whatever she had planned was bound to be delicious. Biting down on her lip, Peyton kept her eyes trained on Hadina, who had picked up the bullet. She held it in front of Peyton's face, twirling the pointed tip around before dropping it to her lips with a raised brow. "Lick it."

Peyton darted her tongue out, wrapping it around the cool metal until it was slick with saliva.

"Good girl," Hadina praised before repeating the action, sucking off the taste of Peyton.

Hadina pushed up Peyton's shirt, exposing her breasts to the cool air. Peyton could feel her nipples pebble further, stiff peaks ready to be toyed with. Hadina clearly had the same thought as she trailed the cold bullet up Peyton's torso, stopping when the tip reached her left nipple. Using the pointed end, Hadina circled the ammunition around her sensitive nipples, moving from one to the other as Peyton writhed beneath her.

The sensation of cool metal against her warm skin was overwhelming and Peyton couldn't handle it. Biting down hard on her lower lip, she swallowed a moan. Hadina was enjoying seeing her come undone, she could tell, and it drove Peyton fucking wild.

"Tell me what you want," Hadina purred, closing her lips around one nipple while playing with the other between two fingers. She twisted the peak slightly, sending a twinge of arousal through to Peyton's core. Peyton could hear how Hadina's breath deepened, and could feel the want matched in everything she did.

"I want you to show me just how cruel the infamous Hadina Adis can be," Peyton panted, shrieking when the other woman's tongue flicked out to incite another jolt of pleasure.

When she pulled back, a string of saliva connected Hadina's lips to Peyton's breasts. Wiping the corners of her mouth with her middle finger before darting her tongue out and breaking the string, Hadina let the wetness drip down onto Peyton's stomach. Her lips curled into a devilish smile, and Peyton could *feel* the sexual tension fraught between them. She didn't know how it was possible for there still to be tension when she was spread bare, but the electricity in the air promised that there was far more to come and she was more eager than ever to find out what was in store for her.

"You should be careful what devils you offer your soul to," Hadina warned, a sexy edge to her voice that had Peyton seeping onto the table below them.

"If you're the devil, consider my soul yours, baby," Peyton replied. She didn't mean for the emotion to clog her throat like it did, but she *did* mean the words. If her soul was to belong to anyone, she

SARAH JAMES

wanted it to be Hadina. There was a darkness in each of them that reached for the other, binding them together. Peyton didn't completely believe in fate, but there was some higher power bringing them together and she understood the importance of that.

Hadina's eyes softened slightly and she paused, her lips parting. She wanted to say something, but Peyton could see the war battling behind those dark eyes and she didn't want to push. Whatever barriers Hadina had, Peyton would stand by the woman's side until she let them drop.

Hadina shifted herself farther back, before pushing Peyton's legs open so she could see her. Then she reached for the bullet again, humming her approval before teasing Peyton's entrance. Peyton gasped, the metal feeling even colder against the scorching heat of her pussy. Her reaction was what Hadina was looking for, those plump perfect lips twitching as she pushed the bullet inside.

"Oh, *God*," Peyton cried out, her knuckles turning white as she gripped the edge of the table.

Spurred on by the moans, Hadina picked up the pace and used the bullet like it wasn't a piece of weaponry. The idea that it was used for something deadly was clearly exciting for them both, Peyton squirming between Hadina's strong thighs as she kept her pinned in place.

Peyton's breathing came out in quick pants as Hadina moved the bullet, scraping the tip against that sensitive spot as she pulled it back out while working Peyton closer and closer to orgasm. When Peyton could feel herself start to shake, her walls tightening, Hadina pressed her thumb against her clit. The added pressure was enough to have Peyton screaming, falling over the edge. Her vision blurred as she trembled through her release, Hadina's name the only thing on her lips.

"I—Hadina—"

"Shh, *mi querida*, don't speak. I know." Entwining their fingers,

Hadina squeezed Peyton's hand, holding tight as the girl came down from her orgasm.

When Peyton's vision cleared and her breathing slowed, a thought pushed its way forward in her mind and refused to move. As much as she wanted to blame it on how well Hadina fucked her every time, she knew it went deeper than that.

Peyton Dimitra was falling in love with Hadina Adis.

Tentadora

CHAPTER 30

PEYTON

Two weeks of rigorous training was enough to have Peyton aching all over—and not in a fun way. Her limbs were heavy and bruised from learning how to use firearms safely and with precision, though she still didn't feel confident in her abilities yet.

The third week was combat training with some of Hadina's workforce. Harris and Hadina watched as Peyton got her ass beat over and over again, her body crumpling to the floor every time her mock-attacker threw a punch her way. One of them was an Asian woman, who said her name was Ume. With her short, black pixie cut and stern stare, she appeared every bit of the fierce warrior Peyton knew her to be. Even after their training sessions, when Ume would help pick Peyton up and tell her she was improving, Peyton was intimidated.

She also kinda wanted to be Ume's best friend.

"Do you think you're ready for this?" Hadina asked on the one-month mark of her training. Peyton had been improving slowly but surely, and Harris had even commented that she could handle herself.

"Yes."

Hadina hummed her disapproval. They had been arguing back and forth for days about whether she was ready to go on her first mission to rescue kids from a shipment that was rumored to be due into port. It didn't matter how many times she assured Hadina that she was ready; Hadina shook her head and told her she needed to train more.

"What about if you just—"

Peyton held up a hand and shook her head. "No. Training can continue *while* we start going on missions together. The only way I'm going to learn is if I'm there with you, seeing it all firsthand."

Hadina looked about ready to argue some more when Harris piped up from where he was leaning on the kitchen doorframe, watching them with an amused smile playing on his lips. He rubbed a hand across his stubbled jaw. "She's right, boss. She'll learn better on the job."

Fixing the man with a death glare, Hadina flipped him off before sighing and slumping into her seat. "Fine. But if she gets hurt, *te cortare las bolas.*" Neither Peyton nor Harris had to be fluent in Spanish to understand Hadina's threat, especially when it was coupled with a mock demonstration.

A SLIGHT TINGE of regret colored her emotions as Peyton got strapped up for their mission. It wasn't that she wasn't ready—she had meant it when she told Hadina that she had to do this—but rather, she wasn't sure she could face seeing all those children with bruised bodies and broken souls. Then again, it was selfish of her to feel like that when those kids had faced everything that brought them there.

The least she could do was wear a mask of bravery and attempt to save them from worse fates.

"You ready?" Ume asked from beside her, handing Peyton a blade before inserting her own into the sheath at her side.

Clearing her head, Peyton nodded curtly at Ume, grabbing the blade and following suit. Then she steadied her shaky hand, pulled her gun from its holster, and held it at her side, making sure it was pointed towards the ground. "Ready."

They had been briefed in the old car lot a few blocks over before they arrived. Hadina had told her that they always made their game plan before moving to the location, so that they could be as quiet as possible on arrival, without rousing suspicion to catch their target off-guard.

Now, they were padding as silently as they could through the forest surrounding the hidden building. Peyton looked to her right and saw Harris nod, motioning with two fingers for them to advance. Her heart pounded in her chest as she crept forward, the heavy breathing and occasional crunch of twigs snapping the only things she could hear. She wanted to look around for Hadina but this was her chance to prove that she didn't need a safety blanket—she could do this on her own.

Ume pulled open a side door and led the way with Peyton hot on her heels. The stench of dampness and mold assaulted their nostrils as they rounded the first corner and landed in a corridor. Dull lights flickered every few feet, casting an orange glow and making it look like something straight from hell. Which, she supposed, it actually was. A man-made hellscape for the torture, distribution, and murder of vulnerable kids. It made Peyton want to vomit.

She was part of the group looking for Ian Lastra, the leader of this fucked-up ordeal. There was a good chance she'd been assigned to this specific group as a test; Lastra was to be killed on sight. There was no information he could give them that they didn't already have, nullifying any usefulness he might offer. While it hadn't explicitly been said, Peyton was to be the one to pull the trigger.

Clearing one room after the other, the team worked their way through the building, looking for Lastra. As they rounded another corner, Peyton heard the grumbling of a male voice. "Ume," she whispered, nodding her head in the direction of the sound.

Ume mouthed, *"Follow me but stay back,"* and headed to see if it was Lastra. Positioning her gun in line with her shoulders, ready to shoot, Ume kicked the door open.

There, sitting behind a desk littered with abandoned papers and a landline telephone from the 80s, was Ian Lastra. Peyton had been shown photos of him for identification purposes, but he looked as though he'd aged a decade. Where his hair had been dark brown in the images, it was now primarily gray. His face was gaunt, wrinkles marring what had once been smooth, pale skin. He looked dirty, like he hadn't bothered to wash in weeks. He must have been living here, though the idea of him being in the same building as the kids 24/7 made Peyton sick to her stomach.

Hadina had explained that while most of the targets they hunted were upper class, using their power and wealth for whatever sick fantasies they had, sometimes they'd have a mark who'd fallen from grace far earlier. Ian Lastra was the latter.

Ian was a silver-spoon, Ivy-league brat who'd been handed everything he ever wanted in life. When he started to show off his unhinged predilections in his teenage years, his parents had shipped him off to military school to straighten him out. And when that didn't work either, he'd been disowned and turned to heroin and meth, squandering his life away on drugs. Somewhere along the way, those old perverted proclivities had turned into his meal ticket. He used the kids to feed his depraved hunger and sold them on, using the cash to fund his out-of-control drug habit.

He was scum, and death would be too good for him.

"Who the fuck are you?" Lastra yelled, ending whatever call he was on.

"The reaper who has come to claim your soul and drop it in hell where it belongs," Ume spat back, grabbing him by the collar. "This one is yours, Peyton."

Ume threw him forward, where he tripped and fell, landing on his knees. He looked up at Peyton with blown pupils and bloodshot eyes. "Please, don't do this."

Peyton ignored his pleas and raised her gun, flicking her safety off. Her hands trembled as she aimed at the man's head. She needed to get it together, calm her nerves, and prove that she could do this— prove it to herself *and* to Hadina.

Her finger moved to the trigger but she hesitated, which was a grave mistake. Lastra sneered and lunged forward, kicking Peyton's legs out from under her. She smacked against the floor, her gun flying out of her hand.

Lastra climbed on top of her, straddling Peyton's hips as he wrapped his hands around her throat. Ume wrestled to get him off, but the skinny bastard was stronger than he looked. Peyton gasped for breath as he pushed his thumbs harder into her skin, choking her.

"What a fucking amateur!" he swore, rearing his head back to smack Ume in the face. She staggered a step, blood gushing from her nose. Lastra grinned triumphantly and returned his attention to Peyton. She punched at him but her consciousness was slowly slipping. "If they want me, they'll have to send people who know what they're doing. Not some bitch playing dress-up." He spat at her, a glob of sickly saliva smacking her cheek. If he wasn't squeezing the breath from her lungs, Peyton would have vomited.

Black spots swam in her vision, unconsciousness beckoning her. She couldn't hear anything but the blood rushing in her ears. She wanted to fight, but her body was betraying her, showing her to be the weak little girl everyone always assumed her to be.

Suddenly she could hear a familiar voice, though it was

muffled, before something hot sprayed across her face. The pressure from her throat was gone and her vision slowly cleared, until the image of Hadina towering over her with furrowed brows came into view. Peyton couldn't figure out if the woman was concerned, angry, or disappointed; but she was glad to see Hadina's face nonetheless.

"Get up," Hadina commanded. With shaky legs and a bout of dizziness washing over her, Peyton pushed to her feet. Hadina caught her as she swayed slightly. "I need you to compartmentalize. The mission isn't over yet—there are still girls to save. Bury whatever you're feeling right now, and deal with it afterwards, okay?"

Peyton steadied herself and took a deep breath, ignoring the burning sensation in her throat. Hadina was right; she had been the one who wanted to do this and she had to see it out until the end. Getting hurt was an inevitable, unavoidable part of what they were doing and Peyton had to learn to be okay with that.

Ume walked past them, throwing a bloody tissue on the floor before patting Peyton's shoulder. "The first time you almost die is basically initiation. Welcome to the team."

"Be strong, Peyton," Hadina said before following Ume out of the room.

Be strong, Peyton. She could do this. She *had* to do this.

Hadina and Ume both stayed with her as they cleared some more rooms, finding each of them empty. Then they caught up with some of the other guys, who had managed to locate a couple of kids and get them out. Hadina ordered them to go and deal with Lastra's body, telling them not to leave a trace.

A thrill ran through Peyton's every nerve ending, even if it was bad timing.

When Hadina split up the groups again, she made sure to have Peyton with her. Which left Peyton feeling conflicted. Sure, she was calmer and felt safer with Hadina by her side, but she also wanted to prove that she could do this on her own.

Reaching the next room, Peyton stopped Hadina when she went to open the door. "I've got this."

Hadina pursed her lips, her dark eyes focusing on Peyton. "You have nothing to prove."

"I do. I have to prove it to myself." Her voice was quiet, vulnerable.

Hadina reached out a hand, entwining their pinkies. "*Yo creo en ti, tentadora.* I believe in you."

Tears sprung to her eyes as she took in the tenderness in Hadina's voice, the affection laced in her Spanish. Peyton offered a small smile, hoping her eyes conveyed just how much those words meant to her and the impact they had on her self-esteem. To have someone like Hadina believe in you was like receiving a gift of courage, and she wanted to keep that feeling bottled up forever.

Hadina released her pinkie and Peyton twisted the handle, pushing the door open. Peyton felt a stab in her chest when she saw a little girl lying on the cold stone floor, her curly auburn hair spread out around her in matted strands. The child cracked her eyes open as they approached, her fear on full display.

Peyton watched as Hadina knelt in front of the girl—the Adis sister's hands held up in submission. While the situation itself was grotesque and heart-wrenching, Peyton was happy to see this side of Hadina. It wasn't often she showed the world the goodness that resided inside her, the softness that she reserved for the people she loved. The fact that Peyton was one of those people and was often on the receiving end of that softness made her heart swell.

"What's your name, love?" Hadina asked, her voice gentle and tentative so as not to spook the child.

Peyton was standing back and didn't hear the response, but Hadina waved a hand and motioned her forward. She took a few steps, slowly, and knelt on the ground beside Hadina. She took in the girl's filthy appearance and sickness rose to the back of her throat at the sight. Not only was she covered in grime and dried blood, but her face was a myriad of colors from bruises on top of bruises, her eyes blackened next to a very broken nose. Peyton had to stop herself from gasping.

"This is Peyton," Hadina introduced. "Peyton, this is Lara. Lara, Peyton and I are going to help you get out of here, okay?"

Waiting until Lara nodded, Hadina and Peyton rose to their feet. Hadina offered her hand to the girl and watched as she took it with a tiny, trembling hand. Hadina then walked the child over to Harris, who waited at the door, before whispering to him. Peyton noticed how his demeanor changed too, his usual stern face softening when he introduced himself to Lara. He gently draped a blanket around the child's shoulders and they walked out of the room together.

Tentadora

CHAPTER 31

PEYTON

So far, they'd been able to rescue twelve girls, all beaten and bloodied and begging to die. Peyton now understood why Hadina had built her walls of ice around her heart, a preventative measure to stop it from being broken every time she found another child who needed to be saved. She knew it would take time for her to be able to compartmentalize her emotions like that, but it still broke Peyton a little more after each rescue too. She had chosen to be part of this, to be part of Adis & Co., but it didn't mean it was easy.

Hadina came over and pressed a warm hand to Peyton's cheek. "Are you holding up?"

Peyton leaned into the heat of her touch, nodding slightly. "Where to next?"

They were in an abandoned building in the middle of the woods, the wild forest hiding the majority of the exterior from prying eyes. It was the perfect place for sick bastards to hide their operations... where no one was around to hear the blood curdling screams that were sure to draw attention.

Hadina had split her team up into four groups, sending two of them to cover the left side of the building. They'd worked their way across each floor, which Peyton realized meant that the basement level was all that was left to check. Hadina gave her a sympathetic look before leading them into the hallway and opening the door to the lower level.

Peyton was sure the building had been a factory of some kind, considering the large pipes that were mounted onto many of the walls. Occasionally, one would groan or thump and Peyton's heart would beat harder in her chest. As they descended the rusty staircase, which clanked beneath their feet, she felt as though she was descending into the mouth of the underworld itself.

Using their flashlights, they split up to look around and try to find the overhead light. Peyton found a switch and flipped it, grimacing as the fluorescent bulbs blinded them for a second.

After their eyes had adjusted, the group looked around and took in the dusty, cold corridor. Harris signaled for the teams to split up, opening up the rows of doors on each side. Hadina and Peyton made eye contact, silently conversing that they would start at the opposite end. Peyton held her breath each time she opened a door, praying she wouldn't find anyone...

"Shh, don't be scared, little one. We're here to help," she heard Hadina say, and quickly stepped into the room behind her. Sitting in the corner, huddled in on herself with a rag doll, was a blonde girl of no more than six. Her blue eyes were startling against the dull light of the room and the grime on her face. Tears welled up in her eyes as Hadina took a step forward.

"Hadi, stop!" Peyton hissed, taking note of the child's fear. Hadina was terrifying—even when she wasn't trying to be—and the girl moved further into the corner. "She's scared of you."

Peyton hated the hurt that flashed across Hadina's eyes before she nodded and took a few steps back.

"Hi. My name is Peyton. Is it okay if I come a little closer?"

The little girl eyed Peyton suspiciously for a moment before finally tilting her head in response. As slowly as she could, Peyton walked forward and stopped when she was close enough to see the girl clearly.

"That woman there is called Hadina. She looks kind of scary, huh?" Another nod. "I promise she's not. Hadina and I find bad people so that they don't hurt anyone again. We found the person who hurt you and he won't be coming back."

Those bright eyes widened as the child regarded Peyton. "Ian is gone?"

"That's right. He won't ever hurt you again."

"But who will look after me?" she asked, pressing her dolly into her cheek.

Hadina stepped up beside Peyton, resting a hand on her shoulder. "We'll find your family for you or we'll take you somewhere safe. Would you like that?"

"Can you tell us your name?" Peyton asked her, her tone soft so as not to spook the girl.

"Amelie. And this is Claire," she said, holding up the doll for them to see. The movement made her sleeve roll down her bony arms, revealing horrific rope burns around her wrist.

Peyton took a staggered step backward as a memory flooded her mind, casting her to a time in her childhood when she had marks just like that.

"I TOLD you to keep your mouth shut, you little bitch!" He shoved the rag into her mouth and tied it tight, the material biting into the soft skin of her cheeks.

"Please stop it," she cried around the makeshift gag, trying to break free from her foster father's grip.

"Stay still!" He smacked her hard across the cheek for her disobedience, and Peyton's vision blurred as she slumped to the floor. "This will teach

you to talk back to me. You should show me some fucking respect, consid-ering I've taken you into my home, given you food and a roof over your head. But, no, you just whine and always ask for more."

Tying rope around her wrists, binding them together, he dragged her down to the dark basement. She was terrified of the basement in this house, of the shadows that lurked in every corner. Sometimes she thought that they were staring back at her, monsters waiting for the right moment to gobble her up.

He dumped her in front of the wooden post in the middle of the room, grabbed the length of rope connected to her wrists, and tied it around and around the pillar. Once he was satisfied that she wouldn't be able to go anywhere, he tied a knot and stood back to admire his work.

Tears clouded Peyton's vision and burned her skin as she sobbed, mumbling how sorry she was over and over. Despite her apologies, her foster father's smile was sadistic as he looked down at her.

"Now maybe you'll appreciate what we give you, huh?" Slapping her again for good measure, he stormed up the stairs and slammed the door shut. Peyton heard the click of the lock as he left her in the cold, dark basement.

For three days, she lay quivering with only the shadows of her night-mares for company. When her stepfather finally returned to untie her, she couldn't feel her hands. She shivered and stared at the burns on her wrists from where the rope had bitten into her young skin, marking the abuse.

She didn't cry after that. Even when he hit her or his biological son crept into her room at night, her tears didn't fall. Instead, she let her mind wander and imagine a day where the monsters in the shadows were hers to control. She would picture the creatures lurching after the ones who had hurt her, eating them whole so that no trace of them was left.

One day, she would think to herself, I will tell my shadows to destroy those who hurt others. They will devour them all.

"Peyton? Are you okay?"

Hadina's voice drew Peyton from the hellish memory she had buried a long time ago. She often didn't think of her life before she was adopted by her parents, instead choosing to bury those years where she was passed around foster carers and abusers. A small part of her, however, relished the fact that she had wished to be able to control the shadows and now she had found *la reina de las sombras*. It was fitting that she had fallen in love with the queen of the shadows, who would burn the world for her if she asked.

Peyton blinked away the memory and blew out a breath. "I'm okay."

Furrowing her brows, Hadina stared back with pursed lips. "Peyton..."

"Hadi, I'm fine," she snapped, turning to Amelie. "Now then, Amelie, would it be okay if we took you upstairs? We can get you a nice warm blanket and some food. How does that sound?"

"Will you give Claire some too?"

Peyton smiled softly. "Of course we'll give Claire some too! We would never leave her out."

Amelie grinned, taking Peyton's outstretched hand. The little girl looked up with hope glistening in her eyes. "Will you really take me back to my family?"

"We'll do our best, baby girl," Peyton answered, squeezing Amelie's hand softly.

By the time they had all the girls fed and sent off to the hospital to get checked over, Peyton felt completely drained. There was so much energy put into pretending like you weren't breaking apart at the sight of the abused children, so much dedicated to containing the fury blazing within your blood when you thought about what they'd endured. Adding in the memory she'd unlocked on top of that was, well, fucking exhausting.

Hadina sighed as she slid into the driver's seat of her car, throwing her head back. She turned slightly so she could look at

Peyton while worrying her lip between her teeth. *"¿Estás bien?* What happened back there? Are you okay?"

Closing her eyes, Peyton contemplated keeping it a secret. But after the day they'd had, she realized there was no one who would understand her more than Hadina. She told the other woman what had brought the memory back, and everything she had suddenly recalled from her childhood. Her voice cracked but she refused to cry, channeling the child who wished to control the monsters. When she finished, she was too scared to open her eyes for fear that she would see pity reflected in Hadina's.

"Peyton, look at me." There was a commanding tone in Hadina's voice that made Peyton slowly open her eyes and look at the goddess beside her. Where she had expected to see pity, she saw anger instead. "You wanted to command the monsters hiding in the shadows, *tentadora,* and that is what I am. Tell me to destroy them and I will make them pay for everything they ever did to you."

Peyton unbuckled her seat belt and leaned across the console, pulling Hadina into a long, slow kiss. "I don't need you to destroy them for me. I want you to teach me how to destroy them myself."

"Convertirse en la oscuridad. Become the darkness, Peyton, and I will be by your side. I will teach you how to devour the entire world."

CHAPTER 32

HADINA

It physically pained Hadina to see the heartbreak in Peyton's eyes during her first mission. She had endured almost being killed and seeing the true horrors of those *bastardos* up close. Her mind was chaotic as she struggled to understand what she was feeling—pride and fear were both eating her alive. Hadina was happy to have Peyton by her side, but she hated how much it felt like she *belonged*. Peyton was a light in the world, and Hadina's life would consume her until all she knew was darkness.

"Why do you look like you want to murder someone?"

Hadina shook her head, looking down at where Peyton lay beside her in bed, blonde hair spread out across the pillows like a golden halo. "I always want to murder someone."

Peyton snorted and smacked Hadina's arm. "You're so fucked up."

Hadina beamed, baring her teeth with the gesture. "Indeed I am."

"Tell me what it was like for you growing up. Before you found out about Adis & Co." Peyton trailed her fingers up Hadina's arm, running soft circles across a white scar marring her skin from a bullet wound.

Hadina let out a sigh, resigned to the fact she would always give into Peyton, would tell her anything she wanted. Hadina would burn the world and stand in the flames if Peyton wished it. She turned to stare straight ahead, looking at the images on the wall. Most of the rooms had family photos framed and displayed, though it made Hadina's heart ache when she looked at her *mama*.

"It was chaotic," Hadina said, a fond smile breaking free, "but beautiful. My mom was *always* in the kitchen cooking, making a complete mess. I used to come home from school and it was like she'd emptied the cupboards out. It didn't matter what she was making, she could never keep the place clean while she did it. *Papi* would shake his head, throw up his hands and say, '*Eres la mujer más desordenada del planeta!*' which she took offense to because, in her mind, she absolutely was *not* the messiest woman on the planet. But then she'd look around her, see the flour covering the surfaces or broken eggshells on the floor, and they'd both burst into laughter."

"You must miss her," Peyton said quietly, linking their fingers together.

Hadina looked at their joined hands, emotion swelling inside her. "*Mucho.* She would have loved you, though I imagine she'd have been throwing her *chanclas* at me for letting you get dragged into this mess."

Peyton squeezed Hadina's hand. "Maybe so, but I'd have convinced her that this is my choice and what I want—just like I convinced you."

"Jury is still out on that one."

"I'm going to beat your ass!"

Hadina wiggled her eyebrows. "Is that a promise?"

"There's something off about this whole thing." Hadina sighed and gratefully accepted a cup of coffee proffered by her father. She had been scouring over CCTV footage for the past two days, desperate to find answers in the hours of video feed. So far, all she had found was more anger and frustration.

"*Confía en tus instintos, mija.* Your gut has rarely ever been wrong over the years, so trust yourself. If you think something is off, keep searching until you find the answers." Her father leaned over and pressed a kiss to the top of her head.

Hadina forced a smile and watched him walk out of the office before burying herself under hours of footage. She wasn't sure how much time had passed before Peyton walked in, a plate of tacos in one hand and a glass of fresh orange juice in the other. Hadina blinked and Peyton let out a soft chuckle.

"It's almost seven, baby. You've been in here for hours and haven't eaten a thing."

Hadina shrugged. "Work is more important."

Peyton rolled her eyes and perched on the edge of the desk, sitting the plate down beside her. "So is your health. You can't help other people if you make yourself sick by not eating."

"That's what my *mama* used to say too," Hadina admitted. A small blush heated her cheeks at the thought. She wished her mother were alive to have met Peyton, knowing she would have adored her. Hadina didn't think anyone could meet Peyton and not automatically love her.

Except Zellie. But she was a bitch anyway.

"Let me take over?" Peyton asked, already pulling up a seat beside Hadina and pushing her to the side. Hadina opened her mouth to argue but Peyton fixed her with a sharp stare. "Eat. I'll watch."

The grumbling of her stomach was the only thing that stopped Hadina from trying to argue further. She looked down at the plate of tacos and found her mouth already salivating. The scent of the spices wafted in the air and she lifted one to her lips, taking a bite as Peyton scrolled through hours of footage.

"*Santa mierda*," Hadina said through a mouthful of food, the myriad of flavors eliciting a small groan. Peyton looked up from the screen, appearing pleased with herself. "Where did you learn to make these, baby?"

Peyton practically beamed as she turned back to the computer, trying to hide the blush on her cheeks. "I found a little box in one of the kitchen drawers and it had a bunch of handwritten recipes. The one for tacos looked like the least complicated so there was less chance of me fucking it up."

Hadina felt emotion clog the back of her throat as she took another bite, savoring the taste. The moment that first piece of beef *fajita* hit her tongue, she knew instantly that it was her mother's recipe. While nobody could replicate her mother's amazing skills in the kitchen—not even her father, who had tried, many times—Peyton had come pretty damn close to matching the recipe. There was something missing, but Hadina felt that even when she cooked herself. Nobody had the talent like her *mama* but the fact Peyton had tried would have been enough to bring tears to her eyes.

"*Tentadora*," Hadina said softly. "Look at me."

Peyton peered up sheepishly, her cheeks tinged pink. Hadina leaned forward and captured her lips, kissing her tenderly. She hoped that the depth of her thanks shone through that kiss, showing just how much it meant to her.

"You like them?"

Hadina nodded, taking another bite. "They're delicious. They taste exactly how I remember."

As the pair exchanged a look, Hadina could feel the tears nipping her eyes as she watched Peyton's glaze over. She was tempted to let them fall, allow both of them a break from being brave. But they had too much to do and too much to fight for; the walls had to stay up for just a while longer.

"Anything yet?" Hadina asked, nodding her head towards the CCTV as she devoured the last taco on her plate.

"Maybe?" Peyton said, self-doubt creeping into her voice.

"Go on."

Moving over slightly, Peyton pulled Hadina back into the desk so she could see the screen clearly. Peyton had zoomed in on footage from four different cameras, watching them on a loop. She pointed to the top right corner on each window, marking the time and date stamp. "Okay, take a look at these dates. This is an hour before and after the last two shipments."

Hadina leaned in, watching the workers walk in and out of the docks, carrying boxes or emptying the containers.

"Now watch here," Peyton said, tapping the screen. Hadina narrowed her eyes, examining carefully. Her mouth opened on a silent gasp as she realized what Peyton was pointing out. "Do you see it?"

"*Eres sensacional!*" Hadina grabbed Peyton by the cheeks and crashed their lips together, laughing into her mouth. "Fucking brilliant!"

Almost invisible to the eye, Peyton had found exactly what they were looking for. On both dates, the cameras caught someone sneaking past the camera. At first glance, they looked like any other dock worker, but if you paid close enough attention, you could see that instead of safety boots, the person wore stilettos.

"It has to be, right?"

Hadina hummed her agreement. "I'm the only person who I've ever seen wear heels on those docks. And those cheap-ass fakes are certainly not mine. This is Regina, or whatever the fuck her name is. You just found proof of her being on our property—we can find this *pendeja* and destroy her."

Tentadora

CHAPTER 33

PEYTON

"I'D KIND OF RATHER YOU NOT SEE THIS," HADINA SAID ON A SIGH.

Peyton rolled her eyes. "And I'd kind of rather you got it into your head that we're doing *all* of this together."

Hadina pouted her pretty lips but relented, handing over a gun for Peyton to put in her underarm holster. She slipped it inside and adjusted it before throwing a silk shirt on, leaving it unbuttoned as it hung by her sides, only just covering her weapons. When she looked up again, Hadina was staring at her with dark eyes and Peyton felt her core heat between her legs.

Harris stood guard outside one of the rusty containers down at the docks. It was used for *storage* apparently, which Peyton had quickly inferred meant *torture room*. It was easy access for them for moments like these, when they needed to grab someone from work without many witnesses.

"He's inside, boss," Harris said gruffly, nodding his head to the side. "He's a slimy-looking little shit, so I think it won't take long for you to get what you want." Noticing Peyton standing beside Hadina, he gave a half smile and another nod of his head. "Peyton."

Peyton returned the gesture, trying not to show how proud she felt to be part of the team. "Adrian."

Adrian Harris was the very definition of tall, dark, and handsome. He was imposing as hell, but Peyton saw the way he always tried to make her feel at ease and help her transition into this new path. He was a good man, she'd concluded, and someone she was beginning to trust dearly.

Hadina glanced at Peyton and raised a perfectly arched brow. "Ready?"

Sliding her dagger from her side, Peyton grinned. "Absolutely."

Harris grabbed the metal door to the large container and yanked it open, revealing the *slimy-looking little shit* he'd described, which was a pretty accurate observation from what Peyton could see. The man's shaggy brown hair was dripping with grease and sweat, clinging to the sides of his face as he hung his head. From where he was tied to the chair with thick rope, Peyton noted the grime covering his clothes—and the needle marks covering his arms.

"*Mierda,*" Hadina mumbled, shaking her head. Her hair was tied up in a slick, tight bun on the top of her head, a stray strand waving with the movement. "What a pathetic sight."

Peyton squared her shoulders and stepped forward, wincing as the smell of stale urine invaded her senses. Moving to the side, she smacked the handle of her knife against the metal wall, the sound reverberating around the small space.

"Wake the fuck up!"

The weasel-looking man shook from his unconsciousness with a jolt, his eyes widening in fear when he took in the sight of Peyton with her shining blade, Hadina poised at her back with a fully loaded gun.

"Please. *Please!* I told that dude I didn't know anything!"

Peyton crouched in front of him, suddenly grateful that her

heeled boots provided her enough height that she was eye-level with him. "I didn't tell you that you could speak." Holding the knife up between them, she tilted the blade so that he could see the freshly sharpened edge. "Here's what's going to happen: either you tell us what we want to know, or I'm going to use this beautiful blade here to practice my butchering skills on you. Are we clear?"

There was a sick, twisted part of her that was excited to use what she'd learned to extract the information needed from the man. She was going to hell for the darkness of her thoughts, but the malicious look in Hadina's gaze made her feel all the better about that. If she was going to hell, Hadina would be waiting on the throne to greet her.

The man gulped and looked to Hadina, tears brimming his eyes as he pleaded. "Ms. Adis, please. Help me! You have to believe me."

Hadina stepped forward, placing a gentle hand on Peyton's shoulder and squeezing lightly. Peyton peered up and saw the devilish thoughts playing behind the other woman's eyes. Leaning down close enough that her lips brushed Peyton's ear, Hadina whispered to her lover, "Show me your darkness, *tentadora*."

Desire and anticipation pulled at Peyton's insides, a delicious shiver running down her spine at Hadina's words. She stood and tapped the handle of her knife against her lips, making a show of her contemplation.

"Well, what's it gonna be?"

"I don't know shit!"

A smile tugged at the corner of Peyton's lips and she sighed dramatically, shaking her head. "Then you really should have paid more attention when you were fucking us over," she cooed, before thrusting her blade into the stomach of the piece of deceiving trash before her.

He cried out, spittle flying everywhere as his blood soaked into his dirty shirt. Satisfied by his screams, Peyton pulled out her knife and admired the crimson coating the blade. There was something eerily beautiful about blood, the way it held someone's entire life force in its rich, colored droplets. She had been scared of the sight when she was a child, but that was before her life had become one big mess filled with blood and bruises. She had let go of her fear the first time her own blood had been spilled at the hands of someone else, and somewhere along the way, it had now become her unhinged fascination. It was hypnotic and psychotic, and she loved it.

"You fucking bitch!"

Peyton tilted her head as she looked at the man before her, noting the way his pants were freshly soaked with piss as it dribbled down his leg. It was laughable that someone who had just been stabbed could be so brave with his tongue.

She tried to emanate Hadina's effortless attitude as she stared him down, hoping that her nerves didn't betray her. Her mind was at war, her thoughts jumbled as she tried to fathom how she could be enjoying hurting someone. One look at Hadina, however, and Peyton realized she didn't care. Whatever was changing within her made her feel powerful and she would not let that go anytime soon. Hadina had been right. She was playing in a den of wolves, but now she was learning to hunt her prey. If the Adis family were the wolves in question, Peyton would happily be part of the pack.

"Here's the thing, buddy," Peyton said, her voice menacingly low. "Your life became worthless to me the moment I found out you helped that woman traffic and abuse children. You betrayed us and allowed her access, helping her fucked-up agenda. Probably in exchange for something more to shoot up, right?"

He didn't bother to look up as Peyton continued.

"Was it worth it? Sacrificing all those innocent kids, just to get your veins filled with whatever bullshit drugs she gave you? Did it help you to get over the fact that you helped kids get raped, beaten, left broken or dead when they're of no use?"

Anger creeped into her bloodstream as she pictured those poor kids, their lives ruined because some junkie wanted his next fix. Addiction was a disease, but it became something far more ugly the moment he chose drugs over children's lives. It made her sick. But the more she thought about it, how his actions had impacted the next chain of events, the more her nausea turned to fury. It burned hot, a white rage consuming her. She let it flow through her, searing into her very being until she was nothing but a weapon, an avenging angel for all the children who didn't get saved. Letting out a blood-curdling scream, she lunged forward and stuck her dagger into the man's stomach again, this time twisting the blade until she could feel it slice through his insides.

"I hope the high was worth it," she spat, drawing her knife back. Blood seeped from his wounds, soaking his clothes. It should have made her feel something, to see what she had just done to another human being. But all she could feel was relief that there was one less person out there willing to help Regina.

"D-d-de–" the man sputtered, blood filling his mouth. Peyton turned to Hadina in confusion, seeing her look almost as taken aback. Hadina stepped forward, leaning down towards him. "D-Demi T-t-reyva..."

Peyton watched as he choked on his own blood, specks of red spitting onto Hadina's cheek. Peyton had barely been able to hear, never mind understand, what he had been trying to say. She grabbed at Hadina's arm, pulling her away. "What did he say?"

Hadina looked haunted as she wiped the back of her hand across her cheek, smearing the victim's blood along the way. "Demi Treyva."

"What does that mean?"

Hadina shook her head. "Not what, but who. Demi Treyva is Regina's real name. I guess your words got to him, baby, because that piece of shit just told us exactly who we're looking for."

Reina
de las sombras

CHAPTER 34

HADINA

Watching Peyton inflict pain on that piece of shit was like flipping a switch inside her. Hadina felt herself finally accept that Peyton was part of this, that she really was invested. Killing someone was never easy; it was a sacrifice that you can't know you're willing to make until you're in that situation, which was something Hadina knew all too well. She had feared that the moment Peyton took a life, she would break. It wouldn't have made her weak, but Hadina would have understood if she wanted to run away after that.

But she'd underestimated Peyton.

Now that she was standing in nothing but lacey black underwear, it appeared that Peyton had found the adrenaline as intoxicating as Hadina normally did. She could see the heat behind those ocean-colored eyes, the desire for a twisted type of romance that only Hadina could provide.

And she was oh so willing to provide it.

Licking her lips, Hadina leaned back in her chair and motioned for Peyton to come to her. "Well, don't you look delicious."

Peyton smirked, walking around the desk to stand in front of Hadina, before brushing some of her blonde bangs out of her eyes while batting those long lashes. "I thought we should celebrate after our little win earlier."

Running a hand down the soft skin of Peyton's curves, Hadina let out a small sigh. "I'm always down for celebrating with you, but I don't think that was a win. *Se avecina una guerra.* There's a war coming, sweetheart, and things are going to get really messy."

Peyton cupped Hadina's cheek, forcing them to meet each other's eyes. "Then we'll ready for battle. You're a survivor and a fighter, Hadi, and we're going to end this bitch once and for all."

Hadina smirked, her insides heating at this new side of Peyton. The anger simmering beneath her words was like fuel to Hadina's desire for her. She leaned forward and pressed a soft kiss to Peyton's stomach, smirking when her lipstick left a stain.

"I do love it when you show me that rage in you," Hadina purred, reaching a hand between Peyton's legs. She felt how hot she was as Hadina pushed the lace of her panties aside, slipping a finger between her wet folds.

"Oh, yeah?" Peyton hummed, her eyes flitting closed.

"Absolutely." Hadina rubbed a finger through Peyton's wet juices, slowly trailing a fingertip over Peyton's clit. Her answering shudder was Hadina's warning that Peyton wouldn't last long if she tried to toy with her like usual. Maybe her little temptress deserved an easy orgasm after the day she'd had.

"Tell me what you want, *tentadora*, so I can make you scream my name as I give you what you need."

Peyton cracked an eye open and peered down at Hadina, her lips pushing out into a tiny pout. She pulled her bottom lip through her teeth, and Hadina felt her nipples pebble beneath her clothes as she recalled how Peyton made a happy little sigh every time she did that exact thing to her.

"I want your mouth on me. I want you to *feel* my entire body scream your name."

This girl was going to be the death of her, but Hadina couldn't think of a better way to die.

Pushing her back, Hadina lifted Peyton's legs up and positioned her on the edge of the desk, slowly dragging her panties down her legs before dropping them to the floor between them.

Hadina lifted Peyton's feet on each armrest, spreading Peyton's knees apart farther so that she was on full display.

"*Dios mio,* I get a little more obsessed with you every time I see you like this. I want to keep you forever."

Peyton lay back, propping herself up on her elbows so she could still see. She looked at Hadina through lowered lashes, a soft smile playing on her lips. "I'm your willing prisoner, *mi reina.* Lock me away for eternity and I will happily be yours."

Mi reina. Something inside Hadina switched onto high alert and she gripped Peyton tighter, pressing kiss after kiss to her inner thigh.

Laughing as she squirmed, Peyton swatted at Hadina. "What is *wrong* with you?!"

"You're a fucking genius is what's wrong with me. *Mi reina.* My queen. My *title.* I'm queen of the shadows, right?"

Peyton's brows furrowed as she sat up a little. "Yeah?"

"Well, if I'm queen of the shadows, Demi is queen of whatever cesspit she crawled out of, in her eyes. *Regina* is Latin for queen. That *pinche puta* is trying to make herself a queen, when she's nothing more than trash."

Peyton grinned, a fierce sight that made Hadina want to kiss her lover senseless. "Then let's find her and remind her just where she came from. The only queen around here is you, Hadina Adis."

"Oh, I'm definitely keeping you forever," Hadina cooed, before dipping forward and pressing the flat of her tongue to Peyton's core.

"Forever," Peyton said breathlessly, gripping the edge of the desk as Hadina lapped at her juices, teasing her entrance with the tip of her tongue.

The sweet taste of Peyton's nectar was like nothing Hadina had ever tasted and she truly couldn't get enough. With every pulse of Peyton's pussy around her lips, she was spurred on by her craving for more. Hadina wanted every last drop, every single taste. She quickened the speed at which she teased, making sure to lick everywhere she could. When Peyton started to tense, Hadina moved her lips to Peyton's clit and sucked, using her tongue to circle the sensitive bud. One last flick had her coming undone.

Hadina held onto Peyton, massaging her thighs as she convulsed through her orgasm. Peyton threw her head back, screaming *Hadi* like she'd promised, with sweat glistening across her skin. From where Hadina sat, it looked like Peyton was glowing, a goddess soaring higher with pleasure from being worshiped. Hadina almost wished she could immortalize the moment, with Peyton's sinful body spread out before her, limp and spent.

But then she'd have to kill anyone who saw her love in such an exposed, tender condition.

"I think you're going to be my destruction," Hadina whispered softly as Peyton stirred.

"Then at least you'll watch the world burn knowing you've been loved."

Tentadora

CHAPTER 35

PEYTON

Peyton hadn't meant to tell Hadina that she loved her, indirectly or not. But every time Hadina brought her to the brink of ecstasy, Peyton found her inhibitions were lowered more and more. It seemed that sex combined with pleasing Hadina—a completely accidental discovery—was the key to make her spill her secret.

While she would normally overthink what had happened and ruminate on the fact Hadina hadn't said anything in reply, there was too much to be done. Hunting down Demi Treyva was top priority if they wanted to stop the increase of trafficking, especially now that she was using Adis employees to get what she wanted.

Taking a seat beside Ume, Peyton turned her attention to Harris, who was standing at the head of the conference table. They had been called into the Adis & Co. HQ, which was effectively just the high-rise building they used for their legal offices. It had a conference space which, according to Ume, they used for meetings when the workday was over. It was seven in the evening now and a soft dusk

257

had begun to settle across the sky, a beautiful sight through the many windows in the room.

"How do we track her?" Jason, one of the members of Hadina's inner circle, asked.

Harris pointed to the screen, which had CCTV footage pulled up from numerous cameras, each dated across the last couple of months. "She's being careless now that the job is getting bigger. Her ego must be huge because that cockiness is in full swing. She thought she could do this shit without us finding out."

Ume spoke up from beside Peyton. "But *how* do we find her?"

Peyton almost laughed as Harris rolled his eyes. "The way we always do. We know her name, which means we now know her business and her territory. It shouldn't be hard to find her. The hard part will be catching her. Now that we're on her tail, she'll know we're coming and her security will double."

"Why don't we set a trap for her?" Peyton surprised herself by speaking out. Apparently she'd surprised everyone else too, because Hadina looked across at her with pursed lips.

"What kind of trap?"

"Well, she obviously wants an empire, right? That's why she's doing all this shit—money and power."

Harris nodded his agreement. "Definitely. What did you have in mind, Peyton?"

Peyton chewed on her lip as she contemplated her plan. She didn't want to sound like a fool in front of everyone, but there was also something in her gut telling her it was the way to go. "We—Hadina, I mean—meet with her. We arrange a place of neutrality and tell her we want to discuss being cut in. We can totally bullshit and say that we've been killing her dudes for coming into our territory, and because we're pissed that we're not part of this."

Hadina and Harris looked at each other, having a silent conversation with their penetrating gazes. A few seconds passed before Harris nodded and they both turned back to face the group. Hadina drummed her fingernails off the table's edge before sighing. "It could work."

She tried not to react, but inside, Peyton was beaming that she had made a business decision which was actually deemed worthy. It seemed that pleasing Hadina and making her proud were slowly becoming two of Peyton's favorite things to strive for.

"Where would we meet?" Ume asked. "There aren't a lot of neutral spaces around here."

"What about *Il Fiore*?" Peyton was quick to reply. Hadina's eyes shot over to Peyton. Peyton shrugged and answered the unspoken question, "I went with Piper."

Hadina visibly relaxed and it was a small victory that the idea of Peyton being out at a restaurant with someone else caused a spur of jealousy.

"It would be pretty easy to get the staff on the inside."

Peyton's brows furrowed. "How?"

Hadina's answering smile was nothing short of wicked. "Because I know that the owner happens to be sinking farther and farther into a hole since he took out a loan from a notorious loan shark. He's drowning in debt of one hundred thousand and I just so happen to have financial stability that could solve all his problems."

"Damn, boss," Jason said, letting out a low whistle. "This is why you're the best in the business."

"Damn fucking right it is. Harris, arrange the meet. Jason, call Zellie and tell her to meet me at the house. We're going to need all hands on deck."

As Hadina stood, everyone else around the table got up from their seats too. It made Peyton think of the President, with everyone jumping to attention whenever the revered leader entered a room. She would never stop being surprised at just how powerful Hadina was.

With their orders given, the group nodded at Hadina and exited the room, leaving only Hadina and Peyton. Glancing over her shoulder to ensure nobody was loitering outside, Hadina made her way around the table and grabbed Peyton by the hips, pulling her forward until they were pressed together.

Peyton smirked and draped her arms over Hadina's shoulders. "Hi."

"Hi."

They stared at each other a moment before Hadina chuckled, capturing Peyton's mouth. It was a slow, sensual kiss that had Peyton's toes curling. Kissing Hadina was never boring and she always craved more, never wanting it to stop.

Sadly, Hadina was too responsible to give into whims, and Peyton knew that the second she pulled back, it was time for more business.

"What's my task, boss?" Peyton asked, entwining her fingers with Hadina's.

Hadina growled, trailing her mouth down Peyton's throat. "Your task is to stay by my side, so that the second we have a free moment, I can devour you wherever you stand."

Shivers ran down Peyton's spine as her core tightened at the promise in Hadina's voice. If Hadina wanted her by her side, that was where she would be. "Orders received, boss."

Peyton yelped as Hadina playfully nipped at the skin of her collarbone, her tongue tracing where her teeth had just been. "You keep talking to me like that and it won't matter if we're alone. I'll fuck you in front of everyone."

"Promise?" Peyton quipped, mischief and desire lacing her words.

CHAPTER 36

HADINA

SHE TRIED REALLY HARD NOT TO HATE HER SISTER, BUT SEEING THAT SMUG fucking smile on her face as she took a seat across from the woman, Hadina couldn't feel anything *but* hate for Zelina.

"So, did you finally realize that you need me because I'm better at your job than you, or did you just miss me, *hermanita*?"

Hadina glared at Zellie, keeping her face schooled. "*Veté a la mierda*, Zelina."

"You were the one who asked *me* here, Hadina. Don't forget that."

Don sighed, shaking his head. "*Hijas, por favor*. This isn't the time to fight."

Piper's gaze bounced to each member of the Adis family. "What's going on?"

"We found Regina," Peyton said, zeroing her own glare on Zellie. Hatred for her elder sister sent a rush through Hadina's veins. It was nice to have someone on her side for once. "Her name is Demi Treyva."

263

Don sucked in a sharp breath, his eyes widening in shock. "Demi did this?"

Hadina shrugged and nodded her head towards Zellie. "It's not like she hasn't come after the business before, thanks to some people." Zellie growled but Hadina continued on, "That being said, it seems like she went from drug running to far darker shit."

"It breaks my heart to think how dark and twisted she has become." Don sighed.

"What's your game plan?" Piper asked, sitting forward in her seat. Hadina was annoyed at having to bring her in, get her involved in any way, but if they were about to go to war, then the entire family deserved to know so they could protect themselves.

Hadina filled them in, explaining that *Il Fiore* was about to get some serious business. For once in her life, Zelina kept quiet while Hadina went over the groundwork of the operation. Their father interjected a few times to ask about logistics, but by the time she was done, they'd all agreed that it was a pretty solid plan.

"So, what are our roles?" Zellie pursed her lips, taking a large drink from her red wine.

"*Papi,* I just wanted to keep you in the loop. Pip, do you think you'd be okay with going to the restaurant and doing the handover?"

Piper leaned forward and squeezed Hadina's hand. "Whatever you need."

"And you," Hadina said, spinning her attention back to Zellie. "I need you with me at the meeting. You're a cold, brutal *perra* and I need that energy if we want to show them that Adis & Co. is untouchable."

Zellie watched Hadina over the top of her wine glass, taking her sweet time before answering. "Okay."

Hadina blinked in surprise. She didn't think she'd heard that right. Zellie was never one to give in easily, and any time she did concede, it made Hadina extremely wary of her motivations. "Okay?"

"You're right. This is more than personal vendettas. If someone is coming after our family or the company, then okay, I'll be there to help."

It shouldn't have been that easy. But, much to her dismay, Hadina didn't have time to argue or reconsider. Peyton looked at Hadina warily, checking to see if she had the same reservations. A small nod of Hadina's head was acknowledgment enough that she didn't trust Zellie either.

Peyton pulled out her phone, checking a text. "Harris says the meeting has been set up. Two days from now, three p.m."

Hadina tapped her hand against the dining table. "Then let's get prepared, *familia*. It's time to defend the Adis name."

THE MEETING last night had gone better than Hadina had thought it would, but she still had a nasty feeling in her stomach. Every time she tried to figure out what was wrong, what the missing piece was, she came up short. Everything was in place and planned out accordingly. Nothing amiss. But it didn't make that feeling go away.

"I want to take you somewhere," Hadina said, walking up behind Peyton.

"Oh, yeah? Where?"

Hadina felt herself smile, though she knew it was one of sadness. "I wanna show you a piece of myself. A place that was mine and *Mama*'s. Will you come?"

"Of course, baby."

Hadina was desperate to feel anything other than that ugly level of apprehension in her gut, and connecting her past with her present seemed like the best way to do it. As they drove downtown, she felt Peyton's eyes constantly on her, questions on her tongue that she was too scared to ask. The thing was, though, Hadina didn't think she'd have the answers anyway. All she could offer was to *show*

265

Peyton a part of herself, her culture—something that was still deep-rooted in her despite the years that had passed.

Pulling into the car lot behind the building, Hadina parked and turned to look at Peyton. "We're here."

"And where is *here*?"

"Market Square. It's one of my favorite places in the world."

Peyton smiled and took Hadina's hand. "Then show me around."

They linked their fingers as they walked, and Hadina felt herself settle. Making their way around to the front of the large stone building, she heard Peyton gasp at her side as she took in the colorful *papel picados* hanging outside.

"Just wait until you see inside," Hadina whispered into Peyton's ear, pulling her through the open doorway.

Stepping into the courtyard was like taking a step back in time to when Hadina was just a kid, holding onto her *mama*'s hand as she discovered her culture, one stall at a time. Everywhere she looked was a familiar explosion of color, from fabric bunting to the fairy lights strung up in rows from wall to wall. Since the courtyard was designed without an overhead roof, sunlight beamed down to illuminate the intricate designs and patterns that lined the little pathways.

"This place is *beautiful*," Peyton said wistfully, spinning around on the spot as she looked up. Hadina could feel a real smile break free on her face at the sight.

"Welcome to the Mexican Market, *tentadora*. My mom would bring me here once a month and we'd spend hours walking from stall to stall, before spending an insane amount of money in the stores. She wanted to show me authentic parts of Mexican culture that I could find here, things that reminded her of home."

Her mom had always been so happy whenever they came, her smile larger than life as she spoke Spanish to all the stallholders. She'd explain to Hadina anything she didn't understand, but had always waited a moment to see what her daughter hadn't picked up.

It was important for the Adis matriarch to know that her children could speak at least some Spanish, something that would connect them to their family.

"Come," Hadina said, dragging Peyton forward. She stopped at one of the first stalls, recognizing the lady cooking. "*Hola, Maritza! ¿Cómo estás?*"

"Ay, Hadina, it is so good to see you! *Soy buena, y tu?*" she responded in a thick accent, beaming at the woman in front of her.

"*Yo tambien soy buena, gracias!*" Hadina gestured to Peyton. "*Esta es mi novia*, Peyton."

"*Ella es hermosa. Se ve amable!*"

"*Sí, sí, ella es.*" Hadina looked at Peyton, squeezing her hand. "Maritza says you're beautiful and look kind."

Peyton blushed and it made Hadina's heart beat a little faster.

"*Gracias*, Maritza. This smells delicious!"

Maritza looked at Hadina and nodded approvingly. Any girl who could say *anything* in Spanish with that natural accent, without speaking the language, was deserving of the approval.

"Could we get some of your infamous *menudo* for Peyton to taste, *por favor?*"

Maritza smiled knowingly and spooned some of the rich soup into a bowl, taking a lemon slice and squeezing the juice in before handing the dish to Peyton with a napkin and spoon. "I hope you enjoy, *cariña*."

Passing some bills to Maritza, Hadina watched carefully as Peyton took her first spoonful. She couldn't help feeling giddy, seeing her temptress try something her *mama* had made for her so many times before. Hadina's mother had always said that Maritza's *menudo* was the only one that could rival her own.

Peyton groaned, closing her eyes as she ate. "This is the best thing I've ever tasted!"

Maritza laughed, clapping her hands together. Hadina thanked the woman and guided Peyton on, walking her through other stalls while she ate. She pointed out some of the other food on display, assuring Peyton that they would get some *pico de gallo* on the way back round.

"You need to teach me how to make this," Peyton said as she finished her last mouthful, wiping the sides of her mouth with her napkin.

Hadina laughed, raising a brow at her. "Are you sure you want the recipe?"

Peyton narrowed her eyes, pursing her lips. "Yes..."

"Absolutely sure?"

"Yes."

"Well, first, you start with the cow's stomach—"

Peyton stopped walking, spinning around to face Hadina. "You start with the WHAT?"

"You heard me, *tentadora*," she said, tears welling in her eyes from laughing so much.

"Oh, you absolute bitch. You could have told me beforehand!"

Hadina rolled her eyes and threw an arm around Peyton's shoulders, pressing a kiss to her temple. "But then you'd have been stubborn and not tried it. It's a delicacy and I knew you'd love it. You really going to tell me that you wouldn't eat it again now?"

Peyton snuggled closer but elbowed Hadina playfully. "It was the most amazing thing I've ever tasted, so you win this time. But I think *you'll* have to be the one to make it."

Barking out a laugh, Hadina conceded, "I think I can manage that."

For the next hour, the duo walked around the outdoor stalls, stopping for Peyton to try foods or look at the jewelry. She'd bought a woven bag, a bracelet, and two scarves before they'd even reached the edge of one row. Every time Hadina spoke in Spanish to the sellers, she caught Peyton watching her with awe. She wanted to kiss every inch of the girl's face when she looked at her like that.

"Let's go inside," Hadina said. "There's a store I want you to see."

Stopping outside the dress shop, Hadina stood behind Peyton, slipping her arms around her waist. Peyton held on, leaning her head back as Hadina pressed a soft kiss to her lips.

"These dresses are breathtaking," Peyton whispered, nodding towards the ballgowns on display.

"They're *quinceañera* dresses. When we turn fifteen, we have a huge party to celebrate the passage of girlhood to womanhood. It's one of the most important events of our lives."

Peyton spun around in Hadina's arms, looking up at the other woman with those tender blue eyes. "What was yours like? What color of dress did you wear? I can't imagine you wearing a dress like that, looking like a princess."

"Sweetheart, I've always looked like a queen," Hadina replied, but her smile faltered. "I didn't end up having my *quinceañera*. My mom died a few months before my fifteenth birthday."

"Oh, Hadi," Peyton said, pressing a soft kiss to her lips. "I'm so sorry. I can't even imagine how heartbreaking and difficult that must have been."

Hadina tried to smile as she brushed a piece of Peyton's hair behind her ear. "It was the hardest thing I've ever experienced in my life. *Mama* was my soul and it felt like losing part of myself."

Peyton nodded. "That's how I felt when Melina died too."

"Anyway," Hadina continued, trying to blink away tears, "I wanted to show you this."

In the next window display, front and center, was the most spectacular dress that Hadina had ever laid eyes on. Layer upon layer of champagne tulle made up the skirt, a layer of lace over the top to create an intricate pattern. The bodice was covered in red lace in a floral design; it looked like red petals were cascading down the rear and onto the skirt.

Peyton stared, her mouth agape. "Oh my. That is... *Wow.*"

"This was supposed to be my dress. *Mama* and I came browsing so many times but I never found anything I liked. Turns out, she had been speaking with the owner and had this dress specially designed for me."

A few tears sprang free from Hadina's eyes and she huffed in annoyance. Peyton reached up, wiping them away softly with her thumbs. "What a special thing to do for you. She sounds like an angel of a person."

Hadina nodded. "She really was."

They walked inside the store and Hadina waved to the old lady behind the counter. "*Hola, Guadalupe.*"

The gray-haired woman smiled, raising a wrinkled hand in a half wave. Hadina wrapped an arm around Peyton's waist, walking them over to the dress inside the shop. From the back, you could clearly see all the extra embellishments that had been added to create the falling petal effect.

"I can't believe how stunning this is. Did you ever get photos taken in it?"

Hadina shook her head. "No. It was supposed to be a surprise at my *quinceañera* so we didn't want to ruin it by letting anyone see it beforehand."

Peyton pouted and it made Hadina chuckle. "I wish I could have seen you in it."

"Me too."

"So, did the owner like the design so much that she added it to her line?" Peyton asked, leaning in to see more of the details. "Oh my God! Is that pomegranate made out of lace?"

Hadina reached out, running her fingertips over the embroidered fruit. "It is. And, no, the designer didn't add it to her line. This dress is *my* dress."

Peyton's brows shot up as she stood straight. "How is that possible?"

"It was one of the last things I got to do with my mom. I couldn't bear the idea of someone else wearing the dress that my mom had poured so much love into. After speaking with Guadalupe, she agreed that I could pay her to keep it up on display. A standing reminder of the beautiful mind that my *mama* had."

Peyton wiped at her eyes, tears streaming down her cheeks. It tugged at Hadina's heartstrings to see her emotional over something that meant so much to someone else. Not just someone. But to Hadina.

"That's the most thoughtful, incredible thing I've ever heard," she sniffled, cupping Hadina's face in her soft hands. "You have a beautiful heart, Hadi. I'm glad I'm the person who gets to see that."

Hadina's chest swelled at the love in Peyton's voice, the sincerity with which she spoke. This girl truly believed she had goodness in her soul, and it made Hadina want to prove her right.

They kissed softly, a light brush of their lips since they were in public. But, somehow, it felt like something far deeper. Emotional. A declaration between them.

"If my heart is beautiful, it's you who made it that way. I'm glad you're the person who gets to see it too."

Reina
de las sombras

CHAPTER 37

HADINA

Hadina hated how quickly her time with Peyton had passed. Sharing the market with her lover was like opening up her soul, inviting Peyton to see the most tender, loving part of the coldest Adis sister. If she were being honest with herself, it was the only way she could show Peyton how she felt without saying the words. It wasn't in her capabilities to say what she wanted, not when she knew there was a possibility this meeting could go to shit and she'd be leaving Peyton alone.

Then again, Hadina was confident enough in herself that she was sure that wouldn't happen.

Still, it didn't hurt to be cautious when it came to the people she cared about.

Just as Hadina was stepping out of the office, Zellie stormed into the house with enough attitude that it could rival a deity's. Her shoulder-length hair had been pinned back, not a single strand out of place. She looked at Hadina through dark lashes, her eyes brushed with smokey shadows and outlined with a black flick. Makeup was battle paint for Zellie, and though it killed her to admit it, Hadina thought her sister looked beautiful.

Pity that her soul was a black void, threatening to demolish anyone who got too close.

"Hadina."

Hadina nodded her head at her sister, brushing past the woman to go in search of their father. She found him in the kitchen, staring out the window somberly at his garden of flowers.

"*Papi?*"

"*Hola, mija,*" he replied, turning round to face her. His weathered face looked older, his eyes tired and puffy. The idea that he'd been crying made Hadina want to tear the world apart. "I have so much faith in you. I need you to know that. But I woke up this morning with such a horrible feeling in my stomach and I can't seem to shake it."

Hadina nodded her understanding, walking around the island to wrap her arms around her father the way she did when she was little. "We're going to be okay, *Papi.*"

Don squeezed his arms tighter around her, kissing the top of her head softly. "I know, but it doesn't make me worry any less. *Ustedes chicas son mi todo.*"

"Don't worry, *Papi,*" Zellie said, trailing into the kitchen with Piper and Peyton in tow. "I'll be there to protect *darling* Hadina."

"Ay, Zelina, please don't start. Today is stressful enough." Don rubbed his brows, letting out a slow sigh. Hadina glared at her sister.

"Anyway." Piper pushed past Zellie. "*Il Fiore* is awaiting your arrival. Everything is set in place."

"Weapons?"

Piper smirked. "Weapons at the door, of course. But I surmise that those tablecloths hide a multitude of sins beneath them."

"Stay with *Papi*, Pip, okay? I don't want you any more involved in this than you have to be."

For a second, it appeared as though Piper was about to argue but then a look of relief washed over her face. She nodded and walked to their father's side, slipping her hand into his. "I'll look after him."

"Ay, I can look after myself. I'm the parent here," Don grumbled.

Piper chuckled and linked her arm through his. "Well, *Papi*, you can look after me then." Don smiled sadly and patted her hand. "Always, *mija*."

Hadina looked at Peyton. "It's time to go."

Peyton smiled, the gesture almost sad. "Then let's go do this."

———

THE OWNER of the restaurant greeted them sheepishly, his forehead already dripping with sweat. Hadina and her team made a show of dropping their weapons on an entrance table, leaving them on display for when Demi arrived. Once she was done and certain that everyone was weapon-free, Hadina turned back to the owner.

"Stay in the back. You already look like you've got *caca* in your pants and Demi will smell that weakness a mile away."

"Y-yes, Ms. Adis."

"Good."

Hadina maneuvered her way through the tables and situated herself in a chair positioned to face the rest of the restaurant. Her team scattered themselves across the other tables, Zelina waiting behind a back door with Peyton and Harris. They had to look as inconspicuous as possible at first, but it didn't mean Hadina was foolish enough to leave her best players behind.

Her ability to remain calm and patient was truly a gift. They had arrived early to make sure everything was in place, and had been waiting an additional twenty minutes since. She tapped her long nails against the table, wishing she had Peyton's comforting presence beside her.

"So sorry to have kept you," Demi said as her guard opened the door, keeping a step in front of her. He moved aside to reveal Regina herself, a beautiful fiend. With curled blonde hair and a statuesque face with sharp angles and strong features, Demi looked like a painting. Even the pinstriped pantsuit she was wearing made her look fierce and dangerous.

But Hadina Adis was the fiercest and most dangerous of them all. She would not be intimidated.

"Nonsense," Hadina said, waving a hand in the air. She smiled, hoping that it showed off all her teeth. "I'm just grateful for you agreeing to meet with me."

Demi snapped her fingers and all her team ditched their weapons on the table. Disbanding across the restaurant, each of her guards taking a seat beside one of Hadina's. Demi moved and sat in an empty chair next to Hadina, which was a smart move. It was silly to turn your back on enemies, even under the ruse of a truce.

"In my family, it's tradition to have a drink for good luck and a successful business venture." Hadina motioned for a waiter to come over. "A glass of the 1811 Chateau d'Yquem, please. And iced water for my team. Please bring out some hors d'oeuvres as well."

"I'll take some of the finest whiskey you have. Water for my team would also be appreciated."

The young waiter bowed his head and walked through the doors to the kitchen. Once he was out of view, Demi turned her gaze to Hadina. "It's a pleasure to finally meet you, Hadina."

"I'm sure."

Demi barked out a laugh. "Ah, are we disposing of the false pretenses so quickly? I do so love openness."

"You say that, but your operation has been running in the shadow of my company. I wouldn't call that open, would you?" Hadina tilted her head. "Oh, and should I call you Demi or *Regina*?"

The woman's answering grin was nothing short of predatory. "You heard of my little nickname, then? I did think it was a nice touch."

It took everything in Hadina not to jump across the table and rip the *puta's* throat out with her teeth. "Cut the shit, Treyva. Tell me what you want."

Demi pretended to ponder for a moment, opening her mouth to speak when the waiters brought the drinks and food out on trays. The waiter who took their order placed Hadina's glass of wine down first, then Demi's, and set a charcuterie board between them. Hadina picked up a cube of cheese and bit down on it, looking at Demi expectantly.

"I want what all women like us want. Money, power, freedom."

"And you think that pushing drugs and abusing children is the way to go?"

Demi sat her glass down on the table without taking a drink. "I think you'll find that I never laid a hand on any children."

Hadina rolled her eyes, taking a swig of her wine. "You don't need to put hands on someone to be an abuser, Demi. Besides, it's the people on your orders and your payroll doing it—in my eyes, your hands are just as dirty."

"You're a tad too sensitive to be the leader of the great Adis & Co., in my opinion. What happened to that pretty sister of yours? She was certainly boss material."

Growling in warning, Hadina gripped the stem of her glass tighter. "Do not disrespect me. Inviting you here was a courtesy that you didn't deserve. I won't be kind enough to let you make a mockery of me."

Demi shrugged. "You allowed me to do that the moment you let things slip between your fingers. I've been using Adis resources and staff for months, and you've done nothing to stop me. You've made a mockery of yourself, Hadina."

Hadina smirked, the deafening silence making Demi uneasy. A spluttering cough from one of Demi's men broke the quiet, his face turning a bright shade of red. Demi turned around in panic, just in time to see him fall from his chair.

"What the fuck?" she yelled, smacking her hand down on the

table. Chuckling to herself, Hadina took a sip of her wine and watched as all the guards choked, passing out where they sat. Demi pushed to her feet, her face pinched up into the picture of fury. "What the fuck have you done?"

At that moment, Zellie pushed through the door and swaggered to their table, a smug look plastered on her face. "Precautions. You didn't really think we'd trust you at your word, did you?"

"Ah, did you need your big sister to come save you?" Demi spat at Hadina, throwing a glare at the two sisters.

Zellie took a seat beside Hadina, swiping the glass of wine and gulping the remainder down. Hadina rolled her eyes, shaking her head at the lack of manners and decorum. "I don't need anyone to save me, dear. But I figured it was only fitting that my sister be here since you two have *history.*"

"You better not have killed my men or I'll gut you where you sit!"

Hadina and Zellie shared a glance, their expressions serious until they both burst out laughing. Wiping at the corners of her eyes, Hadina shook her head. "Oh, you are ballsy. Your men are temporarily indisposed, but if you threaten me again, I'll be sure to have their throats slit while you watch. Your threats don't scare me, Demi, and neither do you." Reaching under the table to the gun strapped below, she pulled the pistol out and pointed it at Demi. "Now, sit your ass down until we're finished talking."

Tentadora

CHAPTER 38

PEYTON

Peyton couldn't see what was happening from behind the door, but a smile spread across her face when she heard bodies drop to the floor. Demi's voice could be heard thundering from where she and Harris were poised, ready to jump into action if they were needed.

"Now, sit your ass down until we're finished talking," Hadina said.

Peyton pushed the door open a tiny creak, just enough to see Demi thump down into her seat. She tucked a strand of her short blonde curls behind her ear, glaring at Hadina as she did so. The venom in the woman's gaze made Peyton want to run out and tear her eyes out of her head for daring to disrespect Hadina in such a way.

"Careful they don't see you," Harris whispered in Peyton's ear, though he was peering over her shoulder to watch too.

Peyton rolled her eyes. "Adrian, they're more likely to *hear* us than see us. So, shut up."

Harris chuckled, quickly covering his mouth with his fist to muffle the sound. "I liked it better when you were a timid little thing afraid of being killed."

"And I liked it better when you were a silent assassin with a dry personality and don't-fuck-with-me expression permanently on your face. But, alas, we're both changed people."

They both locked eyes, a second passing before they each smirked. Peyton was grateful that she'd become fast friends with Harris, that she knew he now protected her because he wanted to, rather than out of obligation because of his orders.

"What is it that you want, Hadina?"

"Your operation to cease. I want you to fuck off back to whatever hole you crawled out of and never come back here. You never sell kids ever again, otherwise I'll hunt you down and make you watch as I kill everyone you love. And then, after you're nothing but a broken husk, I'll torture you until your poisonous black heart gives out."

It was fucked up, but seeing Hadina threaten Demi with such dark intent sent a thrill through Peyton. This woman, fearless and terrifying, was *hers* and she got to see her like nobody else did. Hadina was Doctor Jekyll and Mr. Hyde, and Peyton loved them both equally.

Demi tutted, shaking her head. "Ah, see, this is why your sister should be the one in charge, Hadina dear. Because you don't do your research. I don't have anyone I care about, nobody I love enough that I'd be even a fraction upset if you were to kill them."

Peyton's heart fell a little at that. While she hated Demi Treyva and everything she stood for, she couldn't imagine the utter loneliness one would feel if they didn't have anyone to love. Even during her darkest, most isolated days, Peyton had the love for her sister to keep her going. Melina was dead, yes, but Peyton's love for her sister was strong enough to survive forever. And now that she had Hadina, her makeshift family, friends... she had people that she loved wholeheartedly. She pitied Demi for the fact that she didn't have that.

"But my little birdies tell me that's not the case for you."

Harris tensed behind Peyton as Zellie's eyes widened. Hadina kept her face calm and composed, but Peyton noted the way the woman's grip tightened around her gun, her knuckles turning white. "I already told you your threats mean nothing to me. I'm not scared of you or anything you claim you can do."

"You're not scared of losing that pretty little blonde thing you've been parading around?" Demi asked, picking at her acrylic nails absentmindedly. "I bet your mama would be disgusted with you sullying that oh-so-perfect bloodline, wouldn't she? I mean, it's bad enough that you're fucking a woman, but white trash? Ooooh, I think she'll be rolling over in her grave."

"*Cierra la puta boca!* Don't you dare talk about her like that!" Hadina leapt from her seat, smacking Demi in the temple with the butt of her gun.

Demi cackled, wiping the blood from her wound on the back of her hand as Zellie pulled Hadina back. "*Cálmate, hermana!*"

"*Vete a la mierda,* Zelina! She's disrespecting our mother as much as—"

"It doesn't matter! She just wants to rile you up," Zellie interrupted, motioning to Demi, who was sitting back in her chair with a smug smile on her face.

"I'd listen to your sister, little girl. The first rule of playing with the big fish is making sure nobody can ever have any leverage on you. Didn't dear old Don teach you that? Pity if something were to happen to him too..."

Peyton gasped as Zellie backhanded Demi hard enough that the woman fell from her chair. "You leave my father out of this, *pinche perra puta!*"

Harris shoved past Peyton, running into the room with his gun poised at Demi. Peyton pulled her own weapon out and followed him, willing herself to stop shaking. She wasn't scared; she was furious. She wanted to put a bullet in Demi where she knelt, for threatening Don. Peyton didn't care that the woman had threatened her too—Hadina had told her that it was always a possibility that they could be used as leverage against each other—but the fact that Demi had spoken ill of the dead? It was too much.

This bitch deserved to die.

"Hahaha, has the cavalry arrived? Finally, a real fight." Demi pushed herself up and turned around to face Harris, a trickle of blood marring her chin from where Zellie had burst the woman's lip. Demi saw Peyton storming towards her from the corner of her eye and stopped dead in her tracks, her brows furrowing.

Peyton lifted her gun and pointed it at Demi's forehead. "You don't deserve to live for all the heinous things you've done."

Demi opened her mouth to speak but shut it quickly, her expression changing from confusion to absolute rage. She spun around to Zellie, throwing a hand out in Peyton's direction. "Are you fucking kidding me? You devious, wretched little whore!"

The color drained from Zellie's face as she glanced between Peyton, Demi, and Hadina. The latter had her gun pointed at Demi, but her sights were set on her sister. Peyton could see the cogs working behind Hadina's eyes, trying to figure out what was happening.

"I don't know how you managed to fuck this up so badly, but I'm going to make you wish you had never laid eyes on me." Demi balled her hands into fists, ready to swing for Zellie, but Harris lurched forward and grabbed the woman by the arms. "I'm going to annihilate your whole family! Should I tell your sister exactly who her little plaything is? I'm sure she'd love to know."

A wave of unease washed over Peyton's skin. Once again, there were secrets being kept from her and the fact that Demi was involved made her sick. Her hand trembled and she slowly lowered her gun, taking a step forward. "What is she talking about?"

Zellie shook her head and glared at Peyton. "It's none of your concern."

"She's talking about me, you daft bitch! Of course it's my concern!"

Hadina placed her gun on the table and reached for Peyton's hand, squeezing her palm slightly. "Answer her question, Zelina."

Demi fought against Harris's hold while Zellie contemplated what she was going to do. Both Hadina and Peyton realized a moment too late that Zellie was going to reach for the discarded gun. Hadina pushed Peyton behind her but Zellie aimed at Harris instead. "Let her go."

Harris barked out a sarcastic laugh. "Are you delusional? You're in a room full of armed Adis guards and you think you can call the shots? You're not our boss."

Zellie's lips pulled into an ugly smile. She tilted her head and sighed, before pulling the trigger. The bullet hit Harris directly in his shoulder, weakening his grip on Demi, who wriggled free. Zellie grabbed the woman by the arm and shielded her with her body, blocking anyone from being able to take a clear shot.

Peyton shook as Hadina gripped her tighter, almost as though she were scared what would happen if she let her go. She didn't understand what the hell was happening, other than the fact that Zellie was clearly the evil bitch she'd thought she was since their first meeting, and it appeared that Hadina was equally perplexed.

"*Que mierda estas haciendo?* This is foolish, even for you, *hermana.*"

Zellie grimaced. "*Es complicado,* Hadina." She started to back up towards the exit, making sure Demi was behind her. "We're going to walk out of here without anyone coming after us or taking a shot, okay? Because the only way you're going to get to Demi is by shooting me, and I don't think any of you want to explain that to *Papi.*"

Hadina swore under her breath before sighing. "This is a mistake, Zellie, and you're going to regret it." Looking over her shoulder at

Peyton, Hadina pursed her lips and Peyton nodded slightly, encouraging her. She knew that conceding to Zellie's terms was the only way both sisters survived. "Everyone, put your weapons down. Let them go."

Demi grinned over Zellie's shoulder. "I'll be seeing you real soon, Hadina."

Zellie looked at Hadina and Peyton could have sworn she saw regret in the eldest sister's dark eyes. But with a blink, Zellie's cold demeanor was back on display and she turned, sprinting from the building behind Demi.

As soon as the door shut, Peyton ran over to Harris and pressed a napkin to his wound, applying pressure to stop the bleeding. He winced and grabbed it from her hand, propping himself up against the edge of a booth.

"Are you okay?" she asked, hearing the way her own voice trembled.

He closed his eyes and nodded, his jaw clenched tight. "I'll be fine." He looked up at Hadina, who ran up the moment Demi and Zellie were out of sight. "What the fuck just happened, boss?"

Hadina locked eyes with Peyton and ran a hand through her dark hair. "I have no fucking idea."

CHAPTER 39

HADINA

The door slammed shut behind them as they stormed into the house. Harris was grumbling about his shoulder and—while a part of her deep down did care—Hadina wanted to tell him to shut the fuck up and stop being a baby. She probably would have too, if it weren't for Peyton's fingers entwined with hers, grounding her.

"*Papi? Dónde estás?*" Piper popped her head out of the lounge, her bright smile dropping when she saw everyone's faces. She gasped when she noticed Harris clutching his shoulder. "What the hell happened? Adrian, are you okay?"

"Nothing I can't handle, Piper," Harris said, though Hadina could hear the pain in his voice.

Her father was sitting in his favorite armchair, clutching a bottle of *Jarritos*, the perspiration dripping onto his knee. The sight of Hadina had him out of his chair and clutching his daughter in his arms, concern etched in his face. "*Mija*, what happened?"

Hadina paced the length of the lounge, gripping her hair by the roots. "She double-crossed us. AGAIN!"

Piper flinched at the bellowing but Hadina couldn't bring herself to calm down. Time after time, Zelina had let the family down. She'd abused their trust and now had sided with one of the most vile women she'd ever had the displeasure of meeting.

"Peyton, since you're calmer, can you tell us what happened?" her father asked.

Peyton looked up at him and burst into tears, her whole body shaking with her sobs. Hadina stopped in her tracks and moved to kneel in front of the sofa, where the girl now sat, before clutching Peyton's face in her palms. "Baby, shhh. You're okay. Take a deep breath for me."

Panic seized her at seeing her girl so upset. Ever since they'd met, Hadina and her family had caused Peyton nothing but trouble and now here she was, inconsolable and traumatized.

"Eat this," Piper said softly, handing Peyton a vanilla-flavored *conchas*. "It should help with the shock and give you a sugar boost."

Hadina brushed her bangs out of her eyes and whispered to her while she ate the sweet bread, hoping the physical touch would help calm her. By the time Peyton was finished eating, her sobs had turned to the occasional sniffle, the tears on her cheeks beginning to dry. Hadina breathed a sigh of relief.

"I'm sorry," Peyton whispered, leaning her forehead against Hadina's. "I think I just got a bit overwhelmed."

"You have nothing to apologize for, *tentadora*. It's me and mine who are to blame for this."

"What are you talking about?" Piper asked, looking between them all.

"Zellie helped Demi escape. She literally shielded the bitch with her body and said we'd have to shoot her to get to Demi."

"I should have shot her on the spot," Hadina spat.

Don's eyes widened and he smacked Hadina over the back of the head. "Don't say such things. This family has seen enough loss."

Hadina pushed to her feet and towered over her father, her last thread of restraint finally snapping. "Are you seriously this delusional, *Papi*, or do you just like pretending to be obtuse? Zellie, your fucking daughter, just helped Demi Treyva escape. You know, the woman who trafficked *children* and pushes drugs. She fucking shot Harris! Tell me, how is Zellie any better when she helped to set the *puta* free?"

Piper pushed between father and daughter, creating a divide. "Hadina, calm down. This is *Papi* you're talking to."

Fury boiled in Hadina's blood and she struggled to understand why it mattered anymore. What good was respect if it didn't help the people who needed it?

"Pip, I love you so I'm warning you... Get out of my fucking way and let me handle this."

Movement out of the corner of her eye caught Hadina's attention, and she saw Harris stumbling over to them. He looked pale and sweaty, the blood loss starting to weaken him. He placed a hand on Piper's shoulder, tugging her towards him slightly. "Piper... I need some help here. Let Hadina and your dad talk, eh?"

Piper stared at her sister before nodding, slipping an arm around Harris's waist to help support him as she guided him out of the room.

"Your sister must have had her reasons," Don said, sounding almost defeated. He dropped down into his chair and buried his face in his hands. "She wouldn't have done something like this without good reason, Hadina."

Hadina closed her eyes and willed herself not to cry. Years of anger and frustration were rising to the surface, and she was going to erupt if she didn't get herself under control. She felt arms curl around her waist and opened her eyes to Peyton, her beautiful blue eyes staring into hers. If she needed to find her strength, Hadina only had to look at Peyton and remember the reason she was still fighting at all.

"All my life, you've made excuses for Zellie," she said, allowing herself to be guided by Peyton to sit on the sofa. "She's been a fuckup for years and yet you refuse to hold her accountable. How can you really believe that she has a *good* reason for doing this, *Papi*?"

Her father frowned, clasping his hands in his lap. "Because I know all of you better than I know myself, *mija*, and you all have your mother's heart. Zelina isn't a bad person and I have faith that she will make good of this situation."

Hadina sighed and shook her head sadly. "Then I think you're a fool, *Papi*, and that breaks my heart. She chose to save the woman who disrespected *Mama*, you, and threatened Peyton's life. That's unforgivable in my eyes."

Peyton squeezed Hadina's hand, pressing closer to her. "Demi mentioned something about me, Don. She told Zellie to tell Hadina who I really am. I don't understand what that means. Did Zellie ever mention anything to you?"

In all her anger, Hadina had pushed that part of the evening from her mind. Now she felt chills run down her spine as she saw the panicked look in her father's eyes. Peyton tensed beside her and Hadina knew immediately that she had caught it too.

"What aren't you telling us?"

Her father stood and closed his eyes. "Wait here."

Disappearing from the room, Hadina watched him leave before she turned to Peyton. "I have a horrible feeling about all of this."

Peyton grimaced. "As do I."

They waited in silence until Don returned, a sheet of aged paper in his grasp. He whispered a prayer in Spanish before passing the paper to Peyton, his weathered hands trembling. "I'm sorry."

Hadina watched over Peyton's shoulder as the girl released her grip and opened up the folded sheet of paper. "What *is* this?" Peyton said quietly, her brows pinched together.

A birth certificate. The piece of paper was a birth certificate with Peyton's name. And listed under *mother* was the name Demitria Treyva.

There had to be a mistake.

The paper shook in Peyton's hands as she stared at it, unwilling to tear her gaze away. Hadina looked at her father. "Is this some sort of joke?"

He shook his head. "No, *mija*. Peyton is Demi's daughter."

"I don't understand. My parents said my adoption records were sealed. How do you have this?"

"Because I'm the one who helped facilitate your adoption."

Tentadora

CHAPTER 40

PEYTON

Don's words were ringing in her ears. The room was beginning to look fuzzy, like she was looking through a cloudy lens. Hadina reached for her hand but Peyton pulled away, needing space. She tried not to let the hurt on Hadina's face bother her, even though she knew it would make her upset later.

"I don't understand," Peyton heard herself saying, but her voice didn't sound like her own. The world around her felt strange and deceptive and she wanted to throw up.

"It's a long story, *cariña*," Don said, placing his hand on her shoulder. She shook him off and stood, pacing across the plush carpet.

"*Papi...*"

"Tell me the fucking truth, Don!"

"I knew Demi a long, long time ago. When it was decided that you'd be put up for adoption, I helped make it happen. You were just an innocent kid and I wanted to make sure you were safe."

Peyton stopped pacing and caught his gaze. While he seemed

genuine, her gut was telling her that he was trying to placate her with half truths. She shook her head. "Tell me the full story."

Don sighed. It looked like he wanted to plead with her, but the fiery glare she was giving him was enough to stop him in his tracks. She leaned against the wall with her arms folded—as far away from both Don and Hadina as she could get without leaving the room—and motioned for him to start talking.

"Demi used to date one of my employees. Isaac was one of the most loyal, intelligent people I've ever known, but he let his guard down. During one of our infiltration ops, he came across Demi and the *pendejo* fell in love."

A lump caught in the back of Peyton's throat. "Isaac is my father?"

Don nodded, not meeting her gaze. "They met up in secret for months. He loved her so much, but I don't think Demi has ever loved anyone in her life. Isaac was foolish and didn't see that Demi was just using him, getting bits of information out of him that could help her climb the ranks of the drug world."

"What happened to him?"

"There was a meet that went wrong and Isaac was caught in the crossfire. He bled out before we could save him." Don looked up at Peyton, tears glazing over his eyes. "*Lo siento.* I still carry the pain of his death with me every day."

Peyton felt herself going weak at the knees. She gripped the wall behind her and closed her eyes, pushing her tears down. There was more she needed to hear before she could let herself feel anything.

"Demi found out she was pregnant after Isaac died. She didn't want to be a mother, and I couldn't bear to see my friend's baby come to any harm. So, I convinced her to put you up for adoption."

Peyton scoffed, shaking her head in disbelief. "Demi Treyva doesn't seem like the kind of person to listen to advice."

"She doesn't. But she loves money and power."

"You *bought* me?" Peyton yelled, pushing off the wall. "What the actual fuck?"

Don held up his hands in silent surrender, sensing the rage simmering beneath her skin. "I didn't buy you. I bribed Demi into putting you up for adoption. It was the only way to ensure she didn't ruin your life."

"This is the most fucked-up thing I've ever heard. And what? You've just been keeping tabs on me all these years?" A thought dawned on her then, nausea flooding her system. She looked at Don, horrified. "You knew. That day we met at the hospital... You *knew* me."

He at least had the decency to look ashamed. He glanced at Hadina but her face was stone, her eyes blank as she looked at him. Peyton couldn't bear to look at Hadina for more than a moment, for fear that she'd run over and collapse into the other woman's arms.

"*Sí, lo sabía.* I knew who you were."

Bile rose up the back of Peyton's throat and she doubled over, clutching her stomach. "Oh my God! I can't—you could have told me. But instead, you kept it a secret for all these months. You let me fall in love with your daughter! Fuck, you let me go to that meeting, knowing Demi was my mother!"

Hadina had moved from the sofa to Peyton's side. She began to rub circles on the bottom of her back, and for a moment, Peyton leaned into the touch, desperate for comfort from someone safe and familiar.

But maybe Hadina wasn't safe either.

Peyton lurched back, moving towards the door. Every step Hadina took towards her, Peyton took two in the opposite direction. She put a hand out in front of her, urging her to stop. "Don't come near me!"

Hadina flinched and stepped back as though she'd been slapped. "Peyton, it's me. I would never hurt you. I had no idea about any of this!"

The pain in Hadina's voice was her breaking point, and Peyton finally allowed the tears to fall. Her entire body ached as though it had been waiting for the release. She looked at Hadina through an onslaught of tears, her shoulders shaking as she sobbed.

"I don't know that, though, do I? How can I ever trust a member of this family after everything I've just learned?"

"*Tentadora*, please," Hadina pleaded, her voice cracking on the words. "You can trust me. I promise you that."

Peyton shook her head. "I'll never be able to trust anyone again," she sobbed, wiping her eyes with her sleeves. "I can't be here right now. I need some space."

Spinning on her heels, Peyton ran through the house and out onto the street. She gasped, inhaling as much fresh air into her lungs as possible. She continued to run until she was sure Hadina wasn't following her before collapsing onto a bench. Her chest heaved as she tried to catch her breath, to calm herself long enough to stop her tears from falling.

She didn't know how this was her life. It was crazy to the point of insanity and she was tempted to say that it was all in her head, some elaborate nightmare that she couldn't wake up from. But the look of despair in Don's eyes, the heartbreak in Hadina's... It was too real to be fake.

All her life, she'd grown up in a dysfunctional family unit. The only saving grace was her beautiful Melina. And despite the feeling of being an interloper in her own family, she'd never craved the knowledge of who her birth parents were. When she was old enough to ask about them, she did so only because she knew it was expected. And when she was told that the records were sealed, she was secretly relieved. She didn't want to know about the people who'd given her up, had discarded her like she was nothing.

But somehow the truth that she had so desperately avoided had been flung in her face and it was so, so much worse than she had ever anticipated.

If it weren't bad enough that her birth mother was a psychotic, evil, cold-hearted bitch who was willing to do anything to be on top, her birth father had been a good man and was dead. He'd fallen in love with the wrong person and karma punished him instead of *her*.

And Don knew about it all. For months, he'd comforted Peyton and made her feel like she was a part of his family. Meanwhile, he knew that she belonged to another.

Falling onto the grass in front of the bench, Peyton sat on her knees and retched. Her throat burned by the time she'd emptied the contents of her stomach, her eyes stinging from the tears that wouldn't stop falling. Peyton had no idea what she was going to do. She barely spoke to her parents, and even the mere thought of returning home to Willowbrooks made it feel like she had phantom hands around her throat, choking the life out of her. The Adis family had become hers, and without them, she didn't have anyone.

Her phone rang in her pocket, vibrating against her leg. She sniffled and wiped at her eyes before pulling it out, half-expecting to see Hadina blowing up her voicemail. Instead, the incoming call was from Kaira. Peyton clicked the screen and accepted the call. "Kaira?"

"Peyton! Are you okay? Piper called me and told me what happened. I don't even have words."

"I'm o—" Peyton choked on the words and burst into a fresh flood of tears.

"Oh, honey," Kaira cooed. "It's going to be okay. Where are you? I can get Piper to pick you up and bring you to my place."

Panic seized Peyton's throat. "No! I don't want to be near a single person in that family right now. I don't know what to do, Kaira."

"Okay, here's what you're going to do. I'm gonna text you my address and you'll call an Uber or something to get you here. I promise not to tell Piper where you are. But I need to know you're safe, so you can hide out at my apartment until you sort your head out."

"Thank you," Peyton sobbed into the phone.

Kaira tutted. "It's nothing, honey. That's what friends are for. I'll see you soon."

Once the call ended, Peyton picked herself up from the ground. Her face was puffy and sore, so she could only imagine how she looked. The phone chimed with a text message from Kaira, a drop pin to her apartment. Peyton clicked on the location and saw that it was only a few blocks from where she was presently. She took in a deep breath, the fresh air filling her lungs and helping to soothe her addled brain.

She'd walk to Kaira's. She needed the time to think.

Pulling maps up on her phone, Peyton took off in the direction of Kaira's place. The night air was cold against her raw cheeks, burning into her chest as she breathed. There hadn't been time to grab a jacket or comfortable shoes or any of her stuff before fleeing, and she was now beginning to see how woefully unprepared she was.

Unprepared for a life on the run.

Peyton didn't know if that really was the case or not, but it's how it felt in her heart. She knew that Hadina wouldn't let her go without a fight; she'd told her as much when they'd first met. It seemed like a lifetime ago since she had walked into that office and saw Hadina strapping up, looking like she was preparing for war. If only Peyton had listened to her head instead of her heart and fled the moment Hadina had left that night, she wouldn't be in this fucked-up mess now.

Peyton heaved a sigh and checked her phone. She was only five minutes away from Kaira's apartment, somewhere she could sit and be alone with her thoughts.

Turning the corner onto the next street, she was surprised to see that all the streetlamps were flickering on and off. Unease settled into her gut as she continued on, using the flashlight on her phone to see where she was going. It was a dark evening with no stars or moon to be seen in the sky, making it difficult to see more than a few feet ahead of her.

She swore under her breath when the streetlight above her sparked, the bulb cutting out completely. Chills worked their way down her spine, a thousand needlepoints scratching at her skin. She shivered and wrapped her free arm around her stomach, picking up the pace as she walked.

She'd almost reached the corner to the next street when tires screeched from behind her, making her jump out of her skin. Turning around, she caught sight of a black van speeding down the road. She pressed up against the closest gate, looking for somewhere she could hide. Dread settled in her stomach and adrenaline kicked in, propelling her forward.

Sprinting as fast as she could under the poor lighting and with even poorer footwear, Peyton tried to outrun the vehicle. She knew it was stupid, that she wasn't fast enough, but it didn't stop her from trying. Just like how she knew said vehicle was coming after her.

As she was about to turn the corner, she tripped up over the uneven sidewalk, falling flat on her face. She tried to push herself up but pain shot up her leg, radiating around her ankle. She must have twisted it as she fell. There was nothing she could do as the van skidded to a halt on the sidewalk, the side door flying open.

Two large figures jumped out, their faces covered with black masks. They grabbed Peyton by the arms and hauled her to her feet, shoving her forward with unnecessary force. She fought against them, but their grip on her was iron-tight, and she could feel her skin beginning to bruise already.

"Let me go!" Peyton bellowed at the top of her lungs, kicking her legs out beneath her.

Her struggling made no difference as they threw her into the van and climbed in beside her. There was another hidden figure inside, who leaned forward before shoving a hood over Peyton's head. The material was rough and scratchy against her skin and smelled like sweat and sawdust.

She continued to scream as the door closed and she felt the

vehicle move again. Hands grabbed her by the shoulders and wrists, rope being tied tight to bind her. She kicked out with her uninjured foot, only to have it shoved back.

"You made this too easy, you know," a voice said. It was a man's voice, rough and crackly like he was a chain-smoker.

"Yeah, didn't your mommy ever teach you not to walk alone in the dark?" another voice chimed in, earning a chuckle from Old Smokey.

Peyton screamed and kicked out again, her foot connecting with what felt like a stomach. The man let out an annoyed *oof* and grabbed the hood, seizing a bunch of her hair in the process.

"You little bastard!"

"Go fuck yourself," Peyton seethed, wriggling her wrists to see if she could get free of the rope.

"You'll pay for that," Old Smokey rasped in her ear, before slamming her head into the door. When it was obvious she hadn't passed out, he did it again.

Pain radiated through Peyton's head, her ears ringing. Black spots swam in her eyes and her vision blurred. Slowly and painfully, unconsciousness pulled her under until there was nothing but darkness surrounding her. When her eyes fluttered shut, the last thing she saw was Hadina's face. Peyton was slipping into the shadows but Hadina was *la reina de las sombras* and she'd keep her little temptress safe there.

ACKNOWLEDGMENTS

This book is one of the hardest things I've ever written. It required a lot of work and a lot of research and therefore, it's also one of the things I'm most proud of. I couldn't have done it without my amazing sensitivity readers. Anna, Andrea, Reina, Yvonne, Shania, Stacey, Rosy, Jazmin, Líza, Ana, Domino; thank you from the bottom of my heart for making sure my words were authentic so that I could represent a culture I have so much love for. Y'all are angels and I'm beyond grateful.

My wonderful street team, who have hyped me up and helped me promote Seeds of Sorrow with so much love and excitement. Thank you for all the love, the shares, the time you've dedicated to me and my book.

To my parents, who don't care that their baby girl writes smut. Mum, who always wants to read *everything* I write. And Dad, who sends pictures of my books to family members with a proud smile as he tells them to buy a copy. Thank you for being the first people to ever believe in me, and for always encouraging me to keep writing.

Eliza, my incredible PA and rock throughout this entire process. Being your friend is an honor, but having you show me so much love and hype every single day is something I will never be able to repay. You kept me sane and pushed me when I needed it, while also helping me manage everything behind the scenes so I didn't get overwhelmed. I love you and as thanks, I give you official dibs on Harris. You're welcome.

Domino, baby, this wouldn't have been possible without you. In fact, nothing I write would be. You're so incredible and being your best friend is something I treasure more than anything. You encouraged me to write Hadina how I pictured her, helped me to make sure I was accurate in my Latinx representation, and taught me so much about Mexican culture. This book has a huge part of you within its pages. Thank you doesn't seem appropriate enough, but I trust that you know how much I love you and how grateful I am. You are everything good in the world.

Gabe, you're amazing and I'm so glad you put up with me asking a hundred different questions about Spanish and making you translate things for me. I appreciate all your help and support so much. You're the best, peaches!

My platypi and OG writing besties— Chani, Eri, Dee, Dani, Jesa. Thank you for keeping me sane and listening to me vent about how stressed I am 24/7. Y'all are the most incredible group of people and so insanely talented. I can't wait for all of us to be published and have a shelf dedicated to your books. Love you all!

Jessy, an incredible writer and an amazing friend. You make me smile and are always ready to hype me up whenever I need it. Thank you for always brightening my mood and making me laugh. I'll have your book next to SoS soon and I'm so excited for that!

Reva, my sweet angel. You have been such an amazing help during this process and the reels you've created from me have been outstanding. Thank you for being part of my team, for helping with content and for being part of m y behind-the-scenes team with Eliza. You really are an angel and I love you so much.

Gabs, my hype woman and amazing friend. I am so so grateful for you and your support. Brainstorming with you is always so fun and I forever look forward to endless voice-notes about plotting until we both know what we're doing.

Kat, the best editor in the world! You're an absolute star and one of my favorite people. You make the editing process so much easier and you're so kind and considerate, always reassuring me. Thank you for helping turn my book into something beautiful.

Lastly, thanks to *you*, my readers. You are the reason I get to write and publish, living out my dream. I'll never be able to say thank you enough.

About the Author

Sarah James is an author of dark and smutty romances. She strongly believes that villains do it best and you'll find her usually rooting for them. When she's not writing, editing or designing covers, she'll be trying to get through some of her never-ending TBR or making pinterest boards for all her different book ideas.

Sarah James is a pen name for author *Colby Bettley*.

You can find up to date information or follow her on social media at: https://linktr.ee/authorsarahjames

Sarah James

Printed in Poland
by Amazon Fulfillment
Poland Sp. z o.o., Wrocław

30935138R00186